DONN'S SHADOW

CARYN LARRINAGA

DONN'S SHADOW
Published by TWISTED TREE PRESS

Twisted Tree Press, LLC
PO Box 540836
North Salt Lake, UT 84054
www.twistedtreepress.com

1st Edition | October 2019

The Soul Searchers Mysteries
Donn's Hill
Donn's Shadow
Donn's Legacy

Other Books by Caryn Larrinaga
Superhero Syndrome
Hide and Seek
Galtzagorriak and Other Creatures:
Stories Inspired by Basque Folklore

For Mom & Dad, who taught me the power of a good book

The cabin glared at me through a gap in the trees. Two glassless windows flanked the door like eyes on either side of a narrow nose, their frames sagging downward in an expression that managed to be both accusatory and appreciative. In the harsh light from the afternoon sun, the place looked more dilapidated than I remembered, and wisps of negative energy oozed out from between the rotting logs that made up the cabin's exterior.

I shivered.

"Chilly?" Kit Dyedov reached for the temperature knob on the van's dashboard. "I'll turn up the heat."

I shot her a grateful smile and shrugged deeper into my hoodie. Like the cabin, Kit's van had seen better days, and the crisp October air slipped its way through the cracks and seams in the body to pinch at my cheeks. I told myself the weather was the reason I hadn't yet unbuckled my seat belt, but in truth, this place terrified me.

"Do you want me to drive closer?" Kit asked.

"Do *you* want to drive closer?"

"Not really." She blew a gigantic purple bubble, sucking her gum back into her mouth with a loud snap. "I didn't want to come here at all, remember?"

"Me neither, but a kid almost died," I said.

"I know. But I don't get why we couldn't just finish planning this thing from the kitchen table."

It was the third time today she'd suggested that course of action, and I found myself agreeing with her. We could easily have pulled up the footage from our last two visits to this haunted place to remind ourselves what it looked like. Why had I insisted we drive all the way out here just to stare at it through the windshield?

Because you owe it to that kid, I reminded myself. The uncomfortable lump of guilt shifted from my chest to my throat, swelling until I swallowed it down.

Kit seemed to read my mind and pushed her hands through her wild, green hair with an exasperated sigh. "It wasn't your fault, Mac. Stop blaming yourself."

I silently disagreed.

Five months before, ScreamTV had aired two back-to-back episodes of *Soul Searchers,* the television show Kit's dad produced and starred in. Half paranormal investigator, half sympathetic-but-unlicensed grief counselor, Yuri Dyedov created the show to help people in mourning or distress come to grips with whatever was happening in their home. Sometimes, it was a spirit that needed to move on. Other times, it was the living who needed to do the same.

Kit and Yuri had invited me to join their crew shortly after meeting me the prior spring. I wasn't sure if I was a ghost sensor or ghost bait, but either way, the team caught more apparitions on video than ever before. Spirits like Richard Franklin, who'd been haunting these woods for over fifty years, luring campers and teenagers into dangerous situations that usually resulted in their deaths.

We'd visited the cabin twice, and each time, I'd found the body of one of Richard Franklin's recent victims. The footage thrilled the network, and the episodes pulled in record numbers of viewers. But the executives in Los Angeles didn't have to deal with the nightmares or worry about the consequences of drawing so much attention to a place this dangerous.

I should have come back and cleansed the cabin before the episodes aired, but my last encounter with the spirit here had left me shaken. He'd manifested in the form of swirling dust and leaves, and had somehow conjured a windstorm powerful enough to uproot an enormous oak tree. He'd wielded it like a cudgel, smashing a gaping hole in the roof and nearly killing our entire crew.

Suffice it to say, I hadn't been in a rush to come back here.

Then, two weeks ago, a group of amateur paranormal investigators from the nearby city of Moyard had descended on the cabin with electromagnetic field meters and cell phone cameras. They'd been hoping to record something compelling for their video podcast, but their plans were derailed when a partially downed tree had fallen on top of one of their team members, a nineteen-year-old college freshman named Connor Miles.

Last week, the doctors had downgraded Connor's condition from critical to stable, but he remained inpatient at Moyard General. I checked his family's social media posts obsessively, dreading the day they would figure out what I'd realized the instant I heard about the "accident" on the news: his injuries were my fault. If I'd done my job sooner and forced Richard Franklin's spirit to move on from this place, I could've prevented anyone else from getting hurt.

Coming here today was part of my penance. I'd asked Yuri to let me take the lead in planning this episode, and he always scouted our filming locations in advance... and in person. I owed it to Connor to be brave enough to do things the right way.

Of course, brave didn't mean foolish. That's why we'd stopped before the crumbling asphalt road widened into a graveled parking area. We eyed the cabin from a safe distance.

When I didn't respond to Kit's attempts to lessen my guilt, she sighed again and flipped open her sketchbook. Nestled between drawings of the things I'd seen on our investigations and a diagram of the cabin's interior was a checklist. Tasks like "clear investigation with Driscoll County" and "price additional camera rentals" had already been crossed off with thick, red marker, and only a few items remained.

"Okay, we've got the gear all lined up. I wish we'd been able to find a better field mixer, but I think the sound quality will be fine with the one we have. Um…" She ran her finger down the list. "Oh. Are we filming outside or just in the cabin?"

I squinted through the trees, assessing the space in front of the rotting structure. "We should get some B-roll footage, show the way this place keeps deteriorating. But I don't want to set up lights and everything out here. We can do all the interviews inside, same place as the séance."

She made a note and nodded. "Good. That'll speed things up. How about transportation? Is there enough parking?"

The last time I'd been here, the little parking lot in front of the cabin had been packed with emergency vehicles and swarming with sheriff's deputies.

"Plenty," I said. "Our team will be in the van, and I think the extras are carpooling in from The Enclave."

"And you've got all those people lined up?"

"Yeah."

"Took you long enough."

I resented the jab. Kit had years of experience planning and producing the show, but even she had never pulled together this many people for a single episode. Coordinating with other psychics, especially ones with their own businesses to manage, was like trying to grab hold of a ghost. Options kept slipping through my fingers.

"There'll be four including Graham, right?" she confirmed.

I nodded. I was basing the structure of the séance on the only one I'd ever witnessed in person, which had been hosted by my former mentor, Gabrielle Suntador. She'd insisted on nine attendees. I insisted on the same. Our small crew normally had five members: Yuri and me, who both appeared on camera in most episodes; Kit, who ran the production and typically handled sound; Mark, our camera-man; and my tortoiseshell cat, Striker. I'd convinced my boyfriend, Graham, to join us, which left three slots for outside talent.

"Who'd you get?" Kit asked.

"A few locals. I'd been hoping some of the mediums who come in from New York or Boston for the Afterlife Festival would come back for this, but it's too short notice."

She nodded. "Yeah, this is all way faster than we normally move, even for smaller investigations."

"We have to do it soon," I reminded her. "Somebody else could get hurt."

"I get it, I get it." She held up her hands, palms out, and bowed her head. "Get off your soapbox and just tell me who they are so I can get them the consent forms."

"Do you know Nick and Daphne Martin?"

Kit's head jerked up and her eyes widened. "Nick Martin? How did you manage that?"

"Your dad took me up to their house last week, and we invited them together. They seemed excited, especially since your dad will be here."

"Yeah, they love Dad. But still... This is a huge get." She wrote their names down at the bottom of her list. "Nick is blowing up right now, and Daphne's about to launch this huge traveling psychic circus. The network will freak out when they find out the Martins are on board."

"Yeah, that was your dad's line of thinking too. He wanted some big names to add some extra credibility to the episode."

Kit's body tensed as I spoke. Staring down at her clipboard, and with far too much casual air in her voice, she asked, "Who else?"

"Graham's friend, Stephen Hastain—"

"The Irish dude? Rune caster?" Kit interrupted.

"Yeah. You know him?"

She nodded, and her posture relaxed as she added his name below the Martins. "We volunteered together for the summer art program at the high school. I like him."

I'd known Kit barely half a year, but it'd been an intense six months. We worked together, and her apartment was on the floor below mine. Our friendship had already been tested by lies, arguments, and the discovery of multiple dead bodies. As far as I was concerned, it'd reached "lifelong and indestructible" status, which conveyed upon me certain rights and responsibilities. As her best friend, I had a duty to find out why she'd been so tense a moment before, and, depending on the reason, to make fun of her mercilessly for it.

"Whose name were you worried I might say?" I asked, not bothering to hide my verbal leer.

Her eyes flashed. "I wasn't worried."

"Tell that to your face. And your shoulders. And that pen you're snapping in half."

"I just don't want to screw up the show by bringing on the wrong people."

"That's fair. Who are 'the wrong people?'"

She sat in silence for a few moments, flexing her ballpoint pen between her hands. "Look, this stays between us. I don't want any of this to get back to my dad."

"Deal."

"He's been getting super chummy—"

"With Penelope. I know. It's weird."

Kit made a noise halfway between a gag and a growl, and the pen finally broke. I flinched, bracing for a spray of ink, but it never came. She just threw the jagged halves of the ballpoint down into a cup holder on the floor and moved her hands to the steering wheel where they twisted at the faux leather cover.

"That's not who I'm talking about, but thanks for reminding me."

"Who, then?" I honestly couldn't think of anyone else her dad would get close to. It was strange enough that he'd been spending so much time with Penelope Bishop, the middle-aged deputy mayor of Donn's Hill. Between running the *Soul Searchers* and helping Penelope with her endless projects to increase tourism to the town, I couldn't imagine him having time to spend with anybody else.

"There's this douche magician ScreamTV signed for a new show. The guy is the worst, but Dad just loves him. A few weeks ago, I overheard Dad trying to convince the network to pay for some kind of crossover episode."

I thought back to the people Yuri had suggested I consider for the cabin cleansing. Apart from the ones I'd chosen, there'd been a palmist from Donn's Hill and a medium from Boca Raton. So far as I knew, neither one of them moonlighted as magicians.

"I don't get it," I said. "ScreamTV specializes in horror and paranormal stuff. Why would they want a magician?"

"Why would *anyone* want a magician?" She rolled her eyes.

I shrugged. "I like magic tricks."

"Well, you wouldn't like this guy. He hates psychics and paranormal investigators. He told me, to my face, that we're hacks and scam artists."

"Seriously?"

"Yep."

"Did your dad hear him?"

"Of course not. He knows the network loves Dad, so he pretended to love the show anytime Dad was within earshot." She made a few more notes in her sketchbook before lifting her chin toward the cabin. "Need to do anything else while we're here?"

I hesitated. Ordinarily, we'd go inside the location and scout it for things like electrical outlets, layout, and anything that might require us to bring additional equipment. But we were already planning to run off batteries and had spent more than enough time inside the cabin to know which rooms we'd be using. I gave a firm shake of my head, eager to be away from the strange atmosphere in these woods.

She grinned. "Thank God. Wanna grab lunch? I'm craving fish and chips from the Ace of Cups."

My stomach growled and my mouth watered at the thought of fried cod and salty french fries from one of the new restaurants in town. The Ace of Cups anchored The Enclave, the local occult community's answer to a strip mall that had opened a few months before. Sadly, a prior engagement took precedence over my gluttony.

"I can't. I promised Penelope I'd go check out the renovations on the inn."

The mention of her father's girlfriend sent Kit's ears aflame, and she muttered something to herself as she started the engine. It was too low to hear, but I thought I caught the word "hag" nested between a few choice words of profanity.

"What was that?" I teased.

"You heard what I said."

"I really didn't."

She gave me a one-shouldered shrug. "I don't know what everyone sees in her all the sudden. You two were, like, mortal enemies when you first got here, and now you're all buddy-buddy and checking out her new place?"

This wasn't about my relationship with Donn's Hill's most influential woman. Kit and I both knew it, but the ever-darkening shade of red that spread from her ears and into her cheeks convinced me it wasn't a clarification worth making.

"She apologized for the way she treated me before," I reminded her. "Besides, she's Graham's aunt, and she's doing him a huge favor right now. The least I can do is look at what she's been working on."

"Bet she lured you there with that fancy new coffee maker." Kit narrowed her eyes. "She knows how to manipulate everyone in town."

"Hey! I am not easily manipulated by coffee."

"No, but I heard they serve chai tea and french pastries over there, too."

I opened my mouth to continue my protests—sure, Penelope's invitation had included a promise to show me the new café in her inn's lobby, and yes, I assumed I'd be allowed to sample the goods—but my stomach got in the last word, rumbling audibly and startling us both.

The tension in the van broke and Kit shook her head, grinning at me. "You can't hide your weaknesses from me, Mac. I know your belly calls the shots."

I returned her smile for a moment, but it faded from my face as she coaxed the van into making a twelve-point-turn on the narrow dirt driveway. A view of the rotting cabin filled the passenger side window, and a deep crease formed between my eyebrows as I gazed at the structure. It stared back at me through the trees with defiant window-eyes, zapping the levity from a moment before into nonexistence. We might be pulling away now, but in a few days, we'd be back here. I'd be attempting to banish the most dangerous ghost I'd ever encountered, and I'd be doing it with the largest crew I'd ever worked with.

I wished we had more time to prepare, that we could schedule it at our leisure and I could pull together a dream team of top psychics to help ensure our success. But every day we waited was another potential opportunity for Richard Franklin to hurt someone. Given the ghost's track record, Connor Miles was lucky he'd gotten out of there alive. Franklin wouldn't let that kind of luck ride. Next time, someone would die. Their blood would be on my hands.

Kit took us back toward the highway, and as the woods thinned around us, I broadcast a message to the spirit who lurked in the trees. I allowed my guilt and my hatred for Richard Franklin to amplify the strength of my thoughts, pushing them outward in all directions.

Enjoy your last few days in this place, Richard. Because when I come back, I'll banish you for good.

My mental words didn't seem to intimidate our surroundings. I should've known I was the only one with anything to fear.

CHAPTER TWO

I n a way, Kit was right to be surprised I'd accepted Penelope Bishop's invitation to tour the new inn. I had been hesitant, but not because of the woman who'd invited me.

It was the place that put me off.

Sure, Penelope had tried to bully me into leaving Donn's Hill with my tail between my legs six months before, but that'd been a case of mistaken identity. I'd later found out she thought I was her late husband's illegitimate child, here to cash in on his passing. I couldn't blame her for disliking the person she assumed was living proof of her husband's much-rumored infidelity. Once she realized I was no relation, she'd shed her prickly exterior and started encouraging me to become more involved in the community. I sensed her invitation to tour the newly renovated building was part of her attempt to make amends, so I'd accepted, despite not feeling ready to step foot back into this building.

I fought to keep my expression neutral as I examined the freshly painted walls of the converted attic, hating them for being different than the way they'd been the last time I was here.

"What's wrong?" Penelope asked from beside me. "Is it the color?"

I glanced at her and forced myself to smile, shaking my head. "No, it looks great," I lied.

She beamed at me. "You really think so?"

"Yeah, it's really... great." *Oh, come on, brain. Be a thesaurus for five seconds.*

Penelope didn't seem to notice anything suspicious about my repetitive responses. She folded her arms across the chest of her Christian Dior floral-print blouse and nodded at the surrounding space. "It really came together once I realized I needed to use bright colors. Don't you just love that headboard?"

I didn't, but I could see that she did. Penelope smiled at the furnishings in the newly renovated "King Suite" like she'd just conquered the room in battle. Everything from the oversized striped fabric headboard to the boldly patterned trifold screen by the wardrobe was perfectly in line with her modern, expensive tastes. And truth be told, if this were just an ordinary hotel room, I probably would've liked it. But all I could see when I looked around the space was the furniture that used to be there and the woman who'd originally decorated it.

There'd been a privacy screen in this room before, but it'd been older, made of ornately carved wood with hand-painted maps of Spain between the frames. My friend and mentor, Gabrielle Suntador, had disappeared behind it once and returned with photos of my parents I'd never seen before. Those pictures were the most precious gift I'd ever received.

In the middle of the room, where a chic pair of couches stood atop a faux bearskin rug, there'd been a large, round table. I'd attended my first séance there. I'd accidentally summoned a poltergeist and kind of ruined the evening, but still, it didn't feel right that tourists and business travelers should do paperwork or read magazines on the spot where I'd first seen a full-bodied apparition float through a table and argue with his dad.

"This attic was remarkably livable already," Penelope said.

"Apart from installing the bathroom at the far end, we didn't have to do anything but paint the walls and replace the furniture." She tapped the hardwood beneath us with the toe of her sleek black pump. "Can you believe the floor didn't even have to be refinished?"

My tortoiseshell cat, Striker, sniffed the long, braided cord that hung from one of the paisley-patterned curtains adorning the wide dormer windows. She turned to look at me, her eyes narrowed into squints and her mouth open to display her fangs. It was the same face she made when she smelled something stinky.

"Mac, I swear to God, if she scratches those—"

"She won't." To ensure I was telling the truth, I rushed forward and scooped Striker up into my arms. I'd never seen her scratch anything other than her cat tower and cardboard scratching pads, but her feline sense of humor had a way of getting me into trouble.

"Good. Our first guests arrive tomorrow, so I don't have time to replace anything." She reached out to scratch Striker under her chin, an act that still surprised me whenever I saw it. "Do you want to see the rest of the rooms?"

"Uh…" I hesitated. Seeing the attic like this was painful, but only because of the memories there. I hadn't ever seen most of the other parts of the house, so hopefully… "Sure."

As Penelope led Striker and me around the second floor, pointing out where she'd had to knock out walls to make rooms bigger or add an entire extra bathroom, I marveled at how much she'd gotten done in a few short months.

"This is nothing. We finished The Enclave two weeks early, and that was thirteen buildings. But none of them were this exciting. Here, look at this." She pulled a flat metal oval out of her pocket. A symbol had been carved into it, like a cross with a teardrop for a top.

"Cool, an ankh." I took it from her. Its edges were smooth,

and the silver was darker in some places than others. The metal was cool to the touch.

"I thought you'd recognize it. You and Graham always seem to know about these things."

"Where did you find it?"

"That's the interesting thing. My contractor found dozens of hidden compartments all over the original bedrooms. We left the ones we could in place, like this."

She led me into a guest room papered with intricately patterned fleur-de-lis of varying sizes. She pushed gently on a section of wall above the dresser, and a small invisible door popped open. I gasped, and Penelope chuckled.

"That's the reaction I was hoping for. We couldn't save all the compartments, and some of them are in places too inconvenient to access, but we created one of these little surprises in all the standard guest rooms on this floor. We think it'll amuse the guests. Returning visitors might request a different room than the one they had before so they can discover a new 'Secret Stash.'"

On the other side of the tiny rectangular door, a brass plate explained the provenance of the compartment. Inside, little mints with the inn's logo waited on a paper doily.

"Cute," I told her. "This is where you found the ankh?"

"No, I think this one was packed with sage bundles."

I tried to hand the oval back to her, but she closed my fingers around it.

"Keep it. I have more in my office, and I'm sure Gabrielle would like you to have one." She smiled and shut the door to the hidden cubby. "She told me it'd be best if I left the protective items in place, but we'll be installing more modern precautions."

"You talked to Gabrielle?"

Penelope nodded. "I wrote to her when we first found the compartments. I wanted to be sure we located them all. We couldn't have some hidden place for a guest to hide something that leaves us liable."

"And she wrote back?"

"Yes, she was very helpful. She gave my contractor a list to work from."

I stared at her in stunned silence. Penelope had written a letter to Gabrielle Suntador—the woman currently awaiting trial for killing Penelope's husband—to ask for help? And what's more, Gabrielle had written back with tips to help Penelope make massive changes to her former home? The home she'd been so terrified of losing that she'd gotten mixed up in Penelope's husband's criminal enterprises in the first place? My mind struggled to process the information.

Unfazed by my sudden silence, Penelope led me into the bathroom to show off the faux-granite countertop. "Of course, our website doesn't explicitly say if it's real or not," she said with a wink. "But who can tell from a photo?"

Between the remodeled rooms and designer furniture, the old Victorian felt completely new. Penelope wasn't the first person in town to convert one of the historic mansions into a bed-and-breakfast, but I suspected the rest didn't come close to this level of luxury. It seemed like she was gunning for the top spot on the town's tourism website, which, I remembered, she oversaw.

"I have a feeling you're going to slay the competition," I told her.

She shook her head. "Not with the plans I have for this town. There won't be any vacancy in any inn, any weekend of the year once I'm through."

In the last few guest rooms, her staff was putting the finishing touches everywhere: hanging curtains, making up beds, and counting out the complimentary toiletries. The workers wore sedate black pants and white button-down shirts, but they seemed full of energy as they tossed things to each other and sang along with the pop station on the radio.

We followed Penelope down the stairs to the main floor. At the bottom, she gestured toward the coffee counter at the far end of the lobby. "And now, what I'm sure you've been waiting for most of all: our little French café. Would you care for a latte?"

I glanced toward the espresso machine. Its copper fittings gleamed, and rows of snow white, oversized mugs filled the wall behind it. A college-aged employee was brewing up something that smelled delicious, but the scent triggered a pang of grief that squeezed my heart. An involuntary coo escaped my throat.

It was quiet, but Penelope caught it. "Are you all right?"

What could I tell her? That I missed the smell of nag champa and old bindings that used to fill this room when it was the Nine Lives Bookstore? That I'd give anything to see Gabrielle smiling at me from behind the counter by the window? A fresh-faced kid stood there now, typing something into a computer that sat atop the registration desk. Antique witching supplies should have been on display beneath a sheet of glass; now it was a smooth, modern block of wood with the name of the inn, The Oracle, burned into the front in thick letters.

There was only one thing I liked about the room. Beside the desk, white shelves lined the wall, filled with sculptures by my favorite local artist. Graham Thomas specialized in ancient deities, and busts of Bastet and Hephaestus stared down at me from beside the wide front window. Outside, the trees were shedding tons of multi-colored leaves every day in preparation for the oncoming winter.

My eyes threatened to do some shedding of their own, but I fought to gain control of myself. I'd almost succeeded when Striker reached up a paw and touched my cheek, triggering one traitorous tear to roll down my face and splash onto her fur.

"Oh, Mac. I'm so sorry—I didn't even think." Penelope

squeezed my arm. "This is the first time you've been back here since they arrested Gabrielle, isn't it?"

I nodded, blinking the liquid out of my eyes. "It's okay. Really."

"You know, you can be honest with me. I understand better than you think. There's a reason I'm remodeling this place instead of the old motel."

She walked over to one of the sturdy, square tables that filled this half of the lobby and held up two fingers to the barista as she sat down. I took a seat across from her, holding Striker on my lap.

"What about the diner?" I asked.

Penelope's late husband, Tom, had run three major businesses in Donn's Hill. I'd heard through the rumor mill that he'd only owned one of them on paper, a shipping and delivery company he'd been using to transport stolen goods—things he'd burgled on his many trips out of town.

His other two businesses—a run-down motel called the E-Z Sleep and a diner with arguably the worst coffee I'd ever encountered—had been in Penelope's name. Whether that was for his own protection or because he'd foreseen his fate was anybody's guess. He'd been murdered earlier that year and, though his spirit had lingered long enough to see his killer apprehended, he hadn't been able to answer any questions.

"The diner will open again in a few weeks. We're keeping it simple and calling it Café on Main."

"I like it," I said.

"Thank you. It'll be a good, family restaurant. I'm just a silent partner though." She lifted her narrow chin and smiled up at the ceiling. "This place is my passion project."

The barista delivered the coffees to our table. Penelope took hers black, but I added some creamer and several heaping spoonfuls of sugar. She raised an eyebrow at me.

"You know I only buy the best beans."

"Sorry," I said. "Force of habit. I'm used to Graham's."

She smiled. "Ah, yes. I'm familiar with his preference for high-octane brews."

We sipped in silence for a moment. The coffee was good, but it would've been better with a donut. Or some pie.

"Speaking of new businesses in town," Penelope said, "they're tearing down the E-Z Sleep. The council has approved construction of a newer motel, one of the larger chains. There'll be a swimming pool and triple the number of rooms."

I frowned. "Won't that be bad for your business?"

She shook her head. "It won't be open for at least another year. By then, I expect tourism here to triple."

"How are you—"

A shout from behind us cut off my question. "Penelope!"

I twisted in my seat. Kit was marching across the lobby toward us so quickly that I swear her green hair was flying behind her in a streak. Her eyes narrowed in fury, and I cringed away from her. Kit didn't get angry often, but when she did…

She reached us and slammed her hand down on the table. "Raziel Santos? Are you kidding me?"

She lifted her hand, revealing a small flyer. A man about my age with severe cheekbones glared up at me from the sheet. He was doing something Kit's father Yuri often did, looking over the top of his glasses at the camera as though he didn't even need prescription lenses. His cold, light eyes looked almost as angry as Kit's. Below his photo, blue ink proclaimed RAZIEL SANTOS, FILMING LIVE FROM DONN'S HILL THIS OCTOBER!

"Who is Raziel Santos?" I asked.

"He's that jerk magician I told you about," Kit spat. "He's gotten famous on the back of the occult community. Specifically, by being a prick to psychics and the people who ask for their help."

"He's a world-renowned magician," Penelope said, pointedly

turning toward me as though to exclude Kit from the conversation.

"And paranormal debunker." Kit snatched up the flyer again and whipped it with the back of her hand. "*Why* would you invite him here? He's the opposite of everything Donn's Hill stands for."

Penelope shook her head. "That's not true. The town has a long history of inviting skeptics to the Afterlife Festival. Houdini's visit did wonders for our reputation."

"Raziel Santos is no Houdini," Kit growled.

"Your father seems to think so," Penelope said. "It was his idea to invite him here."

"Bullshit."

"We got to talking one night and…" Penelope tucked a strand of blond hair behind her ear and looked away from us. "And he recommended I reach out to Mr. Santos to invite him here."

Kit's nostrils flared, and crimson heat crept up her face from her collar. "If that were true, he would have told me."

"He knows how you feel about Mr. Santos. He thought—"

"Oh, so you two are talking about me now?" Kit threw her hands up into the air. "Great. That's great."

As they argued, I pulled out my phone and searched for Raziel Santos. The internet seemed to be as divided about him as Kit and Penelope. The top few results were fan pages that called him "mysterious and sexy," but there were also news reports of defamation lawsuits being filed against him and lots of angry forum posts. I clicked the link to his official website and scanned the homepage.

"Raziel Santos," proclaimed the silver script across the black background. "The truth is right here."

Striker rubbed her jaw on the lower corner of my phone. I reached down with my free hand to scratch between her ears. If I didn't pet her quickly enough, she'd bite my phone to get me to put it down.

"Kit, please." Penelope gestured to the empty chair beside her and held up a single finger to the barista. "Won't you sit down and talk about this rationally?"

"What is there to talk about? This guy is literally trying to destroy my father's show and everything we've worked for. And you're throwing him a freaking cocktail party?"

I raised an eyebrow at Penelope. "Cocktail party?"

She sighed and narrowed her gray eyes at Kit. "It's a reception, the kind you throw an honored guest. Mr. Santos and his team graciously agreed to film their next special here. We can't buy that kind of publicity."

Kit snorted and looked away, but I studied Penelope. Her cold eyes and pinched brow made her irritation clear, but she pulled her shoulders backward and kept her spine straight. She exuded confidence, same as she had in nearly every encounter I'd ever had with her. She was a smart woman. Or was shrewd the better word? Either way, I had a feeling she was right.

Penelope turned toward me then. "Speaking of which, dear, I was planning to invite you before you left here. Light hors d'oeuvres and drinks, Friday night at The Enclave."

I glanced at Kit, who was shooting daggers out her eyes at me. "Oh, Friday? Uh... Kit and I were going to—"

Penelope held up a hand. "No RSVP needed. Casual attire is fine if you attend." She stood, cradling her coffee cup in one hand. "If you'll excuse me, I have some paperwork left to do in my office and then a monstrous pile of tasks waiting for me at City Hall."

I moved to stand as well, but Penelope waved her hand at me.

"Stay and finish your coffee," she said. It was one part invitation, one part order. She left us with a final wave, disappearing behind a door near the coffee counter marked PRIVATE.

Kit threw herself into the chair across from me with a huff, reached over, and stole my coffee. She sipped it and scowled. "Of course it's amazing."

The young barista, as though on cue, hustled over to our table with a fresh mug. I reached for it, but Kit slapped my hand and slid my original cup back across the table.

"You ruined it with too much cream," she said.

"I thought it was 'amazing.'"

"Yeah, so I expect it to be mind-blowing when you treat it right."

"So. Want to explain why you're so pissed off at Penelope?"

"What, did your ears fall off? She invited that prick—"

"Come on, Kit," I said. "You told me yourself, your dad loves this guy. He was asking ScreamTV to sponsor a joint episode, right? Is this big special the thing he was asking them to do?"

"No." Her eyes flashed. "He wanted our teams to do something together. Here's the bottom line: Penelope put the idea into Dad's head. She's a manipulative, controlling psycho."

I blinked, taken aback. Her voice was much harsher than it'd been in the van, and her words were razor sharp. "You don't mean that."

"Oh, I mean it." She pushed back from the table and stood up. "Everyone looks at Penelope like she's the queen of this town, but the truth is, she'll be the death of it."

With that ominous proclamation, Kit stormed out of the inn, coffee cup and all.

CHAPTER THREE

Bright spots of late-morning sunlight crept across the floor of my apartment as two slices of bread popped out of my toaster. I spread some strawberry jam on them and pulled my laptop toward me.

Raziel Santos glared at me from the photo on my screen. His dour expression made me laugh; in all the photos I'd found online, he sported the same frown from behind a pair of sunglasses with light, honey-colored lenses. No smiles. No candid shots of him laughing with a friend. It all felt very forced.

I scrolled down to a section that featured recent episodes of his show. Despite only recently joining *ScreamTV*, the view counts on his videos numbered in the millions.

"Holy crap," I told Striker, who lounged in a puddle of sun on the rug. "This guy has a serious following."

"Brrrllll." She punctuated her statement with a yawn then rested her chin back on the floor. She didn't seem to share my interest in Kit's nemesis.

I clicked a video at random. Raziel stood on the sidewalk in front of a Las Vegas casino, trying to talk a passing tourist into being his "assistant." The tourist was a gray-haired older woman who shrieked in delight when Raziel made fire come out of her ears and somehow got her driver's license photo to appear on an electronic billboard down the street. The wailing guitar solos of the heavy metal soundtrack made me turn down the volume on my laptop's speakers.

Judging from the thumbnails, most of the videos were in the same vein. Raziel usually performed outside, impressing small gaggles of passersby with one magic trick or another. But a few rows down, the video image showed Raziel sitting in a maroon wing-back chair in front of a wall made from rough wooden planks. He intertwined his fingers in front of his face. Two stretched upward like a steeple, touching his lips. I clicked on the video.

"Hello, friends." Raziel laid his hands on the armrests beside him, which made him look like a monarch in a throne room. "Welcome to this week's episode. As promised, I'll be giving you a sneak peek at my newest illusion, *The Mage's Hand.* But first, I'd like to update you with some good news from the battlefront."

Battlefront? There'd been nothing in Raziel's bio or my research that mentioned military service or working as a war correspondent.

"The Midnight Lantern has officially ceased operations." Raziel closed his eyes and raised a fist into the air, silent for a moment. Then he looked back into the camera and spoke again. "Victory. Let this stand as a warning to all other ghouls and charlatans—your scams will not be tolerated. We're coming for you. And now: The Mage's Hand."

The video switched to footage of him in his usual habitat, a street corner in Las Vegas, where he appeared to be shuffling cards in midair. I clicked away into a search window, where I typed in "midnight lantern." The top result had Raziel's name right in the headline: *Santos Named in Midnight Lantern Defamation Suit.*

I scanned the article while munching on my toast. The Midnight Lantern reminded me of the shops in The Enclave, where psychics sold incense and tarot cards and offered readings. The owners were suing Raziel, claiming his internet videos about them had been a deliberate attempt to shut down their business. Raziel's legal team countered that he was protected under the First Amendment, and that he was simply a journalist reporting on the unscrupulous practices of a local business. In all the photos, the shop's owners looked devastated. Raziel looked giddy.

"Seems like a real peach," I told Striker.

My apartment door opened, and Graham Thomas strolled across the room like he owned the place. Which he did. Or rather, his father did. Besides cooking me romantic dinners and being my binge-watching buddy, Graham also collected my rent checks every month. He bent his lean frame against my kitchenette and promptly stole my second slice of toast.

"Have you been playing in a giant snow globe again?" I asked him. Flecks of white paint peppered his short brown hair, and larger splotches stained his green coveralls.

He grinned down at me. He was a full head taller than I was, and his thick-rimmed glasses seemed to give him the power to see the world in a much more relaxed way than I did. My heart skipped a beat every time my eyes met his and skipped again whenever he smiled, which was a lot.

"I wish," he said. "That'd be a lot more fun than painting the trim."

My heart skipped a third time, but this was a heavy thud followed by a long stretch of me worrying it wouldn't start up again. When it finally did, I had a request. "Don't tell me you get all the way up on the roof."

Primrose House, as the converted mansion was known, was a three-story tall yellow Victorian, complete with a many-peaked roof and intricate gables. The thought of Graham up that high, balanced on a ladder with a paint bucket and brush, was prime fodder for the anxiety generator in my brain. I'd had far too much death and loss in my life to even fathom losing him.

His smile faded, and he walked around the counter to pull me into a hug. "Hey, don't worry. I'm only working on the ground-level porches. I've hired professionals for the rest."

I pulled away from him, frowning. "Why not just have them do the whole thing?"

"Because I love the smell of paint." He ducked and pushed his hair into my face, shaking his head to tickle my nose. "Smell it. You'll see."

We dissolved into laughter, and he settled onto the stool beside me. Striker immediately jumped up into his lap, correctly guessing that he had a small bag of cat treats in his pocket.

"What are you up to?" he asked as he hand-fed Striker a snack.

I filled him in on Kit's tantrum at the inn, and the corners of his eyes crinkled in a smile.

"Man, she's really not on board with her dad and Penny hanging out together."

"How did you know about that?" Neither Kit nor Yuri had told me about Yuri and Penelope's budding romance; I'd had to put the pieces together from Yuri's frequent mentions of the deputy mayor at *Soul Searchers* jobs and the way Kit's eyes took on a murderous gleam every time the older woman's name came out of her father's mouth.

"I heard about it from my mom," Graham explained.

I should have guessed. Penelope was his mother's younger sister, and his mom frequently filled Graham in on the happenings in his aunt's life. The only thing weirder than my calm, coverallloving boyfriend being related to the most uptight and well-dressed person in town was hearing him constantly call her "Penny."

"How do you feel about it?" he asked.

I shrugged. "Indifferent, I guess? I love Yuri. He's like family. And Penelope's been warming up to me. If they make each other happy, I'm fine with it."

Graham smiled and gave me a gentle punch on the shoulder. "Why, Mackenzie Clair, you big softie. That's a very sweet sentiment."

He spoiled Striker while I returned to my research. On my laptop screen, Raziel Santos was grinning devilishly at the CLOSED sign that hung on the door of the Midnight Lantern. I understood why Kit wasn't excited to see him again.

"So, this is the famous 'jerk,' huh?" Graham nodded at the screen.

"Yep. Check out the size of his fanbase. This video has 1.4 million views, and it's not even a month old."

Graham whistled. "No wonder Penny wants him to come here."

"She's having a cocktail party reception for him tomorrow. Want to come with me?"

His eyes widened in mock surprise. "You don't mean… like, a date?"

"Oh, no. You've completely misread the situation. You'd be the chaperone."

"Right, right." He nodded, pushing out his lower lip in an exaggerated frown. "For you and Striker."

"For me and the food. You know Striker's been officially banned from any event featuring a buffet." It was partially true. After my cat had pulled a tablecloth—and food for twenty people —off a table at last spring's Afterlife Festival wrap party by attempting to climb it, Penelope had politely requested I leave my furry friend at home for catered events. It hadn't been an outright ban, but I read between the lines. If I insisted on bringing my cat to everything, certain tasty invitations would stop coming.

"Where's the party?" he asked.

"The Enclave."

"Oh, good."

I raised an eyebrow at him. "Were you worried it'd be somewhere else?"

"No."

"Liar."

"I wasn't worried," he insisted. "I just thought... you know... she might want to show off the renovations at the inn or something."

"What would be wrong with that?"

He didn't answer.

"I mean, I'll admit, it's super weird being in there now that it's not Gabrielle's store anymore. It's like..." The only similarity that came to mind was when I'd gone back into my father's house after he'd died. The building was the same; even the books on the shelves and the photos on the walls were exactly as he'd left them. But the entire house felt different. Hollow. Just knowing he'd never sit at the table with me again or pull down a volume on North American spiritual traditions and pore over it at his desk—I still couldn't think about it. I swallowed back the hard lump of sorrow that welled up in my throat and shook my head.

Graham wrapped one arm around me in another hug. "That must be hard. Have you heard from her at all?"

I almost admitted that I hadn't heard from Gabrielle since her trial date had been set, then I realized what he was doing. "No changing the subject. Why wouldn't you want to go to the inn? Penelope did a beautiful job, and the lobby is full of your sculptures—oh."

His face tightened at the mention of his artwork.

"Does that bother you?" I asked.

He shook his head. Then he bobbed it in an awkward, semi-diagonal nod.

"Why?" I asked.

"I don't know."

We sat in silence for a few moments while I tried to puzzle out what would make Graham uncomfortable with his sculptures getting some well-deserved attention. He was no stranger to people inspecting and—hopefully—purchasing his work; he had a tent at the Afterlife Festival every spring where tourists from all over the country bought up most of the statues he'd spent the past year creating. His hard work was finally paying off; he'd gotten into a competitive arts exhibition in Chicago, where he'd be selling his creations the following week.

"It just looks nepotistic," he said at last. "I don't want to stand there at the inn with all my sculptures everywhere, and everyone looking at my work and wondering if it's… I don't know…."

"Worthy?"

"Yeah."

"All anyone wonders when they look at your sculptures is how they can get their hands on one. And maybe if you're single. We should probably put up a sign."

He didn't laugh. He just stared down at his hands and pursed his lips.

"Will you go with me?" I asked. "Since it's at The Enclave?"

"Of course." He squeezed my hand. "I'd love to."

"Good, because here's what we're going to do." I stood up to rinse my plate. "Go to the cocktail party, make friends with Raziel Santos, and ride his coattails to true fame and glory. You know, trade nepotism for cronyism."

"Not funny," he said.

"The entire world shall know the great Graham Thomas!" I declared.

I was right about fame following Raziel. But as per usual, I was wrong about everything else.

CHAPTER FOUR

G raham whistled, long and low. "I've never seen anything like this."

We stood at the edge of an unimproved asphalt road in the manufacturing district at the edge of Donn's Hill, admiring the tiny, glowing wonderland that stretched before us. Two streets over, renovations were underway on the E-Z Sleep Motel. But here, another piece of the city had already been transformed.

Originally a pocket of two-story row houses built for miners, the neighborhood had been surrounded by larger industrial buildings in recent decades. Dilapidated and forgotten, the houses rotted on the outskirts of town, waiting to be torn down and replaced.

Then, Penelope Bishop had one of her famous big ideas. She convinced the city council to fund a restoration of the little half-acre lot and converted the run-down buildings into the occult equivalent of an art space called The Enclave.

The Enclave had opened over the summer to instant success with locals and tourists alike. The two rows of clapboard-clad townhomes faced each other across a cobblestoned footpath leading from the road to the pub. Old-fashioned gas lamps lined the path on both sides, and rustic wooden signs hung above every stoop, advertising the psychic readings or mystical products visitors could find inside.

Tonight, hundreds of strings of white twinkle lights crisscrossed between the buildings, reflecting off the cobblestones below and lending an ethereal, almost magical quality to the festivities. Cheerful, upbeat music drifted over the crowd from a jazz quartet stationed by the bar. At least a hundred people milled around the party, peeking in shop windows and snagging canapés and champagne flutes from the college-aged waiters who circulated through the crowd. Every few feet, tall circular tables gave the attendees a place to rest their plates while they stood and chatted.

"What are those centerpieces?" I wondered aloud.

My feet carried me closer to the table nearest the edge of the party, and I recognized one of Graham's statues: the headless body of Laverna, the trickster goddess, who held an elaborate, feathered mask in one hand. On the next table, the stooped figure of The Crone clutched a knobby walking stick. From what I could see, each table held a different piece from the collection of Graham's sculptures that'd been on display at the inn.

Still eying the statues, I asked, "Did you know these would be here?"

He didn't answer. I turned to look at him and realized he hadn't followed me up to the table. He stood at the edge of the asphalt, visibly pale in the twinkling lights. I walked back to his side.

"Hey, are you okay?" I asked.

He stared at the party, where guests were pointing excitedly at his creations. "Yeah. I just... uh... need a minute."

"I'm guessing she didn't clear this with you."

Penelope wasn't the type to ask permission. She wasn't even the type to ask forgiveness later. She was the type to say, "you're welcome," even if you hadn't thanked her for going over your head.

"Nope," he sighed.

"Do you want to go home?"

He thought about it and sighed. "No. We should stay. People have probably already seen us, and it'll get back to her that we bailed. It'll be weird."

"Okay." I stood beside him, waiting until he was ready to step over the invisible line that separated his position of safety on the road and actually entering the party.

He made a good show of staying back for a reason, straightening his tie and pulling out a small cloth to clean his glasses. After watching him complete a few cycles of huffing on the lenses, rubbing them, then holding them up to the lights to squint at them for any signs of smudging, I elbowed him in the ribs.

"I don't mean to rush you, but this sweater isn't really cutting it out here." Through the loose-knit black fabric, the cold pricked my skin. Just a few yards ahead, a group of similarly under-dressed partygoers clustered around a tall propane heater. "Can we put off the inevitable somewhere a little warmer?"

"Sorry." Cheeks flushing, he pocketed his lens cloth and pushed his glasses back onto his face.

"Still nervous?"

He nodded, looking glum.

"Okay, I know she sprung this on you. But that doesn't change the fact that your sculptures are amazing. How many custom orders did you get at the Afterlife Festival?"

"Sixteen," he murmured.

"And how many of your existing sculptures did you sell?"

His face grew redder. "Eighty-four."

"Yeah. Eighty-freaking-four." I squeezed his arm. "Like I said, amazing. You should be proud. *I'm* proud of you, even though I have no right to be."

He pulled me into a tight hug. "Thanks, Mac," he whispered into my hair.

"Hey, get a room, guys." Kit's voice rang out from behind us. "Not at the Oracle, though. I hear it's run by a backstabbing beast-monster."

She stomped past us in a tattered Vandals t-shirt and pushed her way through the crowd until she found a waiter. She grabbed two glasses of champagne and disappeared past another clump of guests.

I started walking toward the party, pulling Graham's hand behind me, but was forced to stop when he didn't move.

"Do we have to stay for long?" he asked.

"We'll leave whenever you want. When you're ready, do this." I lifted my right hand, touched my pinky and third finger together, held my pointer and middle fingers slightly apart, and stretched my thumb out at far as it would go. I did the same thing with my left hand, but flipped it around so that the two shapes faced the same direction. I let them rise and fall through the air a few times, flapping my fingers lightly.

Graham laughed. "What is that supposed to be?"

I scoffed. "A sculptor who can't even see the shapes right in front of him. It's two birds soaring the skies together." I repeated the flapping motion, nodding my head toward the shadow of the birds cast on the ground by the twinkling lights ahead. "As in, 'Let's fly!'"

He was still laughing, but he humored me and tried to mimic the way I held my hands. "Where'd you learn how to do that?"

"My dad." I reached out and helped him make the shapes, pressing his fingers together. "He always dragged me to these boring parties at the university, and he hated it when I'd tug on his jacket and whine to go home." I smiled at the memory. "This was his way of giving me a quiet way out."

Graham's shadow puppets were messy and hardly looked like

birds. We giggled, ignoring the stares of passing guests for a few more minutes before he finally sighed, straightened up, and nodded. He was ready.

As I'd suspected, every single table held one of Graham's pieces. Small metal placards asked guests not to touch the sculptures and displayed tiny prices in the high triple digits. At the far end of the cramped lot, an enormous, wooden bar blocked the entrance to the Ace of Cups. Atop a pedestal in the exact middle of the bar, a huge bust of the Irish god for whom the town had been named scowled at the crowd. A small clump of people had gathered around Donn, the guardian of the afterlife. The onlookers ooh-ed and ahh-ed and restrained themselves from running their fingers down the intricately sculpted details on Donn's armor.

I nudged Graham again. "See? They love it."

He snatched two glasses off a passing tray and handed one to me. "Look, let's pretend none of my work is here. As far as I'm concerned, this is just one of Penny's over-the-top parties."

"Deal."

We meandered up and down the cobblestone path for a while, admiring the way the neighborhood had been transformed for the party. None of the shops were open, but their windows displayed occult supplies, books of folklore and fairy tales, and collections of crystal jewelry. As the champagne glow kicked in, a smile spread across Graham's rosy face. I relaxed, looping my arm through his and pulling him toward a buffet table laden with food provided by the Ace of Cups.

We joined Kit near a tray of bruschetta, but she wasn't much for small talk. She clutched a champagne flute in each hand and glared at something across the party. I followed her gaze; Yuri and Penelope were laughing together near the bar. Kit set down one of her glasses, angrily snatched up a slice of bread, and stuffed it into her mouth. Knowing better than to try to talk her down out of a rage, I grabbed Graham's hand and led him away, leaving Kit to wallow in her own miasma.

"Graham!"

I twisted and caught sight of a tall, thin man in his early forties, side-stepping his way through the crowd with a glass of champagne in his hand. We stopped at a table where a carving of the two-faced god Janus was watching the bar with one set of eyes and the street with the other, and waited for the man to catch up to us. Like me, Stephen Hastain was a recent transplant to Donn's Hill. He'd moved here in June to be part of The Enclave's inaugural set of residents and had made fast friends with Graham, joining my boyfriend on fishing trips and talking to Graham's dad about modern life in Ireland, where Stephen grew up.

The rune caster, who specialized in throwing small objects and interpreting the results, reached us and clinked his glass against each of ours. "*Sláinte!*"

"Cheers," I replied, sipping my champagne. "How come you're not in your shop?"

Not far from our table, the window of a salmon-colored building announced that visitors could seek guidance within Ancient Answers. Like many other residents of The Enclave, Stephen kept his business on the first floor and lived on the second. Tenants could rent units for far below the going rate, provided they practiced some form of arcane art. The only exception was the Ace of Cups, and even they claimed their bartenders were gifted with a psychic ability to sense the drink you really needed, regardless of what you actually ordered.

I'd expected all the stores and psychic parlors to be taking advantage of the large crowd here, but the sign on every shop's door read CLOSED.

"Penelope expressly forbade anyone from working tonight. No unfair competition." Stephen laughed and ran a hand through his long curls, his cheeks pink with excitement. "I don't mind. I'd hate to miss a party this good."

"You're still in for tomorrow, right?" Graham asked his friend.

The Irishman grinned. "All signs point to 'yes.' Who else is coming?"

"The *Soul Searchers*." I elbowed my date lightly. "And Graham."

"Well, I knew that already." Stephen smiled at him. "Thanks again for asking your better half to include me."

"You'll be great," Graham said. "But I'm not sure why she wants me there."

"You helped with my first smoke cleansing," I reminded him. "I'll just feel better if you're there."

He grabbed my hand and gave it a light squeeze. "Then I'm in."

"Who else?" Stephen asked.

I nodded and swept the room with my eyes, seeking out the other two local psychics—more often called "intuitives" in Donn's Hill's social circles—who'd agreed to help. I spotted my volunteers near the buffet and gestured at them with my glass. Daphne and Nick Martin's dark-haired heads huddled together over plates of canapés, their dour expressions at odds with the lively chatter and energetic jazz music that filled the air. Daphne swept her long ponytail back over one shoulder and returned my wave, a small smile creeping onto her face.

"The twins?" Stephen asked.

Graham snorted.

"Twins?" I frowned. Daphne and Nick shared the same thick, straight black hair and heavy eyebrows, but the similarity stopped there. "Aren't they married?"

"They are," Graham said. "Stephen's just being an ass."

Stephen threw up his hands. "Hey, an honest mistake. I'm new in town, remember?" He winked, then nodded at Daphne. "She's read my tarot before. She's good. Very calming demeanor."

The memory of the howling winds and thrashing trees Richard Franklin's ghost had summoned the last time I'd seen him filled my mind and sent a shudder through my body. Calm was what we needed.

"Have you ever seen Nick work?" Graham asked.

Stephen shook his head. "His readings always sell out. By the way, that photo you sent over gave me the heebie-jeebies. The Franklin kid has a real Charles Manson vibe. Crazy eyes."

In preparation for our upcoming investigation, Yuri and I had emailed all the participants a file with details about the location and the spirit who lurked there. We'd included a yearbook photo of Richard Franklin, taken before the budding sociopath had been expelled from his prep school for orchestrating a hazing that resulted in the death of a freshman. He'd been a handsome kid, but the vacancy in his light eyes betrayed a lack of humanity.

Just as I was mentally casting around for a change of subject, Kit pushed her way between us and slammed a hand down on the tabletop. The statue of Janus wobbled. Graham winced.

"What's the holdup?" Kit growled, swaying slightly. "Is this prick gonna make us wait all night or what?"

Stephen raised a salt-and-pepper eyebrow. "Big Raziel fan, huh?"

Kit grabbed a champagne flute from the tray of a passing waitress and snorted. "You couldn't pay me to watch his crap. The only people who follow that *idiot*"—she punctuated the word by banging on the table again—"are idiots."

I stared at her. I'd never seen her drunk before. Her normally friendly eyes had become fiery slits, and the frown on her face erased the illusion of agelessness she usually enjoyed. It was a familiar expression; I'd seen it in the mirror anytime I caught a glimpse of myself remembering what my ex-boyfriend had done to me. It screamed of heartbreak and betrayal.

"Kit." I rested a hand on her elbow and kept my voice low. "Do you want to get out of here? We could—"

She swore quietly, but it wasn't directed at me. Her eyes were fixed on the Ace of Cups. A hush fell over the crowd, and I turned to see a tall, thin man wearing honey-colored sunglasses standing at the open doorway of the pub.

Raziel Santos had arrived.

CHAPTER FIVE

He looked as calculatedly pompous in person as he had online. His thickly lined eyes swept the party from behind his ridiculous glasses, his face expressionless. His thin arms crossed tightly in front of his deep V-neck tee, through which I could see writing tattooed across his chest.

Everyone watched the guest of honor in silence except for the musicians, and I half expected a footman to materialize from beside Raziel to announce His Royal Highness to all the peasants. Instead, a young woman with deep brown skin and a shaved head pushed him gently from behind. His movement broke the hush, and the babble around us started up again. Raziel moved down the steps toward the bar, waving to Yuri and Penelope as the bald woman smiled at the crowd.

I turned back to Kit, expecting to find her glaring at Raziel, but her gaze was fixed on the woman he'd been with.

"Shit," she muttered. "Shit, shit."

"Are you okay?" I asked.

She finally looked at me, her brown eyes wide with panic. "I'm not ready for this."

Without another word, she bolted toward the street. I moved to follow her, but Graham grabbed my arm.

"Stay," he said. "I'll get her home and come back."

"Are you sure?" I asked.

"Yeah, I wouldn't mind a break from all this. And you should stay here and try to network or whatever." He raised an eyebrow and tilted his head forward, indicating something behind me. "Start by talking to her."

I turned around to find Raziel's companion making a beeline for our table through the crowd with a cocktail glass in her hand. Stephen gasped audibly, and I kicked him under the table.

"You're Mackenzie Clair, right?" she asked when she reached us. Her voice was strongly accented.

"I am."

"I'm Amari Botha, Raziel Santos' manager."

"Oh." I shook her hand, then laughed. "This is kind of awkward... I've never introduced myself to someone who already knows my name before."

"Get used to it." She grinned, revealing dimples in both cheeks. "Your show is very popular and growing every week. You'll be a household name before you know it."

In an effort to hide my discomfort, I sipped my champagne. In Donn's Hill, psychic gifts were so normal that even the local sheriff's department didn't bat an eye when the only "evidence" I had to back up my tips were based on a conversation I'd claimed to have with the murder victim.

But I hadn't been living in Donn's Hill long enough to forget what the rest of the world thought of psychics and mediums. Most of what the average person knew came from campy horror movies. Based on the video comments Kit kept telling me not to read, half our viewers only watched our show because they were hoping we'd do something that proved we'd been faking things all along. Very few people were true believers, and they usually kept it to themselves. Publicly believing in religion was one thing. Believing in ghosts? That was something else entirely. Best-case scenario in which I'd become a household name: I'd be a very famous freak.

"This is Stephen Hastain." I gestured to my tablemate, who was currently making a big show of rubbing his shin beside me.

"Pleasure to meet you. And... did I see Kit over here a moment ago?" Amari asked.

"Yeah..." I eyed Amari, trying to read her expression. It definitely didn't match the panic on Kit's face. If anything, she was *too* relaxed. Too casual. "She wasn't feeling well. She went home."

"Oh." Disappointment flashed across Amari's eyes. She cleared her throat, and I waited for her to continue.

She didn't.

"Do you know Kit?" I asked.

Amari flashed her dimples again. "We met in L.A. last spring. We promised to keep in touch, but I've done a bad job of it."

I stared at her. Kit had been in Los Angeles earlier that year; that much was true. She and Yuri had gone to meet with the executives at ScreamTV about the contract for *Soul Searchers*, successfully negotiating an additional season with the network. That was all she'd talked about when they got back. Well, that, and how angry she was that she'd missed getting to see me banish a poltergeist for the first time.

I racked my brain for any memory of her talking about someone named Amari. She had never mentioned her, and given the way she'd nearly vomited all over the cocktail table the second Amari walked into the room, it was odd that Kit had never uttered her name to me before.

Odd... and irresistibly intriguing. I wrestled a grin off my face as I forced myself to stop imagining the grief I was going to give Kit about it later. Once she felt better, of course.

"Well," I said, "welcome to Donn's Hill. Have you been here before?"

Amari shook her head. "It's been on my list of places to visit for a very long time. I was thrilled to receive the invitation from Mrs. Bishop."

I glanced at Penelope; she and Yuri were having an animated conversation with Raziel. She waved her arms at the buildings around us, no doubt explaining how much work they'd put into restoring them.

"And what are you, Australian or something?" Stephen asked. "Your accent's pretty thick."

Amari didn't miss a beat. "You should talk, Irish boy."

I hid a smile behind my champagne glass, enjoying the banter. But Stephen's eyes narrowed; he didn't seem to catch the playful tone in Amari's voice.

"That's no answer," he said.

Amari looked taken aback. After a moment, she said, "Johannesburg."

"Oh," Stephen said.

We all sipped our drinks in awkward silence. Amari stared at her martini. I stared at the cobblestones beneath our feet. Stephen stared at Amari.

After a minute, she swirled the vodka in her glass and smiled at me. "Well, it's been a pleasure talking to you. I need to check on a few things with Raziel. Please tell Kit I said hello."

"I will." I gave her a farewell wave, then whipped my head around to fire a few eye-daggers at Stephen. "What the hell was that?"

"What?" His eyes were wide and innocent, like he honestly didn't know he'd been acting like a total weirdo the last few minutes.

"The gasp? The staring? Asking about her accent in the rudest way possible? Were you trying to make her uncomfortable, or are you that good by accident?"

He laughed. "Didn't you get the memo? Raziel Santos is a class-A arsehole. I don't care if Penelope thinks he's the key to year-round tourism. He's the enemy."

I raised an eyebrow, and Stephen rolled his eyes.

"Come on, don't tell me you're okay with him being here. He hates people like us. Look at his website—he calls us criminals."

"Yeah, I saw it." I nodded toward Amari, who was chatting with another group of people across the room. "But why be rude to her? She's just his manager."

Stephen laughed again. It was a bitter, harsh sound. "She's his biggest disciple. Did you know she gave up a cushy job in Silicon Valley to follow him around like a puppy? She's some kind of marketing genius. The only reason that gombeen has a following at all is because of her."

"'Gombeen?'" I repeated.

"Eh, huckster, I suppose. You know, snake oil salesman." He bolted down the rest of his champagne, burped, and reached for another flute from a passing waiter. "Anyway, he's the devil, and she's the devil's publicist."

A heaviness was building inside my stomach. I didn't like the pattern emerging around me: too much champagne combined with too much negativity. I patted Stephen on the arm then made my way back to the best part of the party.

Two huge buffet tables were laden with food, and I headed straight for the trays of pastries, cookies, and other bite-size sugar bombs. I scanned the offerings for any sign of Penelope's famous lemon bars, then saw a small sign reminding me the pub had provided the catering. I settled for a plate of brownies and several light, fluffy cream puffs, my logic being that they'd combat the anxious weight at the bottom of my belly.

Across the table, Daphne and Nick piled food onto their

plates. Daphne shot me a sheepish grin and nodded toward my stack of cream puffs.

"Careful," she said. "Those things are dangerous."

I returned the smile. "I think I can handle them. Not to brag, but I'm a snacking expert."

"You and my husband both," she said.

Nick elbowed her. "Which one of us put away more shrimp kabobs on the 4th of July, huh?"

The two of them laughed, which accentuated the similarity in their features. I suddenly understood why Stephen had called them twins; they kept mirroring each other's facial expressions and punctuating jokes with the same playful tones. I wondered if they'd had those things in common to start, and that's where the attraction had begun, or if they'd picked up each other's habits unconsciously over time. Would that happen to Graham and me? I counted myself lucky that we didn't already look alike.

"Were you at the grand opening?" Daphne asked me.

I shook my head. "We had to film an episode that weekend."

"Shame," said Nick. "It was a rager."

"If it was anything like this, I believe you," I said.

"This is better, though. All the shops were open that night, so I hardly got to enjoy the party." Daphne popped a cream puff in her mouth and smiled happily.

"Aren't you losing money?" I gazed around at the sea of people crammed into the little neighborhood. It was a bigger crowd than I'd ever seen here, even during the brunch rush at the Ace of Cups. Penelope's decision to close the shops struck me as strange.

Daphne shrugged. "Penelope only invited people who are part of the permanent community here. City council members, the Chamber of Commerce. You know, mucky-mucks. No tourists. Half the people here have never set foot into my shop and aren't likely to in the future."

Heat touched my cheeks as my eyes flicked toward Daphne's shop. Gold ink on the window spelled "Visions" in flowing, vintage script. I'd never been inside or visited any other parlor in The Enclave. Whenever Graham and I came here, we made straight for the pub. The other buildings didn't have any food, so I didn't really see the appeal.

She noticed the chagrined expression on my face and laughed. "Don't feel bad. Readings aren't everyone's cup of tea."

"I'd like to try it sometime," I said honestly.

"You're welcome anytime. First reading's on the house."

"Thanks," I said, following them away from the buffet and toward another tall cocktail table. "I've heard you're great. Both of you. I can't thank you enough for agreeing to do the show this weekend."

"It's our pleasure," Nick said.

"We'd do anything for Yuri," Daphne added. "He's the reason we moved here."

I raised an eyebrow. "Really?"

Nick nodded. "I met Yuri a few years ago at a paranormal expo in Vegas. I was finally starting to get some traction, but I was still unknown. He did me a solid and introduced me to some of his contacts. Really helped me get ahead."

"Six months later, Nick's career took off, and we used the first big check to move here," Daphne said.

"Best decision you ever made," said an unfamiliar voice from behind me.

The muscles in Nick's face tightened, and I turned to follow his gaze. A short, skinny kid who barely looked old enough to drink the champagne in his hand stood uncomfortably close to me, and I quickly sidestepped to put some space between us. He stepped forward, filling the gap and crowding the table.

Daphne's smile didn't reach her eyes. "Mac, this is Kev—"

"Fang," the newcomer interrupted. He saluted me with his

champagne flute then turned to my tablemates. "I hate to steal you away from this lovely young woman," he said, despite being at least five years my junior. "But I need your help. The old hag is complaining about The Enclave to the town council."

Daphne rolled her eyes. "Neighborhood drama. Sorry, Mac. We'll see you tomorrow, okay?"

The adult person who'd decided he wanted to be known professionally as "Fang" pressed his palms together and bowed toward me before straightening up and scuttling after Nick and Daphne.

Left on my own, I people-watched for a while. The air had a good energy, and the music was just loud enough to give the party some energy without forcing you to shout to be heard by the other people at your own table. I returned to the buffet one more time, snagged more cream puffs, and nibbled my snacks until Graham found me.

"Kit get home okay?" I asked. Kit's apartment was in Primrose House too, on the floor below mine. Having your landlord walk you home when you were drunk and angry was just one of the many unofficial perks included in the rent.

"Yeah, I got her settled on the couch." Graham stole a cream puff, popped it in his mouth, and sighed. "I'm worried about her."

"Me too."

"Have you talked to Raziel yet?"

I shook my head. "But his manager came over wanting to talk to Kit."

"Kit?"

"Yeah, there's some history there."

"Well, that explains why she bolted." Graham nodded toward Amari, who'd joined Yuri and Penelope at Raziel's side near the bar. "Do you think that's the real reason Kit was angry they were coming? Because she didn't want to see his manager?"

"Could be. But Stephen hates Raziel too. Maybe he's just that awful." I stuffed the last brownie into my mouth, finishing my thought around the gooey chocolate. "Let's go find out."

I grabbed Graham's hand and dragged him through the crowd, stopping in the shadow of the huge statue of Donn that watched over the party from his position on the bar.

"Ah, here he is now," said Penelope, tilting her champagne glass toward us. "This is my nephew, Graham Thomas. He's one of our most popular local artisans and is responsible for this incredible tribute to our town's namesake."

My heart swelled, and I squeezed Graham's hand. If you'd have told me on my first day in town that I'd want to hug Penelope Bishop, I'd have laughed you right out of the county. *Donn's Hill does strange things to people,* I decided.

Graham's hand tightened in mine. "Thank you, Penny."

"Lovely work," said Raziel. "I especially like your interpretation of the guardian of Hell that's protecting the buffet."

He lifted his chin toward the food where a three-headed puppy with large, circular eyes appeared to be begging for scraps. It was one of Graham's latest pieces and the first that'd ever hinted at his weird sense of humor.

"So whimsical," Raziel continued. "Well done."

The stiffness melted out of Graham's features. He relaxed into his familiar, slouching posture against the bar and smiled. "Thank you. That means a lot."

I hid a smile of my own behind my glass, grateful Kit wasn't here to witness me having a pleasant conversation with a person she hated so much.

Up close, Raziel confirmed most of the impressions of him I'd gathered from my research the day before. He had the same air about him as Penelope, where you could immediately tell he had the money to spend on big-name designer brands. Unlike Penelope, though, his style was less Upper East Side and more upscale goth. Up close, I could make out the letters tattooed across his chest: *Veritas Vincat*. He ignored the trays of champagne, sipping instead from a silver flask engraved with a skull.

"And you must be Mackenzie Clair." Raziel held out a hand. "It's a pleasure."

For the second time that night, I was meeting someone who already knew my name. A warm flush crept up my neck as I shook Raziel's hand, and Amari winked at me from over his shoulder. I got the feeling she was silently laughing at my discomfort. For some reason, that made me feel better.

"Nice to meet you," I said. "Welcome to Donn's Hill. How do you like it so far?"

"It's lovely. I'm staying in the attic suite at the Oracle Inn, and it's full of delightful surprises." Raziel took a swig from his flask and leaned back against the counter, mirroring Graham's relaxed posture, and abruptly changed the subject. "So. I heard you're exorcising the infamous Franklin Cabin ghost this weekend."

"Oh…" I was about to ask how he knew about that, since we hadn't been publicizing it. The only people who knew about it were the psychics I'd invited along and the Soul Searchers themselves. I glanced at Yuri, who looked at me intently but said nothing. I knew immediately he'd told Raziel about the investigation, and there could be only one reason why. I gulped. "Yeah, we are."

"I'd like to come along."

I knew it. I pictured the scene: the nine of us who were already planning to take part in the séance, and now Raziel and his crew with all their extra equipment? It'd be way too many people. Way too much chaos.

Gabrielle hadn't been able to make good on her promise to mentor me before being arrested for murder, but there was one thing she'd taught me at the very first séance I'd ever attended: nine was a powerful number. And when my weekend plans involved visiting a notoriously haunted cabin to summon a

murderous spirit just so I could banish him into the next realm…
Well, I needed to make sure I was at maximum power.

I shook my head. "I'm sorry. I don't think it's a good idea. If
we have too many people, Richard Franklin's ghost might not
show up."

"I won't bring my crew," he pressed. "It'll just be me and
Amari."

I thought about Kit and the way her entire demeanor had
changed the second Amari had walked into the room. Much as I
would derive some eventual pleasure from teasing her, I didn't
want to torture her. Glancing at Amari, I said, "I don't know if
you know the, uh, history between your manager and my
producer—"

Raziel held up both hands to stop me from continuing.
Flaming pentagrams were tattooed into each of his palms. "I get
it. I don't want to cramp your style. Just me, then."

The weight in my belly that'd earlier threatened to ruin my
evening came back. I hated having to say no to people, and Raziel
was forcing me to say it again and again. "Look, you probably
know this better than I do, since you've been in the psychic
community a lot longer than me, but everyone has their methods,
right? The habits that let them tap into their power? Well, part of
my method is that we have nine participants. No more, no less."

Yuri frowned at me, peering at me over the tops of his glasses
the way he did when he was trying to teach me something important. I could tell what was coming next. He was about to overrule
my decision and invite this outsider to the cabin with us. Again, I
imagined us all there. Nine of us in a circle, cameras on tripods
staring down at us from the fringes. Raziel's tenth shape was like
a shadow in my mind, a negative energy distracting me from the
work at hand. It was strange; he'd been so nice to us all so far. His
compliments to Graham were enough to buy him several weeks of
goodwill in my book. But something deep in my gut shivered at

the thought of him joining us for the séance. I knew with a certainty I couldn't place that it'd be better to call the whole thing off than to have him there.

I shook my head at Yuri, wishing I had a pair of glasses of my own to glare at him over. "I'm sorry," I told Raziel again. "It has to be nine. Not ten."

A hard glint flashed into his eyes, but he smiled at me. "Another time, then." He turned to Penelope, gave her a kiss on the cheek, and stepped away from our little circle. "If you'll excuse me, I'd love to meet more of your local talent."

As he walked away, Graham raised an eyebrow at me and mouthed, *Are you okay?*

I nodded at him but raised my hands and formed them into two birds. *Caw!* I mouthed back.

He grinned. I wanted to smile, but I couldn't shake the feeling that—despite Raziel's quick agreement to stay away from the cabin—this wasn't over.

CHAPTER SIX

Two tendrils of steam curled lazily upward from a pair of mugs on Kit's desk, coaxed toward the ceiling by the cool air drifting in from the open bay window. Striker lay on the cushioned window seat there, her tail swishing back and forth as she gazed at the birdhouse hanging from a large sycamore tree.

Kit's apartment sat on the opposite side of Primrose House from mine and one floor down. Like mine, the tiny kitchenette encouraged frequent use of the shared full-sized kitchen downstairs. But unlike my airy studio, which was sparsely furnished and had an open floor plan, Kit's apartment was a tight collection of several rooms, each more crammed with gear and equipment than the last. Two gigantic computer monitors rested on top of her desk, dominating the living room. Right now, video editing software took up the main screen, and footage of Daphne Martin reading a tourist's tarot cards played on the secondary monitor.

Kit's eyelids sagged, and she squinted at the screen. Her acid-green hair was matted on one side, but the rest stood straight up in clumps and spikes. Dark circles ringed her eyes, but I couldn't tell if they were signs of poor sleep or just the remnants of yesterday's eyeliner. I nudged the mug of coffee I'd brought her and took a sip of my own. She followed my example, sipped, and sighed.

"How was the rest of the party?" Her voice was a rough croak.

"Not too bad, except Raziel tried to horn in on our séance." I filled her in on our conversation, feeling proud of myself for standing up to him the night before.

She frowned so deeply I thought she was about to swear and spit on the ground, something she'd told me her Russian grandmother would do when confronted by something evil or suspicious. "I knew that weasel would try something like that. I bet he wanted to bring his crew and film the whole thing so he could edit it to make it look like we're a bunch of frauds."

I studied her face, trying to decide if she was being serious or just hyperbolic. It was hard to make out anything under the layer of exhaustion that muted her features. "Is that what he does?"

"That's *all* he does. He hates people like us. It's his mission in life to destroy us. I think a psychic must have beat the crap out of him when he was a kid or something."

"I don't get it... Why does your dad like him?"

She rolled her enormous eyes. "No clue."

If everything Kit said was true, I couldn't square any of it with the warm way Yuri treated Raziel. Yuri was one of the biggest champions of the paranormal community. He'd been a driving force in attracting new talent to Donn's Hill, and I knew from experience that he truly believed in the positive power psychics could bring to bear in tough situations. Why would he promote someone who seemed determined to put people like us out of business?

"Has Raziel ever gone after your dad?" I asked.

She shook her head. "Not yet. But he will. I can feel it. And when he does, he'll regret it."

We drank our coffee in silence for a few minutes, and I

watched Kit for the telltale signs of caffeine kicking in. Soon enough, she sat a little straighter in her chair. She ran both hands through her hair, which made her look just normal enough that I thought it was fair to bring up Raziel's manager.

"Amari says hello, by the way."

Kit's reaction was even better than I'd hoped. She coughed, spat coffee across her keyboard, and sputtered for several seconds. I grinned at her; she glared at me.

"You meant to do that," she accused, pointing at the droplets of Graham's daily diesel fuel that dotted her monitor.

"Couldn't resist." I got up and grabbed some paper towels from her kitchenette. "Why didn't you tell me about her?"

She shrugged, but a crimson tinge of embarrassment washed over her face as she cleaned up her mess. "We had a lot of other crap going on, remember? I didn't think me going on a single date ranked as high as you banishing a spirit from your apartment for the first time."

"It must've been one hell of a date." I raised an eyebrow as I slid back into my seat. "The way Amari asked about you... seems like you left a pretty big impression."

Kit snorted. "Could've fooled me. She never called."

"Did you call her?"

"Well... no. But she lives in L.A., and I'm out here. Plus, she's Raziel's toadie." She snarled down at her coffee mug. "It wouldn't have worked anyway."

I had to ask the question that burned at me most of all. "Did you know she was his manager when you went out with her?"

"Nope. She didn't tell me."

"How did you meet?"

"Dating app. Dad wanted to go to dinner with the ScreamTV people, but we'd been at their office all freaking day already, and I'd had enough glad handling. I'd heard there was a cool arcade bar near the hotel, but didn't want to check it out alone, so…" She shrugged again. "No big deal."

I smirked. "'No big deal,' huh? Yeah, that totally explains why you nearly threw up on your shoes the second you saw her."

Her blush deepened, but she said nothing.

"I have a theory," I told her. "Want to know what I think?"

She stiffened and eyed me in silence.

"I think you fell for her," I said. "Hard. But she never called, and now you're all sulky."

Kit crossed her arms over her chest. "Yeah, right."

"Hmm. No incredulous snort? No eye roll?" I leaned in and jabbed her with a finger. "No denial."

She turned back to her computer. "I don't have time for this. I'm on a deadline."

When Kit ended a conversation, you could hear the heavy vault door closing and a dozen locks slamming home. If my theory was true—which, in my mind, her reaction proved—then she was still stinging about what'd happened in L.A. I didn't have the heart to keep teasing her about it, so I relaxed into my chair. "Okay. I'll behave, for now. What are you working on?"

"Well, you know how we usually start off the episode with footage introducing the place we're investigating and the people who think it's haunted?"

I nodded. Kit and our cameraman, Mark, would typically gather what they called "B-roll" footage of the town or city and get shots of the family that lived in the house going about their daily business. Yuri would record a voiceover, delivering background information about the location's history and the people that lived there. I never felt like the episode truly began until Yuri actually appeared on screen, arriving at the location we'd be investigating.

"This time, the people we need to introduce aren't the ones who asked us to investigate the cabin since it was our idea to go back there." Kit laughed, looking genuinely awake for the first time that day. "So instead, I'm putting together intro sequences for our guest psychics."

"Oh, cool. Did you and Mark shoot this video of Daphne?"

I indicated the soundless monitor. On screen, Daphne was wearing a thick, brightly colored shawl and flipping over a tarot card. She smiled encouragingly at the tank-top clad teenager in front of her and said something, presumably explaining the meaning of the card.

Kit shook her head. "No, we didn't have enough time. ScreamTV wants this episode next week, which is cutting it crazy close. Luckily, everyone has existing footage for their own websites, so we're just borrowing that."

"Do you have it all?"

"Yeah, we're all set. And Dad already recorded his voiceovers, so I'm just picking the shots to use. I'm hoping to have this part all buttoned up before we head out to the cabin tonight."

I settled back into my seat to watch Kit work for a while. This part of the job fascinated me; she'd watch a long chunk of uncut footage with no sound as she took notes in her sketch-book. Then, she'd go back through and grab sections of video and pull them into a different screen along with a recording of Yuri's voiceover. Watching her tweak the clips to fit Yuri's words was like watching someone work with a literal magic wand.

It was relaxing, sitting there beside her open window, listening to the clicks of her mouse and the chirps of the birds outside. I'd just about nodded off when a sudden burst of laughter erupted from her mouth. Kit shook in her chair, cracking up at a close-up shot of Nick's face. His lips pushed outward in a strange expression somewhere between a frown and a kiss as he nodded slowly at someone in his audience.

"He thinks he looks serious," she gasped between bouts of laughter. "But he just looks like he ate some bad sushi."

I leaned in toward the monitor but didn't find it quite as funny as Kit did. Sure, it was an odd expression, but her reaction...

"Did you stay up all night editing?" I'd thought she'd woken up just before I arrived with the coffee, but now I suspected she hadn't gone to sleep at all. She was way too giddy to have gotten a solid eight hours.

Her laughter subsided, and she wiped at the already-smudged liner beneath her eyes. "Not *all* night. I crashed for a couple hours after the party."

"Geez, Kit. You better take a nap before we leave tonight."

"I will, I will." She waved a dismissive hand then clicked something on Nick's video. "But first, you've gotta see this."

It started over from the beginning, this time with sound. A crowd of about fifty people clapped and cheered as Nick jogged out onto the stage, holding a microphone in one hand. Several women in the audience were crying, but not tears of sadness. They were closer to the tears of ecstasy teenagers produce when they get to see their favorite boy-band live in concert. This crowd adored him.

After a few minutes of "welcome" and "thanks" and reminders about the merchandise table in the lobby, Nick got down to business. The house lights dimmed down to near blackness, and a single spotlight illuminated Nick on the stage. He closed his eyes and raised his free hand high in the air.

"Spirits," he called out. "I feel you with us tonight. Some of you are bound here, bound by the shackles of grief to the loved ones you've left behind. Help us help you. Help us move on, so you can move on as well."

He stood there in silence until it almost felt awkward. Then, he brought his hand down sharply to his forehead, resting his thumb and ring finger on his temples. "I hear you, Jonathan."

Someone in the audience gasped, and a second spotlight shone down on a middle-aged woman who clutched a blue shirt in her hands.

"Is that her, Jonathan?" Nick asked.

The woman nodded emphatically, and Nick contorted his face into that odd expression of concentration Kit had been laughing at before.

She paused the video and grinned at me. "See?"

"Is that what his shows are always like?" I asked. "Some kind of… mass séance?"

"It's called a crowd reading. This is one of his smaller ones, from the Afterlife Festival last year."

"This is *small?*" The crowd measured five times larger than the group of people who'd been at the séance I'd attended in Gabrielle's attic, and that group of nine had seemed difficult to control. Everyone around the table was hoping to see a different spirit, and they were mentally calling out in every direction. How could Nick control a group of fifty people, each hoping he'd contact a different ghost?

"Yeah, he usually does this in Las Vegas, in smaller venues. He's had hundreds of people in the audience at once."

I stared at the paused screen, my face threatening to mirror Nick's strange expression. Hundreds of people. I'd known Nick was famous, but I hadn't connected his name recognition with this level of psychic ability. If he was powerful enough to control the emotions in a room that size and *still* connect with a spirit, Richard Franklin wouldn't be able to resist showing up at our tiny séance tonight.

The thought raced from my mind and into my stomach where it morphed into a tight little ball of anxiety. My presence at the cabin had stirred Richard up so much that he'd manifested as a near-deadly windstorm, and I barely had any power at all.

With Nick there… how far would Richard be able to go?

CHAPTER SEVEN

"This place always reminds me of the witch's house in Hansel and Gretel," I told Kit.

She looked up from our equipment cases and squinted toward the cabin. The sun was setting behind it, casting it in an eerie silhouette, but it was still easy to make out the sagging roof—which now had two massive holes in it, the most recent courtesy of Richard Franklin's atmokinetic ability to conjure storms and control the wind—and the way the two windows flanked the door made the building look like it had two angry eyes and a gaping, hungry mouth.

"Yeah, you're right," Kit said. "Gumdrops on the roof, ginger-bread walls. How'd I never see it before?"

I resisted the urge to push her over since she was holding Mark's camera and I valued my life. "Ha, ha. Hilarious. I mean the way it lures people in."

Over the last several decades, the Franklin Cabin had never had any shortage of willing visitors. Partying teenagers, down-on-their-luck squatters, campers with a ghoulish desire to spend the night somewhere infamous... and now us. I knew the evil power this place held, the risks of being here after the sun had set and darkness swallowed these woods. And yet, here I was, about to enter the cabin for the third time.

And hopefully the last.

I clenched and loosened my fists a few times, trying to muster the courage to walk into the building. The last two times I'd been this close to the cabin, there'd been a body waiting for me. It was as though Richard Franklin liked to leave me gifts. I imagined him standing at the window, gleefully watching me, clapping his hands in excitement at the thought of me finding whatever little present he'd gotten me today.

I shivered, then decided I was being ridiculous. Richard hadn't left those bodies for me. They'd simply been there. I was just the person unlucky enough to stumble across them both times.

Had it been luck? Looking back, it didn't feel like "stumbling" at all. I remembered the way I'd been drawn to the dock on my first visit here, unable to resist sitting at the edge and peering down into the water until Tom Bishop's body floated out beneath my feet. And then...

I frowned, unable to remember if it'd been my idea to seek shelter in the bedroom where we found Brian Anderson's body a week later. We'd been in the middle of a massive windstorm, and I'd never experienced anything so frantic and chaotic in my life. It had definitely been me who'd opened the door to the closet where his body had been concealed. I'd remember that moment until the day I died.

"Play it safe," I muttered to myself. "If you feel the urge to go somewhere, walk straight in the other direction."

Right now, I had the urge to run back to the van. Instead, I took a deep breath and followed Yuri into the cabin.

Inside, the musty stench of rotting wood assaulted my nose. I pinched my nostrils as I gazed around the large, open space that took up the front half of the building. Piles of leaves covered the floor, and a few large tree branches had even found their way into the cabin from the hole in the ceiling. This room had once been easily recognizable as a combination kitchen and living area, but someone had ripped out the cupboards and countertops, leaving behind only traces of glue and pressed wood along the walls.

"Looters," Yuri said, putting down his gear.

I mulled that over while we set up a few folding tables to use as workspaces. "I don't get it. How much can some old cupboards get you on eBay?"

He smiled at me, his eyes twinkling behind his wire-framed glasses. "Do you remember the antique witching supplies Gabrielle used to sell?"

Before Gabrielle's crimes had come to light and she'd sold her home to Penelope to pay her legal fees, she kept rare occult objects in a long glass case where the Oracle Inn's registration desk now stood. Her collection included little pewter cauldrons, silver knives, and rough stone mortar and pestle sets that she claimed belonged to psychics who had died in the Salem Witch Trials. According to Gabrielle, they were incredibly powerful objects.

I nodded to Yuri.

"There's a big market for things like that," he said. "Objects that have been used in rituals or that came from places of great power."

"Seriously? Someone would buy a chunk of a countertop just because it came from *here*?"

He chuckled. "I agree with your skepticism. There are many, many other things I would rather spend my money on. But there are people in the paranormal community who believe psychic energy is like radiation. They think it seeps into the objects around us, powering them up like batteries. And they believe those batteries can be used by other people in their own rituals."

As always seemed to happen when Yuri explained something,

his words became images in my mind. I imagined pale wisps of energy curling away from us like smoke rising from a cigarette. The strands crept up the walls and along the floor, disappearing into the wood. I blinked, and in the instant my eyes were closed, I remembered the grinning, maniacal face of Richard Franklin as he'd appeared to me the last time I'd been here, formed out of wind and dust. His energy wouldn't twist away from him in thin threads; it would pour out of him in thick, noxious ropes and choke out any positive energy we could muster.

Stop it, I chided myself, shaking my head. My confidence was already cracking around the edges. If I kept picturing Richard as some kind of all-powerful super villain, my resolve would shatter entirely.

I forced myself to focus on what Yuri was trying to tell me. "Do you think it's possible? Like, could somebody get a door-knob from the Amityville house and—I don't know—use it in a séance?"

"Oh yes, that's very common. For example, you might use a person's hairbrush to focus on their energy. But someone didn't go to all the trouble of prying out the cupboards just to summon Richard Franklin's spirit. With a poltergeist as present as he is, you don't need a focus object at all."

I pursed my lips into a grim smile, not sure if I was happy or terrified that Yuri thought it'd be easy for us to get Richard Franklin to join us here tonight. "So why take something from here?"

"In theory, to use his residual psychic energy to enhance your own powers."

"Wait… does that work?" I glared at him, suddenly angry. "Why didn't we bring something to make me stronger, to make sure we can get rid of him?"

"To answer your first question: it doesn't work. There's no way to pull energy back out of something. The people who sell these objects are preying on the weak and desperate, like the snake-oil salesmen of the past. And in answer to your second, we did bring something to make you stronger." Yuri smiled and inclined his head toward the open front door, through which we could see Kit and Mark talking together by the van. "Four other people are on the way."

My muscles relaxed, and I unclenched the fists I hadn't even realized I'd made. "Right," I said. "Sorry."

"For what?"

"Doubting our plan." I forced what I hoped was a brave smile onto my face. "I know we'll be strong enough to drive him out."

Then, because my brain kept trying to show me a mental image of Richard Franklin's dark energy oozing out of the walls around us like sap, I left the cabin. Outside, Kit and Mark had unloaded the rest of the gear from the van. Our black equipment cases rested around them in several stacks, but their eyes were focused on a large, rectangular device in Kit's hands.

"Need help with the rest?" I asked when I reached them.

"Uh, yeah," Kit said, not looking up. "Just give me one sec to test this out."

I leaned over her shoulder to get a better look at the thing she was working on. It was a bigger, more complicated version of the field mixer we usually used, with more than double the number of microphone inputs and an intimidating array of controls. Unlike the rest of our scratched and battered equipment, the device in her hands gleamed in the light of the setting sun. Every button and knob was intact and there wasn't a coffee spatter in sight.

"New mixer," Kit said. "We'll have a lot more lavalieres running today, plus I want to set up an extra boom mic."

"Oh, cool. Where did you get it?" I asked.

Kit's head jerked up, and she narrowed her eyes at our cameraman. "Good question. Where did you get this, Mark?"

He coughed and rubbed the back of his neck with one hand.

"Um… I borrowed it."

"Uh huh." Kit put the mixer on top of a pile of cases and folded her arms across her chest. "Appreciate the frugality, buddy, but where did you borrow it *from?*"

He pursed his lips, staring at the ground. "Raziel's crew," he said at last.

Kit's eyes flashed. "Dammit, Mark. Now we owe them a favor!"

Growling, she marched away from us into the cabin. Her loud, furious voice floated back out the door toward us, punctuated every so often by Yuri's soothing tone.

"Uh oh," I said. "You said the secret word of the day."

Mark laughed. "I knew she'd flip out when she found out where it came from."

I cringed. "Sorry I asked. If I hadn't brought it up, she'd have been too distracted by the shiny new toy to even wonder where you got it."

"Don't worry about it." He ran a hand through his mop of curly hair then picked the field mixer back up. "In the end, she'll be so excited about having more audio feeds that she'll stop caring it came from The Evil One."

"I met him last night, and it was weird. The news and Kit's stories about him paint him like a total villain. But then in person, he seems so nice, and if he's willing to loan us his equipment…"

"Yeah, he's a cool guy. He was begging me to let him come with us to the cabin, but I figured Kit would freak out, so I told him no."

"Interesting. When did he ask you?"

"Um…" Mark stared up at the darkening sky, crinkling his brow. "Man, it must have been pretty late. He asked me while I was on my way out, and we pretty much shut the party down. He'd already agreed to loan us the mixer, so I felt really bad turning him down."

"You were hanging out with him?" I asked, quirking an eyebrow.

Mark blushed, which surprised me. "Yeah. I told you—he's a cool guy."

If I ignored everything I'd seen and heard about Raziel and measured him only by my own interactions with him, I couldn't disagree with Mark's assessment. But it bothered me that Raziel had asked my cameraman if he could be part of the episode after I'd already told him no.

A car horn beeped behind us, and I glanced over my shoulder to spot a red SUV pulling down the long driveway to the little clearing in front of the cabin. The car wound its way to us, and soon enough Stephen, Daphne, Nick, and Graham spilled out on to the gravel. Graham held a cat carrier in his hand, and I hurried forward to take it from him.

"How'd she do?" I asked, peering through the metal grate that kept Striker from dashing out into the woods. In the fading light, her mottled black fur blended into the maroon plastic of the carrier, so she was just a pair of angry yellow eyes glaring out at me from the darkness.

"Good." He pulled me close for a quick kiss then turned back to the car to grab a grocery sack full of kitty treats. "She didn't yell too much once I started giving her these."

"Man, she has you trained."

Striker meowed in agreement.

"Let's get her inside before she figures a way out of there," Graham said.

I was anxious to do just that. It terrified me to have her here; she hadn't accompanied me on any of my previous visits because I couldn't fathom having her snatched away by a hawk or mauled by some wild animal. I'd brought her today because I didn't dare attempt something this big without her by my side.

In the cabin, Mark and Kit fitted Daphne and Nick with lavalier microphones in what used to be the kitchen. Stephen leaned against one of the stripped walls, watching as he worked his way through a bag of potato chips. I rested Striker's carrier on a folding table beside him.

"Sorry we're late," he told me.

"It's my fault," Nick called. "I couldn't find my phone."

Daphne rolled her eyes at her husband. "I told you, it's probably in our car."

"It wasn't there," he said. "Or in your bag."

"Why would it be in my bag?"

Nick shrugged. "That thing's a black hole. Everything ends up there."

"Could a thousand dollars magically end up there so we can buy you a new phone?"

"Ha, ha," he said drily.

I looked back and forth between them, trying to figure out if they were just bantering the way Kit and Mark did or if there was some genuine tension flaring up. Their tones weren't as light-hearted as they'd been at the cocktail party.

Daphne opened her mouth to say something else, but Kit cut her off.

"Perfect, you guys. Those levels look awesome." Kit glanced up from her borrowed mixer and gestured for Stephen to join her in the kitchen. "You're up."

I left them to their sound checks and pulled Striker out of her carrier. A purple harness already covered her torso like a little Kevlar vest, and I quickly snapped a leash onto the silver ring at her back.

"Okay, nice and easy." I lowered her to the ground. "Don't make me regret bringing you here."

She glared up at me from the ground, making her feelings about the harness clear. Her fur stuck out awkwardly around the edges and through the mesh, and her legs were stiff as she took a step forward. She sniffed the floor then scorched me with another fiery look.

"Hey, I've seen lots of cats do this online," I said defensively. "They didn't seem to have any issues with it."

In answer, she rolled over on one side and huffed out through her nose. She normally ran all over town with no supervision and no boundaries. I suspected the harness wasn't uncomfortable; the true source of her tantrum was a lack of independence. But how do you explain to a cat that you're terrified of them disappearing into the woods, especially when that's where all the best smells are?

After a few seconds of watching her play dead on the floor, I sighed and picked her up. "Fine, I'll just hold you. But the harness stays on."

Daphne wandered over, tugging a few strands of her long hair out of her lavalier clip. Striker's eyes widened at the sight of the small black hair tie between Daphne's fingers. A sly smile crossed the tarot card reader's lips as she wiggled the tie tantalizingly in front of the cat's face.

Striker earned her name, snatching the tie out of Daphne's hand with such speed and ferocity that the woman leapt back from us with a yelp.

"Crap, did she scratch you?" I asked.

"No, but it was close. She's a hunter. Who's tougher than she looks, huh?" She scratched Striker behind the ears then pulled another tie from her pocket to gather her hair up into a ponytail.

Kit clapped her hands to my left, raising her voice. "Okay everybody, let's take our places. We're ready to go."

Speak for yourself, I thought, hugging Striker to my chest. But ready or not, it was time to face Richard Franklin once more.

Face him, and banish him into the next world for good.

CHAPTER EIGHT

I stared around the circle, trying to swallow down the lump of anxiety gathering in my throat. The candlelit scene around me was familiar, but not in a way that comforted me.

Nine of us sat in a circle on the floor of the cabin's living room. It was the same arrangement as the first time I'd been at a séance, with everyone sitting cross-legged and holding the hands of the people beside them to form an unbroken ring. I glanced down at the light blue tarp below us, which covered the rough wooden planks of the cabin's floor, and winced an apology across the circle at Yuri. I should've thought to bring some fluffy pillows or something for people to sit on.

I also wished we'd brought a nice, large round table with us. It wouldn't serve any practical purpose; it's not like we were playing Settlers of Catan or something. But somehow, I thought it would've been better than staring at the sharp angles of everyone's knees.

Instead of a table, we'd filled the space in front of us with twenty-two stout, black candles. Each flickering light was in memory of someone we knew or suspected Richard Franklin had killed here. I thought the visual might help us focus on the importance of our task. We weren't kids playing with a Ouija board just to see what would happen. If we succeeded tonight, we'd be preventing any other people from joining his list of victims.

The plan was simple. I'd call out to Richard Franklin like I'd done the last time I was here. Once he arrived, we'd use our collective psychic energy to push him into the next plane of existence then cleanse the area with sage to be sure no part of him lingered. A small stack of tightly wrapped sage bundles and a cigarette lighter sat in front of each participant. We'd armed ourselves. So why didn't I feel ready?

From my left, Daphne gave me an encouraging nod. On my right, Graham squeezed my hand and smiled. Striker sat in my lap, her harness secured to my wrist. I realized I wasn't nervous about her running out of the cabin and into the woods anymore. I didn't have any space in my brain to be worried about that, not with everything else that could go wrong. Not when, any minute now, I'd summon Richard Franklin here so he could probably kill us all by bringing the entire cabin down onto our heads.

We're so stupid for being here, I thought. *This is idiocy in action.*

But the alternative—leaving the cabin uncleansed so it could lure more people to injury and death—was unacceptable. I stared at the candles in front of us, pictured Connor Miles' young face, and reminded myself that I owed it to him to follow through with this.

"Ready?" Kit asked. She sat directly across from me, and the lights from her mobile sound board cast her face in a strange shade of green to match her hair.

"No," I said.

Everyone laughed, but I hadn't been joking.

"Well," said Mark from beside Kit. "We're rolling. So, whenever you're ready."

I nodded. Striker shifted slightly in my lap, and I felt the steady vibration of her purr on my legs. I closed my eyes and took a deep breath, letting the silence settle around me.

Near silence, anyway. Outside, tires crunched on gravel. My eyes snapped open, and I frowned. Everyone we'd invited was already here.

"Are we expecting someone else?" I asked Yuri.

He shook his head, and I realized there was only one person it could be. The circle broke as everyone but Graham and I got to their feet.

Kit rushed to the window, peered outside, and spat three times over her left shoulder. "I knew it."

Daphne, Nick, and Stephen joined her at the window, and Stephen began to laugh. "Of course," he said. "He just couldn't stay away."

"Careful with the candles, everyone." I transferred the still-purring Striker over to Graham's lap, unwinding her leash from my arm to loop it around his. "I'll take care of this."

I walked out of the cabin and into the parking area to intercept our uninvited guest. Even in the twilight gloom, Raziel Santos's thin frame was easily recognizable as he crunched his way across the gravel toward me. My eyes adjusted, and I saw that he was wearing a nearly identical outfit to the one he'd worn to the cocktail party: a tight, pocketed t-shirt with a vee that plunged too deeply for my taste and trademark tinted aviator sunglasses that sat right on the tip of his nose so his eyes were completely visible above them.

"Don't worry," Raziel called. "I'm not here to interrupt."

"Too late," I told him, leaving out that I didn't hate delaying the start of the séance. Not one bit.

He closed the gap between us and pulled something out of his pocket. In the dim, flickering light from the cabin window, I could just make out the rectangular shape of a cell phone. "I'm just here to return this. It's Nick's. He left it at the party last night."

I held out a hand. "Thanks, I'll give it to him."

Raziel didn't pass me the phone. Instead, he made it disappear behind his hand with a small flourish. He craned his head to the side and peered around me in an exaggerated way. "Well... Since I'm here..."

"We were just about to get started, and the cameras are rolling," I said, stepping slightly to the side to block his view. I cast my mind around for the phrase I'd heard Kit use on nosy neighbors at other investigations. "And it's a closed set."

Raziel straightened up and arched an eyebrow at me over his shaded sunglasses. I smothered the urge to rip them off his face—it was night, and the stupid things were doubly unnecessary if he wasn't even looking through them—and raised my eyebrows back. We stared at each other silently for a few moments in the cool, still air. Our lack of movement proved too much for my team to handle in silence, and I heard feet on the gravel behind me.

I broke eye contact with Raziel to toss a worried glance over my shoulder. Graham waved at me from inside the cabin where he stood at the window with Striker in his arms. Behind me, Kit, Yuri, Mark, Stephen, Daphne, and Nick stood in a line like a makeshift wall erected specifically to keep Raziel from crashing our party. Yuri held one of our electric lanterns aloft. Beside him, Kit's eyes burned with fury, and Stephen rolled up the sleeves of his sweater dramatically. I turned back to Raziel, fighting the urge to laugh at the mental image of everyone behind me leaping forward to attack the intruder in a cartoonish action sequence.

"Fine," Raziel said at last, holding up his hands in surrender. "I'll go."

"Thanks. I'm not trying to be rude or anything."

"I get it." He flashed me a wide, mirthless smile, then snapped his fingers. The phone reappeared in his hand, and he held it out toward Nick. "I believe this is yours."

Nick stepped forward and took it, his eyes narrowed. "Thanks. Where'd you find it?"

"Oh, I didn't find it." Raziel tucked his hands behind his back and his grin widened. "I lifted it from you last night at the party."

"You picked my pocket?" Nick's face flushed.

"I meant no disrespect. Isn't it a sign of respect among thieves to share our skills with one another?"

"Excuse me?" Nick moved in toward Raziel. "Are you calling me a thief?"

"And a liar." Raziel beamed at him, his hands still clasped behind his back.

"Hey," I began. "You can't just—"

Raziel cut me off. "Come on, Nicky-boy. Don't tell me you're in that much denial. You steal from people all the time and lie to their faces while you do it."

"Wh... I don't... You..." Nick sputtered.

"I'll give you credit for being a skilled cold-reader," Raziel said. "It'd be impressive if you used it for something less despicable than fleecing the grieving family members of the recently departed."

I stared back and forth between them, dumbfounded. And I wasn't the only one; nobody spoke at all, not even Nick. His eyes went wide, and the red tinge of anger that'd invaded his face seconds before faded into an ashy gray.

"Be honest with us, Nick," Raziel said, his voice low. "Has a spirit ever actually spoken to you?"

"Of course they have," Nick growled.

Raziel shook his head and made a low *cluck-cluck* sound. "I've crashed your little shows in Vegas, man. Most people can't spot a spotter, but me?" He thrust his arm out to the side and a playing card—the ace of spades—appeared in his hand. "A trickster can always see behind the curtain."

My curiosity got the better of me. "Spotter?"

"It's a thieving term," Yuri said from behind me. Sadness filled his voice. "Someone who picks marks out of a crowd, so the nearby pickpocket knows who to steal from."

"Exactly." True happiness crept into Raziel's smile for the first time. "In Nick's case, they scan the crowd in the lobby and move around the seating area, watching and listening for clues. Clues like tattooed names, or initials engraved on something someone is carrying. And they're just the tip of the iceberg. How many researchers do you have backstage, stalking ticket buyers online, Nick? Again, it's almost impressive. But social media makes it too easy these days."

A vein throbbed in Nick's forehead, and he clenched and unclenched one fist in time with his pulse. I stared at him, thinking back to the video Kit had shown me. The woman in the audience had been holding a blue shirt. Could it have been a work shirt? The kind with a sewn-on name tag?

"Is it true?" I asked Nick. "Are you a fraud?"

My question seemed to break some sort of spell on him, and he lurched forward. "Screw you," he told Raziel. "I don't need this."

At first, I thought he was about to push Raziel or try to attack him. Instead, he breezed right past everyone, marched off to the SUV, and climbed inside. A moment later, the engine roared to life, and he sped away into the darkness.

"Uh... He was our ride," Stephen noted.

I turned around to check on Daphne, expecting her to look angry or upset. She just rolled her eyes.

"Typical. Just typical." She headed back into the cabin, calling over her shoulder, "Are we doing this or what?"

"I'll just let Amari know I'll be here for a while." Raziel tapped something into his cell phone.

Unable to control myself, I snorted when I noticed the artwork on his phone's case. A hyper-realistic painting of his own face, one eyebrow raised menacingly, glared at me from the back of his phone. Red flames glowed behind him, and the words *"veritas vincat"*—the same words he'd tattooed across his chest—arched above his head.

Raziel tucked it into his shirt pocket and clapped me on the back. "Lucky I'm here. You said you needed nine, right?"

He followed Daphne into the cabin, leaving me to stare after him in shock.

CHAPTER NINE

"Did you know?" I asked Yuri. "About Nick?"

My voice held no accusation. Yuri cared deeply about the trust our clients had in us; he wouldn't knowingly bring a fake psychic onto the show. It was a stupid question, but I'd felt compelled to ask it, anyway.

As I expected, he shook his head. "There were rumors, but there are plenty of rumors about us too. There are always doubters. I'd hoped he was as genuine as his wife."

Across the room, Daphne whispered to Stephen in the flickering candlelight. Raziel watched them from a few feet away, a sickeningly satisfied smile on his face as he sipped from a silver flask. Kit didn't bother to hide the looks of disgust and loathing she shot at him as she and Mark reset the cameras. Graham sat on the floor with Striker, feeding her an inappropriate number of treats. The cat gobbled them up greedily, oblivious to any human drama.

"What do we do now?" I frowned up at Yuri, needing him to take over the decision making. I'd planned this séance as carefully as I knew how, and it'd gone completely off the rails before it even began. Clearly, I was not experienced enough to pull this off. "Do we reschedule? Wait for Raziel's team to leave Donn's Hill?"

Yuri sighed, took off his glasses, and cleaned them with a small cloth while he deliberated. "We could. But that may be more than a month."

"A month?"

"They've booked an extended stay at Penelope's inn while they film his next special."

Waiting that long was out of the question. It was already early October, and the closer we got to Halloween, the more likely it became that adventurous teens or amateur ghost hunters would visit the cabin. Connor Miles had already been injured because I'd waited this long to finish what we'd started. We had to do this now.

"Okay," I said. "Then we'll shoot with just eight. I'm sure it'll be fine."

That was a lie if ever there was one. At Gabrielle's séance, she'd been so reluctant to continue with only eight participants that she'd pulled me in when one of her clients dropped out. The results had been disastrous, but her determination to have nine of us in the circle had to mean something.

"Mac, I made you a promise that you could run this episode. I hope you don't feel I'm about to break that promise." Yuri pushed his glasses back onto his face. "Nick was a risk from the start. I'd heard the rumors. But I'd been willing to take a risk on him for one simple reason: he has far more name recognition than we do, which would help the show immensely."

He watched Raziel for a few moments before continuing. "I don't care for Raziel's methods. I know you don't either. He likens himself to Robin Hood, a thief acting in the best interests of the poor. Or in his case, the grieving. In his mind, the end justifies the means."

I knew where this was going. "Just like including him would

be justified because his millions of fans would watch the episode."

Yuri nodded, but he pursed his lips momentarily. "More than that, did you ever ask Gabrielle why she favors nine participants?"

"No. I never had the chance." A light note of bitterness crept into my voice, and a lump of now-familiar guilt strained at my stomach. It was true that I'd never had the chance to ask her before she'd been arrested, but how many times had I thought about writing her a letter and not followed through with it?

"There's a superstitious numerical pattern among the psychic community in Donn's Hill," Yuri continued. "Two, four, nine, twelve."

"I don't get it."

"Like most of Gabrielle's methods, it was something she traced back to ancient witches. It ties to nature. Two, for night and day. Four, for the seasons. Twelve, for the months."

"And nine?"

"Nine is a powerful number. Mathematically magical, strangely compelling, and an ender of cycles. Nine precedes ten, and what is ten but zero all over again? Nine lends strength to séances because the goal is to end one cycle and begin another by helping a spirit move on to the next life."

I bit my lip and reviewed the group I'd selected to be part of this. Yuri, Kit, and Mark were obvious; they were the Soul Searchers. The four of us formed the foundation of this entire endeavor. Graham and Striker were obvious as well; nobody alive gave me strength and confidence like those two. Stephen, Daphne, and Nick had filled out the last three slots on Graham and Yuri's recommendations, and truth be told, I hadn't had strong feelings about them from the start apart from Nick and Daphne's crowd appeal.

Wasn't Raziel just another Nick? Why did I hate the idea of

him being here so much? Was I so shallow that I'd exclude someone just because I genuinely hated the way he wore those stupid sunglasses everywhere, even at night? Or was I so devoted to Kit that I'd refuse to let Raziel take part just because he'd insulted her?

What we were doing was more important than petty rivalries and prejudices. Richard Franklin had to go, and if that meant rewarding Raziel for his little scheme to get here, so be it.

"Ok," I said at last. "He can stay. Let's do this."

HERE WE GO AGAIN, I thought, staring at the flickering candles. I focused on them until I couldn't see the faces and cameras around me, using their irregular pattern to help steady my thoughts. It was easier once I made myself forget that I was being recorded. This was just a séance, something Gabrielle had done so regularly she'd become famous for them. This was no more difficult than playing a musical instrument once you'd learned how.

After several minutes of focus, my heartbeat slowed and my muscles relaxed. I was ready to begin.

"Everyone, please join hands."

I felt, more than saw, my companions comply. Kit had traded places with Daphne, and I gripped her cool, dry hand with my left. Graham's held my right, and the purring Striker sat in my lap. As everyone connected, an unexpected hum of energy coursed through me, startling me and nearly making me drop Graham's hand. I hadn't felt that before at Gabrielle's. Was I feeling it this time because I was taking the lead?

"Clear your minds," I commanded sharply, suddenly afraid. I envisioned our circle as a ring of light, a glowing electrical current only kept in check by our collective focus. If anyone's mind strayed, I imagined an arc of lightning might bolt outward and pull who-knows-what back into this space. Breathing deeply, I concentrated on strengthening and steadying the ring before continuing.

"Think about Richard Franklin," I told the team. "Picture his face in your mind."

Try as I might to see him as the young, prep-school expellee from the photo we'd shared with our guest psychics, all I could picture was a face made of leaves and dust and wind. It was the same face Richard Franklin had shown me through a window while he was attempting to cave the cabin's roof in from the outside.

Much as the memory made my palms sweat, I latched onto it, forcing myself to remember the way it'd made me feel. He had transformed debris into his image and twisted the darkness into a grin, and I'd never felt so defenseless in my life. I needed to lean into that vulnerability. I needed to lure him in, and just when he got close, he'd find out how much I'd changed since the last time I'd been here.

Back then, I'd only been thinking about him for a few moments before he arrived. That's how hungry he was, how rabid. This time, the minutes ticked by until my legs ached from sitting on the hard floor, and I tried not to wonder how long we should sit here before acknowledging defeat.

Striker growled. My heart skipped a beat.

This is what you want, I reminded myself.

Is it? my gut countered.

This wasn't the time for internal conflict. Richard Franklin knew what I was up to. He'd been eager to manifest himself before because he knew we were unarmed. Easy pickings. But this time, we'd prepared. We'd brought backup. It'd been foolish to assume he'd just waltz right out and let us banish him. I had to find him, find him and drag him out of whatever metaphysical cranny he'd hidden himself in.

An idea popped into my head from somewhere deep in my memory. Shortly before my mom had died, I'd been having an anxiety attack. To calm me down, Mom sat beside me, rubbing her hand back and forth across my forehead. Her touch had lightened until it disappeared completely, but I'd still felt the direction of her fingers—left, right, left, right—above my eyebrows. She later explained that she'd been sending healing energy through me, and her own life force was washing away the negative energies that clouded my mind. I'd fallen asleep within minutes.

I realized the electrical current I'd imagined coursing through our joined hands a few minutes ago was more than just a mental image to guide my thoughts. The nine of us were truly connected. Could I pull on that energy? Use it to bolster my own ability? Was that the true benefit of a group séance?

"Everyone, lend me your strength," I said aloud. "I'm going to try something… something I've never done before."

"Are you okay?" Graham asked.

Still keeping my eyes closed, I squeezed his hand. "I'm fine. Just focus—send your energy my way, okay?"

My mental image shifted. The current no longer swirled around us in a clockwise circle. Instead, I pictured a beam of energy flowing from each participant's heart directly to my own.

Richard Franklin, I called silently. *I know you're here. This is Mackenzie Clair. Come forward. Show yourself.*

I implored him again and again, pushing the words out into the ether with every ounce of my strength. Like an SOS call, I repeated the same message until the words followed the natural rhythm of my beating heart. *Rich-ard-Frank-lin. Thud-thump-thud-thump. Mac-ken-zie-Clair. Thud-thump-thud-thump.*

The surrounding temperature plunged. The muscles in my back tensed and my eyes shot open. Small puffs of steam from everyone's mouths were just visible in the candlelight, and behind me, the floor creaked.

It's nothing, my brain automatically decided. *Just an old structure settling.*

I was falling back into old habits by trying to rationalize away the supernatural. I'd seen more than enough evidence of ghosts and hauntings to know that sometimes, a creak is more than just a creak. Enough evidence to make me angry at myself for even attempting to explain away something *during a séance* as nothing more than naturally expanding wood.

Another creak sounded, and Striker growled again. Slowly, I twisted my torso until the fireplace behind me came into view. Wet, cold remnants of a few burned-out logs sat on the rusting grate. A bitter, weedy smell tickled my nose, but nothing else seemed out of place. Why, then, did every hair on the back of my neck feel like it was being yanked outward by an unseen hand?

Had I imagined it, after all? I turned back to the center of the circle, searching the faces around me for any sign that someone else felt what I felt. Everyone gazed back at me, their expressions ranging from Stephen's mild interest to Yuri's concern to Raziel's naked disdain.

Everyone except for Daphne. From her position directly across the circle, she watched something behind me with wide, terrified eyes.

My skin rippled, goosebumps bursting to life up and down my arms. I hadn't imagined it. Gripping Kit and Graham's hands tightly, I twisted around again. At the last moment, out of some childish instinct to spare myself from seeing something frightening, I closed my eyes.

Are you crazy? I internally screamed, and I forced myself to open them.

A tall figure stood before me. He faced away from the circle, his head twisting back and forth between the half-destroyed fireplace and the window like he was trying to get his bearings. From his size, I knew I wasn't looking at Richard Franklin. This man's huge frame reminded me of a linebacker or a nightclub bouncer, and the breadth of his shoulders and tall, straight posture screamed, *Don't mess with me.*

His clothing was strange; he wore a waist-length cape and a low top hat, like he'd just walked off the set of a Dickens play. But despite the oddness of his appearance and the clear feeling the figure didn't belong here at all, something about this moment was familiar. A wave of déjà vu slammed into me, and I squeezed Graham's hand to steady myself.

"Do you see something?" Yuri whispered.

"Yes," I whispered back.

The instant the syllable left my lips, the apparition twitched. Slowly, he turned, but not the way someone might turn around in a narrow hallway, one foot at a time. No, he *rotated*, like a piece of cake in a diner's dessert display.

Instinctively, I recoiled. But I couldn't flee; not only was I sitting down, but my legs were numb from sitting on the hard floor for so long. My inactivity had trapped me here, leaving me no choice but to watch his face come into the candlelight one inch at a time.

In the flickering light, I had trouble making out his features. His brimmed hat cast his face in shadow, as though there was a light I couldn't see above him. But two things stood out, even darkness. The first was his mouth, which curled upward into a satisfied sneer, as though something had just made him both very pleased and very proud. The second was his eyes, which burned a deep, haunting crimson.

"Hello, Mackenzie," he said, his voice as deep and smooth as melted chocolate. "I've been looking for you."

Striker moved, jumping past me and emitting a horrible, shrieking howl. Every candle went out at once, snuffed by some invisible force. I screamed. The circle broke. As soon as Kit's hand slipped out of mine, the energy in the room dissipated.

"Sage!" I shouted, fumbling in the dark for the bundles in front of me. My left hand had just closed around a lighter when a spark burst to life at my side. Graham had been faster than me. He re-lit one of the fat black candles and used it to ignite two bundles of sage at a time. The air filled with the sweet, strong scent of the cleansing herb as Graham lit and passed more bundles around the circle.

Someone else lit more candles, and the room brightened. I leapt to my feet and swept the room with my eyes, but the ghost had disappeared.

I rounded on Daphne. "You saw him too, right?"

Her face was pale, and she nodded as Stephen pulled her into a standing position. She swayed for a moment, rubbing her temples. "I need to lie down."

She looked the way I felt, or at least the way my body felt. Exhaustion tugged on my limbs and the room fuzzed at the edges of my vision, but my mind clicked away at double speed, struggling to process what we'd just seen. My plan, which had been cracking at the edges since Raziel arrived, shattered completely.

"Was it him?" Yuri asked, switching on an electric lantern and holding it aloft. "The Franklin boy?"

"No. But whoever he was..." I stared at the spot in front of the fireplace where this new spirit had said my name. "He knows me."

CHAPTER TEN

"You're sure he's gone?" Yuri eyed me over his glasses, a deep frown of concern on his face.

Yuri, Graham, and I stood in the cabin's former kitchen. Striker snuggled in my arms, purring as though it was her job. Which it sort of was.

I watched Mark pack up the camera gear. He'd been reluctant to tear everything down, but I'd been firm. The night was over. Our plan didn't make any sense anymore. A few feet away from him, Kit watched the footage from the seance on a small field monitor, already making notes on her sketchpad so she could dive into editing the minute she got home.

"Richard Franklin isn't here," I told Yuri. "I can't feel him at all."

His frown deepened. "I wonder who it could have been."

"The man in the hat?" I whispered. I'd been wondering that, too. I wanted to ask Daphne if she recognized him. It was comforting knowing she'd seen him too. Had she heard him speak my name? But as soon as we'd switched on the lanterns, she'd stumbled toward the more intact of the back bedrooms to rest while we packed up.

"In the hat?" Yuri repeated. "What hat?"

"Wait, who's the 'who' you're talking about?"

"The psychic who came here and took care of Richard Franklin. Someone must have come here after Connor Miles' team and banished the poltergeist."

That made no sense to me. Now that I knew Nick was a fake, I couldn't think of any mediums in the area powerful enough to handle Richard Franklin alone. And the ones from farther away, who travelled to Donn's Hill just for the Afterlife Festival every spring, would have announced they were coming.

But Yuri had been in this business far longer than I had. His theories were worth considering, so as far as I could tell, there were three possible explanations for why I hadn't been able to summon Richard Franklin during the séance.

First: Richard Franklin's spirit was still here and I just couldn't feel it. As soon as the idea entered my mind, I dismissed it. The last two times I'd visited the cabin, he'd been eager to show me his powers. The sadistic side of him couldn't resist scaring us before trying to harm us.

No, he'd gone. No shred of him lingered here. I'd never been so certain of anything in my entire life, which left only two possibilities in play.

Could Richard Franklin have detached from the cabin on his own? Moved on or become attached to something—or someone —else? As I knew all too well, poltergeists could haunt a person just as easily as they could haunt a physical location. I didn't find it likely that he would up and depart for the next plane of existence after having clung to this cabin for so long. But I could see him latching onto a potential victim and following them out of the woods.

The thought made me shiver. Graham pulled me into a hug and rubbed my shoulders. Striker continued purring between us, and I leaned my head into Graham's chest, closing my eyes as I considered the third possibility: Yuri's theory that a psychic had come here and done our work for us. They would have had to come here sometime between the night Connor Miles nearly died and tonight. And if they had, they'd kept it quiet.

Why would someone come here in secret? Because they didn't want credit, like a humble hero in the movies? Maybe they were filming a competing television show, so they were keeping everything under wraps until the premiere. We always asked our clients to sign forms saying they wouldn't tell anyone what had happened while we were there until after the episode aired, so it was very possible some other team and crew had done the same here.

"Are you okay?" Graham asked.

I bit my lip then nodded. Physically, I was fine. But I'd be lying if I tried to pretend this hadn't all left me feeling extremely shaken.

"Did you see anything?" I asked.

"No." He leaned down and kissed my forehead. "But I was scared. Your scream…. I've never heard you make a sound like that before."

"Can you tell us what you saw?" Yuri urged gently.

"Wait!" Kit shouted. She set down the field monitor, wrestled a camera back out of its case, and hurried to my side. "Turn on your lav."

Yuri sighed. "Kit, for goodness—"

"Hey, are we paranormal investigators or not?" she demanded, attaching the camera to a tripod. "Our psychic saw something. We need to record her experience while it's still fresh. For science."

Finished with the camera, she walked over and grabbed my shoulders.

"You get it, right?" she asked.

"Yeah," I said. "You're right."

"Good." She clapped me on the back, and we ran through a quick audio check before she gave me a thumbs up.

I took a deep breath and recounted what I'd seen, describing the man, his odd clothes, and his red eyes. As I spoke, Graham wrapped his arms around his torso and stared at me. When I got to the part about the man saying my name, he shivered.

"He knew you," he whispered.

I bit my lip. "Maybe. I was putting my name out there, thinking it over and over to get Richard Franklin to recognize me. This other spirit could've just picked up on that. But…"

"What?" he asked.

"Well, it's weird. He seemed familiar, but I can't place from where."

I had a suspicion about it, though. When I was a child, dozens of ghosts had visited me, none ever staying for very long. My mother had dubbed them "The Travelers." I'd been so young… I was sure I'd forgotten more of them than I could remember. Could one of them have found me again? If so, was it by chance, or had he really been searching for twenty years? The thought gave me the chills.

"Here." I handed Striker to Graham. "Do you mind cajoling her back into her carrier? I want to finish cleaning up and get the hell out of here."

He nodded, and I returned to the living room. I was kneeling on the tarp and packing up candles when Raziel reappeared from the cabin's back hallway. He folded his arms and watched me put the last few unburnt bundles of sage into a large plastic tote.

"That was some performance," he said.

I stood and dusted my hands off on my jeans. I was exhausted and more than over this arrogant party crasher, so I didn't bother trying to hide the irritation in my voice. "Why am I not surprised you'd call it an act?"

He smirked. "Why am I not surprised you'd pull out all the stops?"

"All the stops?" I nodded toward the tarp on the floor. "Yeah, this is a real classy affair. The caviar and champagne will be here any minute."

Raziel rolled his eyes. "You know what I mean."

"I really don't."

"Sure, you're masking it under this rough-and-tumble camping vibe, but all the elements are here. The candles, the sage, even the general air of dilapidation that surrounds us. It's stage setting."

An exasperated sigh mixed with a low growl escaped my chest. "What are you talking about? This cabin is a hundred years old and nobody's taken care of it in decades, so it's not like I went to some special effort to get it to look this way. The sage is to cleanse the area and drive out the spirit. The candles—"

He cut me off before I could explain that each flame represented one of the spirit's victims. "Let me guess: candles are just how it's done, huh?" Raziel smirked and pulled a quarter out of his pocket, then held it in front of my face with his right hand for a moment before flipping the coin back and forth across his knuckles. "Let me explain something to you, since you didn't pick up on it outside when Nick ran off with his tail between his legs. You're a scam artist, just like him. Know how I know? Because *I'm* a scam artist. I know all the tricks, all the strategies. It's all about setting expectations."

As he spoke, he continued to move the coin. Left to right, right to left. It was mesmerizing, like a swinging pocket watch. Despite wanting to glare at Raziel, I couldn't look away from his hand.

"Once you've lured them in, once they're transfixed on the thing you want them to be looking at…"

Raziel abruptly made a fist with his right hand, trapping the quarter inside. With his left, he snapped his fingers next to my ear. I jumped, startled by the closeness of the sound, and jerked my head to one side. I hadn't even seen him move that arm. In his left hand, he pinched the coin between his fingers. I glanced down at his right; it was empty, palm open towards the ceiling.

He leaned in close, his nose an inch away from my own. "That's when you get them. And they give you all they've got."

I backed away from him. "We don't take anything from the people we help. We don't charge fees or even accept donations."

"Maybe not, but you're still culpable. You still feed into the whole system and keep people clinging to hope that if they just find the *right* psychic, if they just spend *a little more*, they'll get to see the people they love again. And either you're playing into it on purpose, or you're getting used by the people who are."

"That's not—"

"So, which are you?" he interrupted. "Complicit, or just stupid enough to buy into all the smoke and mirrors?"

"I am *not* a fraud," I growled.

"Fine, then you're a fool."

My mouth and brain stopped communicating with each other at that point, leaving me unable to do anything but gape at him while the insult sank deep into my skin. Daphne emerged from the dark hallway behind Raziel, her eyes narrowed.

"What's going on?" she asked.

"Raziel thinks I'm making all this up," I said. "He doesn't believe I saw anything. But you saw the spirit too, right?"

She nodded, and a shiver passed down her body. "I've never seen anything like that before."

Raziel folded his arms across his chest. "Oh, this should be good. Do tell, tarot mistress. What did you see? Jacob Marley, rattling his chains?"

Steel flicked across Daphne's eyes for a moment as she gazed at Raziel.

"Ignore him," I said. "Just tell us what you saw."

"Oh, for the love of all that's creepy!" Kit shouted from the kitchen. She bustled into the living room, carrying a small condenser microphone on a stand. "How many times do I have to tell you people to save it for the show?"

I glanced down at my shirt, remembering the lavaliere microphone Kit had pinned there. At my hip, the red light on the transmitter box glowed, reminding me that everything I said to Raziel was being recorded. At least Kit would edit out anything we didn't want our viewers to hear.

"Okay, you're all set," she told Daphne a second later. "What did you see?"

"A shadowed figure." Daphne pointed to the space behind me with a shaking hand. "It stood between Mac and the fireplace, looming over her like a dark omen."

"Could you see his face?" I pressed. "His eyes?"

She shook her head. "No. It had the height and width of a man, but it had... Well, the only way I can describe it would be to say it had the opposite of a glow, as though he was sucking light into himself. Is that... normal?"

I wanted to laugh. *Normal.* I'd left normal behind months ago, the day I'd seen a ghost in the Grimshaw Library and discovered my psychic abilities. To my eyes, the spirit had been a young woman with dark hair and a shy smile. But to the cameras recording me, she'd been a shimmering blur, a shapeless blob of white light.

The spirit that day had been friendly. According to the library staff, she never harmed anyone. She just wanted to spend eternity reading books on a sunlit window seat on the second floor.

The spirit I'd seen today had known my name. And to Daphne, he'd been a shadow, as opposed to being made of light. What did that mean? And had the cameras picked up the same thing?

"Did you see anything like that in the footage so far?" I asked Kit.

She glanced at Raziel, then lowered her voice. "Not yet, but I'm sure we got something."

"What's that?" Raziel cupped a hand to his ear and leaned toward us. "Let me guess: the footage is conveniently dark, so you can't prove anything conclusively."

My hands balled into fists at my side. "I'm not making this up. If you'd seen what I've seen—"

"Oh, right," he cut in. "All the hauntings and séances. Remind me, where were you the first time you saw someone summon a 'spirit?'" He crooked his fingers in air quotes around the last word.

I narrowed my eyes, sensing a trap. We'd never talked about this before. How could I remind him of something I'd never told him?

"Ghost got your tongue? Well, I heard it was at one of Gabrielle Suntador's famous—or should I say infamous— séances. And where is she now?" He frowned and scratched his head in mock thoughtfulness then snapped his fingers again. "Oh, that's right. She's awaiting sentencing for robbing her clients blind and killing her co-conspirators. Sounds real trustworthy. I'm sure she'd *never* fake a summoning."

My fingernails dug little grooves into my palms. "You're wrong."

He smirked at me.

"I hate what Gabrielle did." My voice hitched in my throat. "I *hate* it. She has a gift—a beautiful, powerful gift—and she threw it all away. But her mistakes don't invalidate what I do. What *we* do."

Raziel opened his mouth to reply, but I held up a hand. I wasn't finished. Not by a long shot.

"We help people. We're there when they're at their lowest, when they think they're losing their minds. And we *help* them."

Mark, Yuri, and Graham joined us in the living room and flanked me, wordlessly backing me up. I straightened my spine.

"Know what I think? You go on and on about how you're a thief and we're the same, but *you're* the only thief here. You steal hope. You steal livelihoods. Why are you so desperate to prove you're right about everything? Why are you so scared to see proof of an afterlife?"

Raziel stiffened, and I knew I'd struck home.

Yuri placed a hand on my shoulder. "Mac—"

But I was already pressing forward. "What did you do, Raziel? Afraid to pay for your sins?"

He glared at me then laughed again. The sound was hollow and forced. "Nice deflection. Your acting skills are impressive. Gabrielle taught you even better than I thought."

I lunged at him, not sure what I was about to do. Graham grabbed my arm and pulled me backward, and Raziel laughed again, genuinely this time.

"Hey, take it easy, champ." He patted his shirt pocket, which still held his cell phone. The camera lens was just visible above the lip of fabric. "I don't think the network will be too happy if a video of you attacking me goes viral, do you?"

My breath caught, and I stopped struggling against Graham's grip. "You're recording this?"

"All night long, kid." Raziel strode to the door, tipping an imaginary cap toward us. "Thanks for the show, everyone. See you online."

CHAPTER ELEVEN

My mother's backyard glowed in the light of the setting sun. The flowers in her garden bloomed vivid pinks and yellows, and the low hum of summer sounds droned around me: insects, a light breeze, and music from the open window of a passing car.

I knew it was a dream. It'd been twenty years since I'd been back to this place in the waking world, but my unconscious mind regularly pulled me here. I didn't mind. The patio was peaceful, and my limbs felt heavy against the hard metal chair of my mother's old bistro set.

"How can I be sleepy when I'm already asleep?" I wondered aloud.

Nobody answered. The backyard was a solitary place. Occasionally, on nights past, my mother would appear on the fringes of my vision, just out of sight. I'd always wake up before she came into full view. I was content to sit here, alone, relaxing in the evening air. I closed my eyes and leaned my head back.

A sudden chill chased goose-pimples up my arms. I opened my eyes in near darkness; a single candle guttered and spat from the center of the table, and the rest of the backyard was obscured by a black mist.

Two red dots glowed from the shadows. The ghost from the cabin materialized across from me, his pupils burning like embers in a campfire. He leaned forward, bringing his face into the light, and I shrank back into my chair, squeezing my eyes closed.

"Wake up," I told myself. "Wake up!"

When I opened my eyes, I was still in my mother's backyard. The shadows had disappeared and the sun once again warmed my skin. The red-eyed spirit had left, chased away by the return of the light and replaced by a somber-faced Yuri.

"It's over, Mackenzie," he said. His voice echoed oddly, as though we were in a large arena filled with loudspeakers. "ScreamTV has cancelled *Soul Searchers*."

"No!" I covered my mouth with one hand. "Isn't there anything we can do?"

Yuri shook his head slowly. "My dream is dead. You killed it."

The patio spun, and I faced the back of my mother's house. Over Yuri's shoulder, the ghost from the cabin stood at the kitchen sink, grinning at us through the open window. He cocked his head back and began to laugh, the brim of his top hat ringing his face like a dark halo.

As he laughed, the chair dropped out from beneath me and the ground shook. I looked around in panic, hoping to grab hold of Yuri to steady myself, but couldn't find him. The patio groaned, cracking and splitting in two. I dove to one side, clinging to the trunk of an ash tree.

My mother's house crumbled. Oddly, I was relieved. The ghost had been inside. Surely, he'd been trapped by the rubble. He wouldn't be able to frighten me anymore.

In the distance behind the ruined house, two shadows appeared. One shimmered in gray light, reaching out a hand.

"Mackenzie!" my mother's voice called. "Wait for me!"

But it wasn't up to me. My feet didn't move. The surrounding scenery rushed past as though blown by a strong wind. The second shadow in front of me grew bigger, filling my entire field of vision. As his face came into focus, his red eyes glowing harshly in the gloom, the red-eyed spirit opened his mouth.

Larger and larger he loomed, finally swallowing me whole.

CHAPTER TWELVE

I stared sullenly down into my mug, watching the flakes of instant coffee dissolve in the swirling water. This wouldn't be strong enough to chase away the lingering fragments of my nightmares. Again and again, the red-eyed spirit had stalked me through my dreams until my subconscious had grown tired of that particular game. Then, it switched to something much more terrifying in its plausibility: visions of a California conference room where ScreamTV was cancelling our show, citing my behavior and the fact that I was "wildly unpopular with our viewers" as reasons to terminate Yuri's contract and leave him with nothing.

A pair of light snores drifted across the apartment. Graham was asleep in my bed, and Striker loafed on his chest. Her high-pitched, nasal wheezing was the exact inverse of his low, purring snuffle. The sight was just cute enough to prevent me from waking Graham and begging him to go down to the big kitchen to make me a better cup of coffee. I'd never been able to recreate his method; his brews were atomic strength, enough to knock the sleep out of you for weeks, but they still tasted good. Especially with something sweet and tart, like the box of raspberry danishes I knew Kit had hidden above the fridge.

Besides, even if I woke him, I didn't think he'd be able to help me work through either of the things that were really bothering me. He wasn't a psychic. He wouldn't be able to confirm why Richard Franklin's ghost hadn't appeared or how I could figure out who that other spirit had been. I wished I could just pick up my phone and call Gabrielle. Even if I wrote her a letter, who knew how long it would take her to get back to me.

As for the second concern, there was only one thing that would make me feel better. I'd crossed a line last night with Raziel. I knew what I needed to do. And though it was still early, I knew I was putting it off. It should have been the first thing I did: the moment my feet hit the floor beside my bed, I should've marched straight over to the Oracle Inn to apologize for trying to attack him—and beg him to delete that video.

My reflection glared at me as I brushed my teeth and tried to flatten my hair into submission. I finally gave up and showered, marveling at the paradox of trying to look nice for a person whose definition of "dressing up" was wearing an extra revealing V-neck. I'd rather spend the entire day picking litter up off the side of the Moyard highway than spend another two minutes talking to Raziel, but if I didn't do this, the entire *Soul Searchers* crew might have to find jobs doing roadside maintenance. Once Raziel was through with us, I was certain another network would never touch our show again.

I left Graham and Striker to slumber on without me and dragged myself to the inn. It was a sunny fall morning, and the scent of freshly fallen leaves filled the air. I cut through the square on Main Street, pausing to throw a few coins into the fountain at the center. The floral-themed water feature with its upturned petals catching the rays of the sun always reminded me of my mother. She'd been a horticultural hobbyist and could never resist the superstitious act of wishing on fountains. I stood there for a few moments, regarding my reflection in the rippling water. That, too, was a constant and comforting connection to my mother, whose genes had made a strong claim on my features.

Is that where you got this absurd impulse to tackle anybody who offends you? I asked the girl in the water. She shrugged, and I went on my way.

Wafts of pumpkin spice drifted out from the inn's open windows, and I promised myself a steaming mug of chai tea and a pumpkin cookie as a reward for putting on my big-girl pants and extending the olive branch to Raziel. Whether he accepted was on him. A smile flitted across my face as I imagined what he could do with that proverbial branch if he didn't want to erase his video.

The inn was quiet at 6:00 a.m. on a Sunday. Few guests were up this early, and none had yet made their way down to the café at the far end of the lobby. The barista, the same dark-haired college student who'd served me during my tour with Penelope, leaned over the counter, reading the paper. His espresso machine gleamed tantalizingly, but I sternly told myself that rewards were best enjoyed after you'd finished your chores. Especially if the chore was this distasteful.

I made my way up the inn's grand staircase. On the top floor, the door to the attic suite had a shiny bronze '301' drilled into it. The light reflected off the numbers unevenly, and as I got closer, I realized the door was ajar.

"Raziel?" I knocked softly on the doorframe, not wanting to push the door open any farther. The thought of walking in on him changing—or worse, with some fangirling groupie—made the last of my instant coffee rise in my throat.

There was no answer.

"Raziel?" I tried again. "Hello?"

An unmistakable shiver of dread passed over me. Something was wrong here. I could feel it. Swallowing, I pushed the door open, revealing...

Nothing. The cozy cluster of couches and their little table

were undisturbed, and the heavy curtains hung unruffled. The wardrobe doors looked firmly closed, and the trifold screen zigzagged beside it. Across the room, the bathroom door hung open, and my reflection stared back at me from the mirror above the sink. A rush of relieved air escaped my lungs, and I laughed quietly.

"You and hotel rooms," I told myself. "Are you ever going to get over that?"

I leaned into the room to grab the knob and pull the door closed, and something strange caught my eye. In the gap between the privacy screen and the floor, something shiny glinted. I moved closer; Raziel's honey-tinted aviator sunglasses rested on the hardwood.

"Raziel?" My voice quavered, betraying my strong desire to not see what was behind that screen. But I'm nothing if not morbidly curious, and the need to know beat out my want to stay ignorant. My hand reached out on its own and pulled the screen back.

Raziel lay face up, his vacant eyes staring at the rafters above us. Red marks covered the lower half of his neck, and the braided tassels of a curtain's cord snaked around his throat.

He was dead.

The coffee in my stomach bubbled up again, this time getting all the way up to my mouth as I stumbled backward. I tripped over my own feet, landed on the rug and coughed, struggling to swallow so I could suck in air.

My throat cleared, and I gasped in enough air to scream for help. After another scream, footsteps pounded up the stairs outside the open door.

"In here!" I yelled.

As the footsteps grew closer, I looked once more at Raziel's lifeless body. He'd been so convinced there was no such thing as ghosts that he'd dedicated his entire life to destroying psychics and mediums. Now he was dead and knew better than any of us what truly waited on the other side.

Wherever he is, I thought, *he can't deny the afterlife anymore.*

CHAPTER THIRTEEN

"There she is." Deputy Alicia Wallace strode across the cafe floor and set her brimmed hat on my table. She tucked her thumbs into her belt, tugging her utility pouches and holster forward.

With her tall, sturdy frame, Wallace towered over me even when I wasn't sitting down. That stature, combined with her ever-present firearm, had intimidated me since our very first meeting. Now, even though I considered us friends, her presence still made me a little nervous.

"Donn's Hill Body Magnet Strikes Again," she said, dragging her hand across the air in front of us like she was revealing an invisible newspaper headline. "I can't wait to hear what you were doing in Raziel Santos' hotel room at five-thirty on a Sunday morning. Aren't you with Graham Thomas?"

"Yes." Heat rushed into my face, heat that had nothing to do with the chai tea in my hands. "And this isn't what it looks like."

She chuckled and clapped me on the shoulder. "It never is. Look, I still need to go check out the scene and conduct some interviews. The sheriff is taking the lead on this case personally, due to the high profile of the victim. And when he does something 'personally,' it means I do it."

I stared up at her. "What?"

"Never mind. Bad time for a joke." She patted my shoulder again, more softly this time. "I know finding a dead body isn't easy. Do me a favor: stay here. I'll come back and go over your statement once I've been upstairs."

I nodded, and she left me in the company of my own thoughts. The flush faded from my face, and I pulled out my phone to text Graham. The last thing our fledging relationship needed was him hearing about this from someone else, especially anyone who might've made the same insane assumption as Deputy Wallace.

He called immediately. "I'm coming to get you."

"I'm fine," I told him. "Stay there. Go back to sleep."

It took several minutes of arguing back and forth before I finally convinced him there was nothing he could do here apart from getting in the way, and he agreed.

"Call me if you change your mind," he said. "I love you."

"I love you too," I murmured before hanging up.

From my table in the cafe's corner, I watched as the lobby filled with chaos. A line of people waited at reception as a frazzled college student checked them out. The other guests in the café, most of them holding suitcases or rolling luggage, sat in somber silence until their travel companions had paid their bills. Then, barred from leaving by the Driscoll County deputies who controlled the area, they sat over steaming cups of coffee and whispered to each other. The collection of low voices blended together into an irregular hum, and I let my eyes close.

"Mackenzie, you're going to spill that."

Penelope's voice startled me back from the edge of sleep. My mug of tea rested in my lap, barely upright. I gingerly lifted it back up to the table as the older woman sank into the chair beside me with a deep sigh.

"What a morning." She signaled the barista for a cup of coffee then eyed the line of guests at the registration desk. Her eyes were bright and alert, and she looked sharp as always in a flowing silk blouse. Only the slump of her shoulders hinted how tired she must be.

"I guess this is pretty bad for business," I said.

She shrugged. "Most of my guests were weekenders and would have checked out in a few hours, regardless. I've offered those that are here for longer stays a steeply discounted rate. Most of them seem to be fairly understanding of the situation."

The situation. It was such a mundane way to describe what had happened. Raziel was dead. Someone had killed him.

I felt numbed by those two facts. I'd seen him less than twelve hours before; how could he be dead? I searched my teacup for answers as I remembered our last conversation and recalled the flash of pain in his eyes just before he'd stormed off. He'd died before I'd had time to clear the air between us. It was an uncomfortable truth that made my stomach hurt.

"Oh, is Kit here to collect you?" Penelope asked.

"Hmm?" I raised my head; Kit was indeed walking toward us across the inn's lobby. "Oh. Graham must've told her."

"Hey, Mac." Kit locked her eyes on me, pointedly ignoring Penelope. "What are you doing here?"

I frowned. "Waiting to be interviewed by the deputies."

"What? Why?"

"She found Raziel's body," Penelope put in.

Kit's eyes went wide, and all color drained from her face. "No," she whispered. "Again?"

When I nodded, she swore under her breath and bent down to pull me into a hug.

"Holy crap, it's like you're cursed," she muttered into my hair. "Are you okay?"

"I'll be fine." I pulled away from her, studying her face. She was wearing a glossy nude lipstick that brought out the warmth in her olive skin, and she smelled faintly of mandarin oranges. I raised an eyebrow. "What are *you* doing here?"

"Um…" Blood surged into Kit's face from her neck. "I heard about… well, Raziel… and everything… and I called Amari." She cleared her throat and jerked her head toward the barista's counter. "I thought I'd take her some coffee."

Penelope nodded. "Good idea. Coffee is on the house today, for everyone. Please be my guest."

Still refusing to acknowledge Penelope, Kit squeezed my shoulder. "Are you sure you're okay?"

"I've been through this before," I reminded her. "I'll be fine."

As Kit left us to hustle away toward the barista's counter, Penelope sighed. "She's still upset."

It wasn't a question, nor did it need to be. Kit broadcasted her emotions more clearly than anyone I'd ever met. When she was angry, an invisible black cloud formed around her, casting a shadow on everything around it. On the flip side, her good moods were as contagious as the flu.

"She'll be okay," I said.

We sipped our drinks in silence for a few minutes, watching the ebb and flow of activity in the lobby as guests finished checking out and giving their statements to the deputies. Before long, the tall figure of Deputy Wallace appeared at the bottom of the stairs and she made her way toward us, dropping into the chair across from me with a *clunk*.

Wallace shot Penelope a meaningful look, one eyebrow raised.

Penelope took the hint and stood. "I've got to go check on some guests. Excuse me."

As the innkeeper left us, Wallace turned to me, her expression darkening. She flipped to a new page in her tiny notebook and examined my face with narrowed eyes. "Okay, Mac," she said. "Let's hear it."

The story spilled out of me in a rush. I was eager to share it, to get the memory of finding Raziel's body out of my mind by way of my mouth. "We had an argument at the old Franklin cabin last night. Things got heated, and I said some hurtful things. I came here to apologize, and that's when I found him." I described the attic suite as I'd found it that morning, with the door ajar and Raziel on the ground behind the folding screen.

Wallace nodded as I spoke, jotting down notes and asking no clarifying questions. When I finished, she folded her hands in her lap and exhaled slowly through her nose. "Did you see anything else up there? Take anything?"

"No, why?"

"Some of his personal effects are missing." She narrowed her eyes. "I hope you understand that we'll need to verify your alibi with Graham Thomas and talk to the rest of the crew you had at the cabin."

"Alibi?" I repeated. "Am I a suspect?"

Wallace waved a dismissive hand. "Suspect is too strong a word, but I'll be frank. You're a person of interest, and with Mr. Santos' celebrity status, this is a high-profile case. The Sheriff has made it clear we'll be sticking to the book on this one."

"As opposed to?"

"We won't be using any outside consultants this time. Because of your involvement with the deceased prior to his death, I can't share any information with you."

"Oh." I wasn't sure how I felt about that.

Wallace believed in the paranormal even more than the average Donn's Hill resident. She hadn't batted an eye when I'd told her about seeing the ghost of a murder victim in the spring. Instead of calling me crazy like I'd expected, she'd encouraged me to reach out to the ghost for information to help find his killer.

She was making it clear now that this time, things would be different. She wouldn't be sharing any inside tips with me the way she'd done before. If I was being honest with myself, I didn't care. The fact that Raziel was dead still hadn't permeated my consciousness; it still felt unreal, like a rumor I'd heard but couldn't verify. Had it really been his body upstairs? Had I really found it? Was I even awake?

These were the questions that pressed against my forehead, not "What can I do to help solve this case?"

Wallace stood and placed her felt hat back atop her head. "Let me know if anything else comes to mind. Don't talk to the press. And don't leave town."

She left me, and I stared stupidly after her for a few seconds. After a while, her last sentence finally made it through the mess of confused information that cluttered my brain. *Don't leave town.*

I swallowed drily, forgetting the tea that sat on the table in front of me. She'd called "suspect" too strong a word. So why did I feel like that's exactly how she thought of me?

THE MEDIA CIRCUS descended on Donn's Hill within twelve hours. Camera crews arrived from every major station in the state, and even a few cable news channels were represented. The Driscoll County Sheriff's Department was being tight-lipped about Raziel's death, refusing to even call it murder, but that didn't stop the press from speculating about everything from possible motives to reasons Raziel might have taken his own life. Penelope warned us to steer clear of the Oracle Inn, where journalists had checked into most of the rooms.

"I can't tell if she's happy or upset at how busy the inn is," Graham admitted to me over dinner the next evening.

We'd taken advantage of the good weather while it lasted.

Graham had built a picnic table out of leftover lumber from around the house, and he'd dragged it onto a patch of asphalt in front of the garage. He grilled while I sat backward against the table and let the sun warm my face. It was chilly enough in the shade to want a hooded sweatshirt, but on this little impromptu patio, it felt warm enough for a t-shirt. Music drifted through the open garage doors, and I tapped a hand against the table to the beat of a Silversun Pickups song.

"Not to mention the national attention Donn's Hill is getting," I added, lifting a hand and squinting at him. I regretted leaving my sunglasses inside, but I was far too comfortable to go get them. Plus, Striker had taken up residence on my lap the instant I'd sat down. Her black fur baked in the sun until it was hot to the touch.

"Oh, Penny's thrilled about that."

Graham set a pair of plates onto the table, and I scooted around to face the proper direction, careful not to dislodge Striker. She sat up anyway, her little nose twitching at the scent of freshly grilled fish and veggies. One stealthy paw snuck up onto the tabletop, aiming for an asparagus spear.

I batted her away. "You don't even like vegetables."

Graham pulled a sliver of fish off his plate and reached over to the cat, who snapped the morsel from between his fingers. "I saw the inn on the news this morning. The sign was in the background for the entire story. You can't buy that kind of publicity."

"They should film in the lobby," I said. "Where your sculptures are."

As expected, his face flushed. Despite the positive comments about his work at the cocktail party, he still seemed to suffer from imposter syndrome. But at least doubt hadn't paralyzed him; through the open doors behind Graham, the evidence of his frenzy to get ready for the Chicago show was everywhere. Finished pieces crowded the shelves and tables, but they were arranged haphazardly instead of in his normally neat rows. Even the band posters on the back wall above the sink—souvenirs from Graham's younger days, when every weekend meant trips to Moyard to see touring acts—looked askew.

"Are you all ready for your trip?" I asked.

"I think so. I just need to get all my inventory into my new credit card app and pack everything in bubble wrap so it'll survive the ride in Dad's trailer."

"Need any help?"

He looked startled then pursed his lips. "Uh... well... I kind of want to do it all myself. Make sure I know for sure where every piece is... and everything."

I raised an eyebrow at him. There was an underlying implication there that if I helped, he wouldn't be comfortable with the outcome. But his short hair was a mess, his flush had faded into irregular red splotches, and he hunched over his plate like a cat who couldn't find a comfortable place to sit. He was stressed.

Still, I couldn't let him off the hook for not trusting me entirely. I teased him a little, hoping to pry a smile out of him. "I'll cross my fingers that your work ends up on channel five."

He granted my wish, flashing a weak and nervous smile at me. "Penny keeps saying there's no such thing as bad publicity."

The words hit me strangely. I'd heard the phrase hundreds of times, and it rang in my head over and over like a catchy song. But something about it made me feel suddenly ill. I rubbed my stomach and frowned.

"Something wrong with the food?" Graham asked.

I shook my head quickly. "No, it's delicious. I just feel kind of... I don't know. Anxious, I guess."

He twisted in his seat to check the old public-school style wall clock that hung over his band posters. "It'll be dark soon. How about we head inside and watch a movie?"

"Sure." I smiled, though my belly twisted in knots. "That sounds nice."

Graham cleared our plates and ushered me upstairs to the couch in his living room. He put on a movie to distract me, but my mind drifted. I finally realized what'd been bothering me about the old adage about publicity; it was a lie, and Raziel's show proved it. Most people had never heard of the Midnight Lantern before Raziel's exposé. It'd become famous just in time for Raziel's legions of fans to rejoice in its demise.

Was that what would happen to us if his team posted the video of me going off on him at the cabin? The *Soul Searchers* would become a household name then cease to exist entirely? I petted Striker absently, chewing my lip as I tried to imagine life without my team, without new investigations to look forward to. It was a dreary thought.

Not for the first time, I kicked myself for losing control of my emotions at the cabin. I'd just been so raw from my failure to reach Richard Franklin.

No, it wasn't a failure, I decided.

Sure, I didn't contact the spirit I'd been hoping to banish, but I had reached out into the space between worlds and something had reached back. By that measure, I'd succeeded.

And I couldn't ignore what I'd felt at the cabin. Richard Franklin no longer lurked there. I felt the truth of his departure with a certainty that helped mollify my guilt about what'd happened to Connor Miles. Even if it hadn't been me who banished Richard Franklin's spirit, he was gone.

The question was: who'd beaten us to it?

Yuri's theory that a competing team had cleared the cabin didn't sit right with me. They'd have bragged about it to someone. The paranormal community was a small one, and it was even smaller within Driscoll County.

It also didn't feel likely that his spirit had left on his own. He seemed gleefully happy with his situation; I didn't picture him growing bored with hunting, scaring, and ultimately killing thrill-seekers and campers who wandered within his range.

There was only one thing I knew for certain: someone had visited the cabin between Connor Miles' injury and our attempted séance. The cabin hadn't stripped itself, and Richard Franklin hadn't left me any of their bodies to find on my subsequent visit. The dots connected in my head, and I felt like an idiot for not putting things together back at the cabin.

Whoever had stripped the cabin had also banished Richard Franklin.

But who on earth would do both things? And where did the spirit who *had* appeared fit into all of this?

"What was that?" Graham asked.

"What?"

"You just muttered something about fitting in."

"Oh, sorry."

I didn't elaborate. He looked at me askance but didn't press me. I squeezed his hand and snuggled into his shoulder, looking at the TV, but my eyes unfocused and I was soon back in the maze of my thoughts.

I'd reached out to one ghost and another answered. The spirit in the hat had known me. He'd said my name. Had he been at the cabin all along, watching us on our prior visits? Did ghosts talk to each other? Maybe he'd learned my name from Richard Franklin, who'd learned it from our past attempts to contact him.

On top of that, something about him had been so familiar. I'd seen him before. I knew it. But where?

Unable to wrap my head around that mystery, I bounced back to the other question that hovered in my mind. Raziel's death happening so soon after the séance couldn't be a coincidence. Had the spirit in black been an omen? Was he... responsible?

"Mac, you're bleeding." Graham touched my lip with his

thumb. A smudge of red shone on his skin when he pulled his hand away.

"Oh."

He stood up. "I'll get you a tissue."

When he returned with a box of Kleenex, he turned off the TV and faced me. His eyes narrowed behind his thickly framed glasses, and his mouth was set in a deep frown. "Do you want to talk about it?"

A smile quirked the edge of my mouth as I realized he hadn't bothered to ask if I was okay. He wasn't one to waste words by asking questions to which he already knew the answers.

"I'd rather do something about it," I admitted.

His frown deepened. "Deputy Wallace told you not to get involved."

"I'm not going to 'get involved.' It's not like I'm going to run around and start asking people where they were the night of the murder or something. I just…"

I trailed off, not sure what I was even considering doing. A vision of a séance hovered dimly on the edge of my mind, too abstract to come into focus. I didn't know how large it should be or even who I should try to contact. Raziel? The man in black? My parents?

I blinked, startled by my own thoughts. I had to be pretty tired for an idea like that to bust through the protective wall I'd built around their memory.

"I know what you're thinking." Graham's voice was soft. "I know you, Mac. You're thinking of summoning somebody. You're practically lighting the sage in your head right now."

I didn't answer.

He leaned forward and stroked the small scar that sat on the side of my neck. "Isn't that exactly what you were doing when you got this?"

A frustrated groan escaped my throat, and I shoved myself off the couch, dislodging Striker. She hopped into Graham's lap and the two of them stared at me, their four eyes wide with concern—and a teensy bit of accusation.

"What am I supposed to do?" I asked. "Keep going like nothing's wrong?"

"No, but—"

"You know what's crazy?" I interrupted. "The last two days have been so insane that I actually forgot a spirit forced its way into a séance—uninvited—because I found a dead body the next day. I mean, was this town always so dangerous?"

It was his turn to answer with silence. I knew from our conversations that, despite its slogan as "The Most Haunted Town in America," Donn's Hill was an uneventful place to live. People worked. They farmed or ranched or made things, and once a year they cut loose at the Afterlife Festival, getting just crazy enough to give themselves something to talk about for the next eleven months.

Wallace's nickname for me—The Body Magnet—was eerily accurate. I didn't like it. In the short time I'd lived here, I'd found three bodies. *Three.* That wasn't normal.

I balled my hands into fists and struggled to put all these thoughts into words, eventually dropping into a chair and cradling my head in my hands. A moment later, Striker pawed my knee and a large hand squeezed my shoulder.

"Okay," Graham said. "This will sound like a punishment, but I have an idea that might help."

"What?" I peeked up at him through my fingers.

"Sometimes, when my head feels like a mess, I'll organize something. Like clean out my car or inventory my studio."

"You're not tricking me into cleaning out that Geo."

"Oh, I like you way too much to make you do something like that. But I have a project I could use an extra pair of hands for. I was saving it for tomorrow, but we might as well get a jump on it."

"What is it?"

"Cleaning the butler's pantry. Phillip left it in good condition when he moved out, but it could use some sprucing up before Amari can move in."

"Wait—what?" I stared at him, my brain failing to translate my thoughts into something my mouth could work with. I was forced to repeat myself. "What?"

The corners of his eyes crinkled when he laughed. "Okay, that's my fault for assuming Kit told you. Amari isn't comfortable staying at the inn with all the reporters and everything. She's renting a room here for a while."

"How long is 'a while?'" Despite it coming out of my own mouth, the question surprised me. What did I care how long she was here? She was just another tenant.

Except… she was more than that. She'd been here less than a week, and I could already feel a distance growing between Kit and me. The recognition of that distance put a stone in my stomach, though I couldn't say why. It didn't feel like jealousy, but whenever I thought about Amari, a clump of worried energy the size of a boulder seemed to balloon to life inside my chest. I rubbed the skin below my collarbone. Maybe it was just indigestion.

Graham reached out a hand and pulled me to my feet. "Come on. I'll let you pick the music."

Striker and I followed him down the stairs to the main floor, and I scrolled through his iPod. My mood called for some '90s grunge, and I was pleased that he had plenty of Alice in Chains. I was just debating whether *Jar of Flies* or *Dirt* would be a better choice for housework—both titles felt thematically appropriate— when Graham abruptly stopped on the last stair. I bumped into him and tipped backward, but he caught me by the elbows.

"Look," he started, "I know you're going to do whatever you're going to do. But promise me something. If there's anything I can do to help, tell me."

"Of course," I said. "You're the most helpful guy I know."

He ignored the flirtatious tone in my compliment. "And promise me you won't do anything dangerous."

I frowned, unsure where that was coming from. As far as I knew, I'd never done anything dangerous. Well... apart from hitchhiking. And staying in a seedy motel by myself. And trying to talk to ghosts on a professional level.

As I opened my mouth to answer, a pounding sounded at the front door of Primrose House. Graham stepped off the last stair and opened the door, revealing a pair of Driscoll County Sheriff's Deputies. I recognized them from the inn's lobby the day before, but I didn't know their names.

"Mackenzie Clair?" one of them asked, leaning around Graham to address me.

I swallowed. My heart pounded in my chest, and my hands twitched at my sides. For some reason, my first instinct was to run. I forced my feet to stay where they were and answered. "Yes?"

"We need you to come with us."

The pair of them stepped forward, intending to push past Graham, but he held his ground, blocking the doorway with his tall frame.

"Is she under arrest?" he demanded.

"Not yet," one of them said.

"But she can be, if that's what it takes to get her down to the station." The second produced a pair of handcuffs and dangled them in front of Graham's face. "Sir, move aside."

I have absolutely no idea where I summoned the courage to step around Graham and face the deputies. "Will Deputy Wallace be there?"

The first one nodded. "She's who asked us to come get you."

That felt odd. Why hadn't she just called? I'd have gone to the station right away, no questions asked. Why had she sent these strangers here to collect me?

Instead of voicing these concerns, I simply nodded and followed the deputies outside. Graham hustled along beside me, and Striker ducked back and forth between the deputies' legs, nearly tripping them several times on the walk to the curb where a black SUV with the seal of the Driscoll County Sheriff's Department waited.

"I'll follow you," Graham said as the deputies helped me into the vehicle.

I swallowed again, trying to clear the lump of anxiety from my throat. All I could do was nod as the heavy door clunked shut, locking me in the backseat.

CHAPTER FOURTEEN

I'd thought I had good reason to be nervous the last time I'd visited Deputy Wallace at the sheriff's station. That time, I'd traveled there on my own two feet, not contained in the backseat of an SUV by a thick sheet of bulletproof glass. And I'd met with Wallace in a comfortable, well-lit conference room.

This time, the deputies led me into a small interrogation room. The gray cinderblock walls stretched high above me, touching a flat, featureless ceiling at least ten feet above the steel table. My cold, metal chair had been bolted to the concrete floor. There wasn't much to look at apart from my reflection in the window-sized mirror across from me, and I hated the way my wide eyes and unhealthy pallor made me look. If I didn't know me and saw a photo of this woman in the paper, I'd assume she was guilty of anything they said.

When Deputy Wallace walked into the room a few minutes after I arrived, I knew she was thinking the same thing. Her eyes held no trace of the warmth from the inn. There was no sign in her stiff, official manner that we were friends. She dropped heavily into a chair and let a thick manila folder fall onto the table with a loud *fwap!*

I opened my mouth to speak, but she held out a hand to stop me, shaking her head. A moment later, a heavyset man about Yuri's age walked into the room. He wasn't as tall as Wallace, but he looked like he weighed enough to take her down in a fight. His bushy mustache covered his mouth, making it difficult to tell if he was smiling or frowning. He tucked his thumbs into his belt as he considered me from the doorway. Then he sighed, removed his brimmed hat, and set it onto the table as he lowered himself into the chair beside Wallace.

"Miss Clair, this is Sheriff Harris." Deputy Wallace gestured toward the man beside her. "I don't believe you've met."

I shook my head. He didn't offer his hand, so I left mine pinned beneath my thighs.

"As I hope the deputies made clear, you're not under arrest. We just have a few questions for you." Wallace folded her hands on the table. "Let's start with this: why didn't you tell me you assaulted Raziel Santos the night he was murdered?"

"*What?*" The question exploded out of my mouth. Assault? What were they talking about?

"We have a witness who claims you attacked Mr. Santos following an attempted séance at a cabin near Lake Anam," Wallace said.

"The same cabin where, I might add, a friend of yours killed two people earlier this year," the Sheriff put in.

"Wha—I—" I sputtered, unable to find anything untrue about his statement but wholly unsure what Gabrielle's crimes had to do with Raziel's murder.

Deputy Wallace rested a hand on the Sheriff's forearm. "Look, we know you had nothing to do with those earlier deaths. But I find it strange and, to be honest, very disconcerting that you did not mention your confrontation with Mr. Santos when we spoke yesterday."

"I did!"

"No. You told me you 'argued.' You made zero mention of a physical altercation."

"There wasn't—"

"Let's skip to the part where you tell the truth, Ms. Clair." Sheriff Harris leaned forward and spoke in a low, calm voice. "Did you, or did you not, attack Mr. Santos at the lakeside cabin?"

"No!" I paused. "I mean, not really. I sort of lunged at him. But that's it! Graham pulled me back and calmed me down."

"That must have been very frustrating," Sheriff Harris said. "Is that why you visited the inn that night? To finish what you started at the cabin?"

My mouth fell open, and I stared at him, too stunned to speak.

"See, there are a few holes in your story." The sheriff leaned back, mirroring Wallace's posture. "You claim you arrived at the inn at six o'clock in the morning, but we can't find anyone who can corroborate that."

The wheels in my brain finally started turning again, and I wracked my mind for anyone or anything who could back me up. Striker was the first creature to come to mind, but her communication skills with humans were pretty much limited to demanding treats. "What about the barista? Or cameras? The inn had to have cameras, right?"

Wallace shook her head. "The barista doesn't remember seeing anyone that morning. And unfortunately, Mrs. Bishop's contractors are still behind on the camera installation."

"A weakness in the inn's security system," Sheriff Harris said, "that we believe you knew about prior to Mr. Santos' arrival."

Had I known that? My mind spun. I couldn't be sure.

"We also have statements from a witness saying you threatened to harm Mr. Santos if he didn't," Wallace consulted her notes, "quote: 'get out of town.'"

"*What?*" The word erupted out of my mouth at top volume. "Who said that?"

"You seem agitated, Miss Clair," Sheriff Harris said. "Why do you want to know the names of the people who've come forward? So you can try to intimidate them, too?"

"No!" I stared at Deputy Wallace, begging her with my eyes to shed this callous shell and revert to the person I'd befriended over the past few months. Didn't she know me well enough by now to know I could never kill someone? "I just want to know who would lie about me…. and *why* they would lie about me."

The sheriff snorted, and Wallace pressed her lips together into a thin, hard line.

"Where's the phone, Ms. Clair?" she asked.

I hated the way she kept calling me that. She hadn't called me "Ms. Clair" since before I'd confided in her about my psychic abilities. She'd offered to make me a police consultant that day, and she'd called me Mac ever since.

The biting formality when she addressed me, coupled with the stony expression on her face, made the truth painfully clear. We weren't friends. Not right now. Maybe never again. I was just a suspect, someone who might have information Deputy Wallace needed to do her job. When she finished with me, she'd go home and take off her hat and turn into regular old Alicia Wallace in front of the TV.

When I didn't answer, she asked her question again. "Where is Mr. Santos' cell phone?"

"What cell phone?" I asked.

"The one Raziel filmed you with. We hear he threatened to share a video of you attacking him with your network." She gazed at me from across the table for a while with cold, calculating eyes. "We've searched his room, his luggage, even his team's gear, and there's no sign of his phone. Somebody took it. Probably the same person who killed him."

"I don't know where it is," I told them honestly.

They exchanged glances. Wallace leaned forward and rested her elbows on the table. She held her hands out to me, palms upward.

"Mac," she said. "Help us out here."

Oddly, when she finally said my name, it felt even harsher than hearing "Ms. Clair." She'd chosen to use it, to make me think we were pals. My eyes narrowed.

"All we want is the truth," she said. "Here are the facts. Someone murdered Raziel Santos. You had a fight with him the night before he died. You were at the inn the morning his body was found—"

"Yeah, by me!" I shouted.

The sheriff's mustache twitched. "You've got quite a temper. Raziel made his name exposing fake psychics, right? What would you have done if he'd posted that video and painted you as a violent fraud?"

"I don't know. I guess I'd hope people who know my gifts are genuine"—I nodded at Wallace—"would back me up."

She blinked and momentarily ducked her head. Then she stood up, gestured for the sheriff to follow her, and the pair of them left me alone again in the interrogation room.

I sighed and rested my head on the metal table. All I wanted to do was go home. It had to be after midnight by now, and Striker would be livid about the lateness of her bedtime meal. I closed my eyes and thought about my soft bed and my cozy apartment, and the way the cold air tickled my cheeks if I left the windows open at night. I breathed in deeply, imagining I could smell the fallen leaves outside my window.

When I opened my eyes, I half expected to be sitting at the window seat in my apartment. But I was still in the strangely proportioned room, trapped by the gray cinderblock walls. When

I sat up, my red, tired eyes gazed back at me from the reflection in the large mirror across the table.

Eventually, Wallace came back. The door swung closed behind her, leaving the two of us alone in the small space.

"Okay, Mac," she said. "You're free to go."

I stood slowly. Part of me expected her to shout "Gotcha!" and slap a pair of handcuffs on my wrists, but she just pulled open the door and watched me exit the room in silence.

Graham waited for me in the station's lobby. He leapt to his feet when he spotted me, closing the distance between us in a few quick bounds so he could gather me up into a tight hug.

"Are you okay?" he whispered into my hair.

"I'm fine," I lied, pressing my face against his chest. It was an ineffective way to hide my tears; they gushed onto his Sonic Youth t-shirt, soaking it on contact.

Wallace cleared her throat. Graham and I pulled apart, and he stepped in front of me, partially blocking my view of the deputy.

"Thanks for coming down," Wallace said, seeming to ignore Graham's protective stance. "You've been very helpful."

"Great," I said. "Glad I could help, I guess."

"Listen, remember what I said. Don't leave town. And Mac…" Her dark eyes bore into mine. "Be careful."

CHAPTER FIFTEEN

Morning sunlight warmed the best room in the entire world: the kitchen at Primrose House. Large and airy, it was the opposite of the tiny interrogation room in every meaningful way. I sighed as I leaned against the counter with a mug cradled in my hands. Through the wide windows at the back, I watched Graham ferry sculptures out of his garage-turned-studio and onto a pair of long folding tables he'd set up on the driveway. He often liked to sculpt outside on sunny days, but today he was working with finished pieces, wrapping them in layer upon layer of bubble wrap to ensure they'd survive the trip to Chicago the next day.

Beside me, Kit poured coffee into a pair of simple mugs from the collection of Graham's creations he'd deemed "unsellable." She added her usual splash of vanilla-flavored creamer into one and gave the second cup a hearty pour from the milk carton. I raised an eyebrow at her.

"Don't start," she told me.

"I wasn't saying anything," I murmured into my mug. I took a sip of coffee and glanced at the closed door to the butler's pantry.

"I was just wondering what to get Amari for a housewarming gift."

Kit glared at me and I cracked, allowing a chortle to escape my nose. Her foot connected with my shin, just hard enough to send a message.

"Ouch!" I balanced on one leg so I could rub the other. "Be nice to me. I had a rough night."

She grimaced. "Ugh, sorry. I still can't believe Wallace treated you like that. I thought she was cool."

I thought back to Wallace's apologetic explanation just before I'd left the station the night before, and her warning. After a good night's sleep, it was easier to see things from her perspective.

"She's still cool," I decided aloud. "I think she means well. The sheriff, too, even if he is callous as hell. They just want to find Raziel's killer."

"Are you really a suspect?" Kit asked.

"I honestly don't know. They let me go, but..." I remembered the way they'd badgered me. "It sort of feels like I'm the closest thing to a suspect they've got." Looking for a happier topic, I asked, "What are you up to today?"

"I'd been planning to edit the episode, but the network nixed it."

"What?" I let my mug clunk onto the counter, splashing a few droplets of coffee onto my shirt. "Why?"

She shrugged. "The cameras didn't pick up anything. Our thermometer registered a drop in ambient temperature, but that's it. The footage just isn't super compelling. Put that together with it being Raziel's last night alive, and..."

It made sense that the network would want to delay airing anything recorded the night Raziel had died, but the other half of Kit's news sent a wave of disappointment washing over me. I'd been hoping the red-eyed spirit would've shown up on the footage, even if he just appeared as a dark shadow the way

Daphne had seen him. He'd seemed so... *present*. It was weird that a spirit would show itself to me so clearly yet make little impact on our instruments.

Strangest of all was that Kit didn't seem to care. She eyed the door to the butler's pantry, then grinned at me. "So instead, I'll take Amari to lunch."

At the mention of Raziel's manager, my stomach twisted. "Is she planning to stay long?"

"She's leaving tomorrow morning to take Raziel's body to Reno, where I guess his family lives. She'll be there a few days for the services. She's coming back after that."

"For how long?"

Kit pursed her lips. "We haven't talked about it. I sort of don't want to ask."

I nodded but said nothing. The unidentified rock that seemed to accompany any thought or conversation about Amari dropped back into my belly. I still wasn't sure where it came from. Irrational anger at Penelope aside, Kit was a good judge of character, and she seemed to have strong feelings about Amari. Even now, as she stared at Amari's closed door, her facial expressions flitted back and forth between happiness and apprehension like a TV on the fritz.

Deep down, I worried about my friend. She'd boomeranged from stress puking at the sight of an old flame to looking forward to spending as much time as possible with that same woman. How long before Amari returned to her real life in Los Angeles and Kit sank back into the low end of that spectrum?

She seemed to sense that something was off and elbowed me gently. "Hey, are you sure you're okay?"

"I'm fine."

The flat look Kit gave me declared it'd been a pointless lie. She'd been with me when we'd found a corpse in a closet at the Franklin cabin the previous spring, and she knew from experience that finding a dead body wasn't something you just slept off, especially when you'd been dragged into the sheriff's station for some late-night conversation afterward. But she'd also been part of my life long enough that she didn't push me to talk about it. Instead, she followed the Katerina Dyedov method for comforting friends and family.

"So, which apartment will it be?" Her brown eyes glimmered mischievously over the rim of her mug as she took an unnecessarily long sip. It gave me the distinct impression that she wasn't drinking her coffee; she was drinking it *at* me.

"Apartment?"

"Yeah. You know, when you two lovebirds move in together. I need to know if I'll be stealing your cute turret room or just expanding into Graham's place."

I rolled my eyes, but the telltale heat in my cheeks gave away my embarrassment. Try as I might to resist, my eyes locked on Graham's tall form in the backyard. It was true; we didn't spend many nights apart these days. If I wasn't sleeping in his bed, he was sleeping in mine. But despite already living in the same house, consolidating apartments was something I firmly defined as a Next Step. It was one down from getting engaged, and there was only one step left after that. The thought sent a thrill of excitement and a jolt of fear down my spine.

I'd only ever moved in with one other person before, a choice that currently held the title of Worst Mistake of My Life. In my heart, I knew Graham would never betray me the way my last boyfriend had, but...

"You should move into his place," Kit said. "I like your apartment better."

"Maybe you should move into the butler's pantry," I countered.

It was her turn to blush. In answer, she dipped her fingers into her mug and flicked a few droplets of coffee onto my face. I blinked in surprise, startled for a moment. Then inspiration struck. Diving past her, I grabbed the spray nozzle from the sink and knocked the faucet to full blast. Kit ducked, but she wasn't fast enough to avoid the stream of cold water I shot her way. Shrieking, she dove around to the other side of the kitchen island. I steadied my firing hand, ready to spritz her again whenever she popped her head above the counter.

Just then, the door to the butler's pantry opened. I knocked the faucet back to the "off" position and let the spray nozzle retract into its housing, hurrying to compose my features into an expression of maturity. Kit shot upward from the floor and took a seat at one of the tall barstools that lined the far side of the kitchen island. By the time Amari appeared in her doorway, I was the picture of a calm adult. Kit's face was equally serene, apart from a murderous twitch in her left eye.

"Morning," I chirped.

"Good morning." Amari padded barefoot into the kitchen and took a seat next to Kit. She was dressed much more casually than she'd been at the cocktail party, in an oversized University of Johannesburg t-shirt and orange leggings.

Kit handed her the mug of coffee she'd prepared, and Amari squeezed Kit's hand. Feeling suddenly like a third wheel, I pulled out a frying pan and got to work whipping eggs in a bowl.

"How did you sleep?" Kit asked.

Amari ran a hand over her shaven head and sighed, but it was a deep sigh of happiness. "Very well. Thank you for suggesting I come here. It's much quieter than the inn."

I chewed my lip as I dropped a few pats of butter into the pan. Had Amari heard I was a suspect in Raziel's murder? Did Kit already tell her about last night's interrogation? I had to assume that, even if she'd heard the news, she didn't believe I'd killed Raziel. No way would she be able to sit here with a smile on her face, sipping coffee in the company of someone she thought killed her boss.

That, or she was better at hiding her true feelings than I could ever hope to be.

The three of us sat in silence. The only sounds in the kitchen were the sizzle of butter and the faint strains of Soundgarden from Graham's studio. We watched him work for a few moments.

"He's very talented," Amari said. "Does he do well?"

"Yeah, he sells a lot of pieces at the Afterlife Festival every year." I poured the eggs into the pan. "And then I helped him make a website this summer. He's been getting some custom orders through that."

Her eyes brightened. "Can I see it?"

"Sure. It's nothing fancy. I'm not a professional or anything." I pulled out my phone, found the website, and passed it to her.

"No, it's very good," she said, scrolling with one long finger. "If you like, I could help you with the SEO." She noticed Kit's raised eyebrow and translated, "Search engine optimization."

I took my phone back. "I couldn't ask you to—"

"Please." Amari's dark eyes were intent. "For Graham. He's doing me such a favor and won't charge me rent. I would like to do what I can."

"Um… sure. That stuff is way above my head."

"It sounds like Amari's specialty," Kit said, a note of pride in her voice. "She's the marketing genius that made Raziel famous."

Amari shook her head. "I shone a spotlight, that's all. He did the rest."

A hundred questions about her now-former boss sprang to mind, but I pushed them away, focusing instead on grating a block of cheddar. The kitchen filled with the smells of eggs and cheese, scents that never failed to remind me of my mother. Like my ability to see the dead, I'd inherited my limited culinary talents from her. Scrambling eggs was something I pulled off with a medium success rate.

I divided the eggs onto three heavy ceramic plates and carried one to the kitchen table. Kit followed my lead, bringing over plates for herself and Amari, and I tried to word questions in my mind as we ate.

At last, I settled on, "Do you mind if I ask what Raziel was really like? I've seen his videos—was that him, or a persona?"

"That was him," Amari said. "He was truly that passionate. It's why I wanted to work with him."

"How did you meet?"

"I was in San Francisco, working at a software firm. They hired Raziel to perform street magic at the employee appreciation party. We talked afterward, and he told me his idea for launching a web series. I immediately wanted to be a part of it."

Kit had grown quiet and stared down at her eggs.

"So, you're a fan of magic?" I asked.

"The opposite." A slight edge sharpened Amari's voice. "I hate it."

I tried to catch Kit's eye, but she ignored me. A muscle in her cheek spasmed.

"I don't understand," I admitted. "Why be part of his crew then?"

"Raziel's show wasn't about magic. His goals were to show how easily people allow themselves to be duped and to expose the villains who prey on the grief-stricken."

"People like the Midnight Lantern?" I asked, remembering the video I'd watched before the cocktail party.

Her eyes flashed triumphantly. "Exactly."

"I didn't read the specifics. Why did Raziel go after them?"

"Because they 'specialized'"—she emphasized the word with air quotes—"in finding lost children. Parents from all over the country would pay the owners to locate runaways. We hired six actors to go in with photos of their supposed children. The Midnight Lantern demanded three hundred dollars up front from each customer, and in most cases, these so-called psychics told our actors their children were dead." She paused, and her dark eyes steeled. "The Midnight Lantern advised them to stop looking."

My stomach tightened. "That's awful."

"I've seen worse."

I waited for her to elaborate. She said nothing.

Eventually, Kit cleared her throat. "More coffee, anybody?"

While Kit refilled our mugs, Amari and I eyed each other. There was another question about Raziel I needed to ask, but I didn't know if I could handle the answer. Her shoulders were tense, as if she dreaded what I was about to say.

Kit saved me from doing the impossible. In her typical style, she simply said what needed to be said. "He thought you're a fraud, but Amari disagreed."

Amari's eyes widened and her shoulders relaxed. She confirmed Kit's pronouncement with a small smile.

"You believe me?" I asked.

"Yes."

The simple endorsement stunned me. Despite her friendliness at the cocktail party, I'd been sure she was firmly in Raziel's skeptical camp.

"*Why?*" I blurted.

She answered my question with one of her own. "Do you know about real magic?"

I exchanged glances with Kit, who shrugged.

"I've travelled the world, and I've seen true magic," Amari said. "Things that can't be explained in modern terms. Astral projection. Miraculous healing. Once, I even witnessed telekinesis."

"I don't understand. If you know those things are possible,

why are you so…" I trailed off, narrowly avoiding an unintentional insult.

Amari inferred it anyway. "Hostile toward psychics? I have nothing against the genuine article. But we came to Donn's Hill for a myriad of reasons, chief among which is that you are swimming with frauds. And I've seen firsthand how dangerous they can be."

Dangerous? I remembered Raziel's argument with Nick at the cabin. Raziel had said Nick was all smoke and mirrors, and Nick hadn't denied it. But Nick couldn't be dangerous… could he?

"How do you know there are fakers here?"

"That's the easiest part of my job. There's a simple difference between a fraud and a true intuitive: the fraud will advertise their abilities. Someone with real power guards that secret jealously. It takes months of research for me to find them, and they wouldn't talk to me if they knew I worked for a celebrity like Raziel, because the spotlight is deadly for someone with true, raw *power.*"

"That's not true," I protested. "I've seen real power. I watched Gabrielle Suntador summon multiple spirits last year."

"Yes, I'm familiar with her work. For the sake of argument, let's say she has a legitimate gift and is one of the rare ones who dared to profit from it. She still betrayed the trust of the people who came to her for help. Psychic or fraud, she did the same amount of damage either way."

I hated to admit it, but she had a point.

"And what about what we do?" I asked. "Are we dangerous?"

Amari's eyes softened. "I don't take quite the hard line that Raziel does… did. I adore Yuri. Raziel had a fair amount of respect for him, as well. I know your goal is to truly help people heal, and I admire that."

"Raziel made it clear what he thought of me," I said, folding my arms on the table. "But I still feel awful about what I said to him."

"It might not be too late to apologize," she said.

My head snapped up. Was she serious? There was no hint of sarcasm or humor in her voice.

Kit stared back and forth between us. "That's an awesome idea. I'll get it set up."

"No." I shook my head. "No cameras. No crew. Just me."

"What?" Kit's eyes flashed. "Why?"

"This can't be for the show," I said. "We can't exploit Raziel's spirit that way."

If Kit had been a cat, I swear her hackles would have risen. "We don't *exploit*," she nearly spat the word, "anyone with our show."

"I know that. But Raziel thought differently. And if I was him and someone tried to reach me while a camera was rolling…" I shrugged. "I wouldn't reach back."

Amari rested her hand on Kit's shoulder. "Please, Kit. Mac is right. Recording an attempt to reach him would be an insult to his memory." She glanced at me. "I trust you'll let me know how it turns out."

She stood and retreated to the butler's pantry with her mug in hand. Kit followed, and I stared after them, wondering what else Amari had seen in her travels. She'd said there were things worse than telling frightened parents their missing child was dead with zero evidence to back that up. The still-digesting eggs in my stomach politely requested I refrain from imagining what those things could be.

As I cleared the table, a rough plan began to take shape in my head. If last night was any indication, the only evidence Deputy Wallace's team had pointed firmly in my direction. There was only one person who could point me toward the real killer.

And lucky for me, I knew just how to reach him.

CHAPTER SIXTEEN

"Why don't you come with me?" Hope glimmered in Graham's eyes. He pulled on my arm, tugging me toward his father's pickup truck. "It'd be like a little vacation."

I shook my head. "Wallace was super clear. They don't want me leaving town."

"It's just Chicago," he said. "It's not like it's across the country."

"Somehow, I don't think going to a city with a nice, big international airport would look good for me right now."

I expected him to laugh, but his face darkened.

"I don't like this," he said. "Screw the expo. I'll stay here."

"Are you serious?"

He nodded. "I can go next year."

"No. No way. You're going to that show."

The early morning sun cast the driveway in golden light as we stared each other down. His eyebrows drew together above his glasses, and I could see the wheels turning behind his eyes as he cobbled together an argument that would justify skipping out on the opportunity of a lifetime.

Before he could say anything, I reached out and closed his hand around the truck's keys.

"If you miss out on that show because of me, I'll never forgive you." I kept my voice quiet and my tone light but pushed steel through my eyes. "I won't pretend it didn't scare the hell out of me, getting questioned like that. But I'm innocent. I know it, you know it, and Wallace knows it."

"Does she?"

I didn't allow myself time to mull it over. I had an argument to win. "I hope so. But even if she doesn't, there's nothing you can do here. Please, go to Chicago."

It took several more minutes of convincing and me threatening to cry before he finally climbed into the truck and left. I watched him pull out of the driveway with all his sculptures in tow. For a wild moment, I wanted to run after him, arms waving, and tell him I'd changed my mind. A huge part of me agreed with him. What if I got arrested tomorrow and he was all the way in Chicago? What would I do then?

But it wasn't fair to keep him away from something he'd been working toward on a "what if." He deserved a shot at greater success. If I kept him here and nothing happened, I'd never forgive myself.

I stood in the backyard for a few minutes after the back of his trailer disappeared down the street. I wrapped my arms around my torso, rubbing my arms against the chill of the oncoming winter. Once I was certain I could trust myself to move without chasing Graham down, I went back into the house for a sweater, some sage, and his car keys.

Graham fondly called his faded yellow Geo Metro "Baxter" and had been nursing the aging car along since high school. Baxter and I were not on good terms. More stubborn than a spoiled cat, the car never cooperated when I was at the wheel. If I didn't know better, I'd think it was territorial and didn't like me spending so much time with its owner.

Striker shared my feelings about the vehicle. I put her on the passenger seat, closed the door, and walked around to the driver's side. The second I opened my door, she shot out of the car like a tiny racehorse. She hunched on the picnic table, glaring at me.

"You don't want to come?" I asked.

Her angry yellow eyes informed me she did not.

Hands on my hips, I considered her for a few minutes. I could trick her into following me back into the house by shaking a treat bag then pop her into the cat carrier and be done with it. But then I'd have to drive to the inn with a howling cat beside me, carry that same raging creature up three flights of stairs, and pray she wouldn't take her ire out on Penelope's expensive furnishings.

I sighed. "You win, as usual. Stay out of trouble."

For a moment, I was pleased with myself for being the bigger person and avoiding unnecessary confrontation. Then, I remembered about the car.

It took several tries to start it, an abnormality Graham never seemed to experience. Then, muttering and swearing under my breath, I coaxed Baxter down our road and onto Main Street. Despite the cold, I cranked the window open and let the breeze swirl through the car, stirring up the clay dust and cat hair that covered every inch of the upholstery. In the end, it took me about the same amount of time to get to the center of town as if I'd walked.

Vans and SUVs bearing the logos of various news stations crowded the curb in front of the Oracle Inn. Camera crews stalked up and down the sidewalk, thrusting microphones into the faces of passing residents. One of those faces was familiar, framed by long curls and dominated by rosy cheeks. Stephen Hastain was gesturing wildly and grappling with a reporter for control of their mic.

"Oh, boy," I muttered, parking Baxter against the curb and clambering out of the small car with less grace than I'd have liked.

"*He* was the fraud!" Stephen shouted at the reporter as he swayed on his feet. "Are you going to report on the lives he ruined? Well? Are you?"

"Sir, let go of that!" The reporter wrenched the microphone from Stephen's grasp, then ran his fingers through his hair and straightened his tie.

The cameraman swung the lens in my direction as I jogged up to them. I blocked my face from view with the palm of my hand, feeling a teensy bit like a celebrity trying to get some privacy in Hollywood, and turned my back on the reporter.

"Mac?" Stephen squinted at me, blocking the morning sunlight with one uplifted hand. "What are you doing here?"

I wasn't stupid enough to admit I'd come here to contact Raziel's spirit in front of a rolling camera. Wishing Graham was here to ferry his friend home, then remembering Graham had already done that for Kit two days before, I realized I couldn't just leave Stephen here to fend for himself against the media. I put my arm around him and steered him away from the news crew. "I'm taking you home."

The reporter's voice followed us up the sidewalk. "As you can see, these events have shaken members of the local psychic community and left a deep divide—"

I supported Stephen as he staggered toward the car. Praying he wouldn't do anything that would make Graham suspend my Baxter-borrowing privileges, I buckled the rune caster into the passenger seat. Stephen rested his cheek on the open window frame, letting the breeze lift his curls as we cruised to The Enclave.

I parked Baxter in front of an enormous building housing a

wood furniture manufacturer, and we made our way down the cobblestone path. The sun hadn't yet cleared the top of the tall warehouse to the east, which cast the two rows of houses in a cold shadow. Without the strings of twinkling lights from the cocktail party, the little neighborhood felt a little less magical, but quirky charm still radiated from the stoop of each brightly painted building and every old-fashioned gas lamp.

We passed Daphne's shop, Visions, where she read tarot. Another sign hung from the second-story window advertising massage and reiki sessions, and something called "furrapy." Small CLOSED signs sat in the front windows on both floors; none of the businesses here were open yet, though the curtain in the massage parlor's window twitched as we passed. Clairvoyance appeared to be a strictly nocturnal activity.

Stephen led us to his pink building where he threw runes under the banner of Ancient Answers. He rattled the doorknob and swore under his breath.

"No keys?" I guessed.

He didn't answer. He gave the building a little kick and hopped off the stoop, stumbling on the landing. Then he banged on the door of the lime-green building beside his. "Fang!" he shouted. "I'm locked out!"

After a few minutes of banging and shouting, the door opened and a sleepy, black-haired kid poked his head out. I recognized him from the cocktail party; he'd pulled Nick and Daphne away because of some neighborhood drama. The boy, who looked too young to even be out of high school, ducked back inside for a moment before returning to the door and dropping a key in Stephen's hand. Stephen blew him a kiss and came back to his own porch to open the door.

"Bless that boy," he muttered as the deadbolt clicked back and the door swung open.

"He had a key to your building?"

"I've got one to his too, and about half the other shops here. This place is like a dormitory. Everyone's in each other's business, coming and going"—he jerked his thumb toward the windows above Daphne's shop, where the curtains twitched again —"and spying. It gets on your nerves, and quick, but it's downright useful having a couple spare keys floating about."

Inside, a small square vestibule presented us with two options. The glass door to our right was etched with the same logo as the window out front. Stephen ignored that one, unlocking the solid wooden door in front of us that guarded the staircase up to his apartment.

Short ceilinged and uncomfortably narrow, Stephen's space on the second floor felt even tinier than my studio apartment at Primrose House. But his kitchen boasted more built-in appliances than mine, and he had enough room for an overstuffed couch and flat-screen TV. Dim light from the shadowed street glowed through the edges of the black curtains that hung from the window in front of his dining set. I pulled them open, and he winced.

"Come on, Mac." He yanked them closed again. "Have a heart."

I got to work scooping grounds into his coffee maker while he cleared a pile of mail and paperbacks from the black-clothed table. Within a few minutes, he was scowling down at the mug in his hands and picking at a sleeve of saltines I'd found on the counter.

"Are you going to be okay?" I asked.

He stuffed a few crackers into his mouth and chewed them for a long time, finally swallowing and mumbling, "I'll be fine."

I let him eat and drink in silence for a few minutes and studied the tablecloth. A silver circle about the circumference of a dinner plate was embroidered in the center, and four silver lines divided the circle into equal quarters. The pattern was familiar, and I thought I might have seen it on one of Graham's sculptures.

After Stephen finished the crackers, he ran his fingers through his long, unwashed hair and rubbed his eyes. The bags beneath them had me wondering if he'd gotten an early start on the booze today or if he just hadn't stopped since last night.

After his second cup of coffee, the alarming crimson flush he'd been sporting at the inn had faded back down to his normal level of floridity, and I felt he could handle another inquiry.

"What was that back there?"

He shook his head. "God, I was really off the rails, wasn't I? How embarrassing."

"It's okay. I mean, who hasn't gotten drunk and tried to steal a reporter's microphone?"

"I'm not drunk," he protested. "Just tired. I was up all night listening to tourists sing Raziel's praises. You know how they're talking about that bastard? You'd think he saved a bunch of kittens from a fire." He crunched angrily into another cracker. "After I closed up shop, I got on the news sites to read what the press is saying. They're worse than the tourists, but worst of all are the comments. All these sheep, bleating about how Raziel was some kind of saint."

I'd learned the hard way that internet comment sections were dangerous places. After my first episode of *Soul Searchers* aired, ScreamTV viewers had seemed to care more about my physical appearance than about the ghostly figure that'd appeared next to me on a library bench.

"Do you know if he posted the video?" Stephen asked.

"Which video?"

"The one from the cabin." Stephen flashed me a wicked grin. "Where you almost punched his lights out."

"I haven't seen it anywhere," I said. "Hopefully it stays that way."

"I'll drink to that." He gulped down the rest of his coffee and got up to refill his mug. He'd stopped swaying, and for the first time since he'd gotten into Graham's car, I felt confident he wasn't about to throw up on me. "God, that guy. He had it out for everyone."

"Did he ever accuse you of anything?" I asked. "Like with Nick?"

He plopped back down into the chair across from me. "No, but my profile is a lot lower. I don't think I even registered on that prick's radar."

"What would you have done if he had?"

"I dunno. Changed my name and kept going, or maybe thrown in the towel and retired to Corpus Christi. Who knows?"

"You wouldn't have fought back?" I persisted. "Tried to prove him wrong?"

"How can you prove something like that? Plus, here's the irony. Nick is a fraud. No question about it, and I've known it for a long time. But he's huge. His following is massive, and they've got too much invested at this point. Imagine you're at one of his readings, and you think you'd spoken to your dead wife or something, and in some weird way that brings you peace. Then you hear a rumor Nick was just a con artist. Pride alone would keep you from believing you got fooled."

"So Raziel outing him wouldn't have hurt his business?"

"Maybe he wouldn't see many new customers. But he's been around long enough to keep going. He'd probably stop selling out the huge venues he's been doing, but he'd bring in enough cash to keep himself up."

I chewed the corner of my thumbnail. Just one week before, I'd assumed everyone in town had gifts as genuine as my own, but the truth was becoming clearer by the hour. Raziel had known before coming here that not everyone was on the up and up. He hated psychics—he'd made that clear—so why had he accepted Yuri and Penelope's invitation to come to a place like Donn's Hill?

The answer leapt into my head the moment the question finished forming. He'd come here looking for his next Midnight Lantern, somebody new to debunk. Had Nick been his primary target?

Had I?

That answer wasn't as obvious. Raziel hadn't secretly recorded Nick performing a séance. He'd reserved that distinction for me. Nick had been a pawn, someone Raziel could knock out of the way so he could weasel his way into the cabin that night. But I wasn't a tenth as famous as Nick or half as well-known as any of the intuitives that had regular clients at the festival. I wasn't even as established as anyone who rented space in The Enclave. And Amari had said there'd been a "myriad" of reasons they'd decided to film here, so it couldn't be just me.

If Raziel hadn't been killed, I'd probably have gotten skewered on his new show. My career as a psychic would've been over before it began. I glared down at the black tablecloth, realizing my career could already be over. If I went to prison for Raziel's murder, my entire *life* would be over.

Something tugged in my gut. Alive, Raziel had been a threat to someone, just like he'd been a threat to me. Was that reason enough to kill him?

For someone, it may have been. And if I could figure out who they were, I'd be able to clear my name.

"Do you think any of the psychics here are genuine?" I asked my host.

Stephen frowned, and he pulled back the curtain, letting in the gray light from outside. From this vantage point, all the houses on the opposite side of the narrow street were visible. He looked up and down the row of buildings and eventually shrugged. "At least half."

Half? That was it?

Seeing the look of dismay on my face, he said, "You're a good kid, Mac. Keep your optimism. Don't let the odds get you down. Focus on the folks who are here for the right reasons."

"How can you know who they are?"

He shrugged. "You can't."

"There has to be some way," I pressed. "How did Raziel know about Nick?"

"Well, that's sort of the paradox. You can't know for sure if someone is telling the truth. But Nick got big enough and sloppy enough that he proved he was lying." Stephen cocked his head to one side and considered me. "I know that's not what you were hoping to hear."

"I just want..." I stopped myself before admitting I was a murder suspect. "I just need to know who I can trust."

"Trust your gut."

"I don't know *how.*" I winced at the petulant whine in my voice.

Stephen inhaled deeply and closed his eyes for a few moments. Then, he rapped his knuckles on the table. "Okay. Let's start easy here. Do you think I'm a fraud?"

I opened my mouth to say no, but he held up a hand to stop me.

"Don't give me the polite answer. Really think about it. Weigh the evidence. Listen to your instincts." When I hesitated, he said, "You won't offend me."

"It's just... I've never seen you work. I don't really have anything to go on."

"Fair enough. But here's the thing: I've seen *you* work. I was at the cabin for that séance. I've watched every episode of your show. I'm sitting across from you right now, and I *still* wouldn't stake my life on you being the real deal."

His words stung like a slap in the face. He'd been in the room when I'd made contact with that spirit at the cabin, and he still didn't believe in me? I'd expected to face skeptics, just not from within my own community.

"Why did you come with us to the cabin then?" I tried to ask it in a normal voice, but it came out in a childish half-whisper.

He reached out and squeezed my hand. "Hey, you're taking this all the wrong way. I believe you are what you say you are, Mac."

That made me feel an ounce better, though in the back of my mind, I wondered how much the free publicity from our show played into his decision to be part of the cleansing.

"I'm just saying we can never really *know*," he went on. "I think it's healthy for everyone to have a little skepticism, and it's even more important for people like us. Understand?"

I didn't, and the confusion had to be plain on my face.

He sighed and stood up. "I see you're the type who has to learn by doing. Wait here."

He retrieved something from a table by the door. It was about the size of a box of donuts but made of dark, sweet smelling wood.

"Brazilian rosewood," he explained when I sniffed the air. "People find it soothing."

From inside the box, he pulled out four black velvet bags, each cinched closed with a different colored string: red, green, blue, and yellow. He lined them up on the table in front of me.

"Any of those speaking to you?" he asked.

I glanced down at the bags and back at Stephen, doubting his earlier claim that he wasn't drunk.

"Just pick up whichever one you feel like picking up," he urged.

Feeling foolish, I considered the bags. They were just bags; I didn't even know what was inside. How could any of them "speak" to me?

But the expectant expression on Stephen's face made me reach out a hand. I almost grabbed the bag with the red string, but felt a sudden warmth from the one with the yellow tie as my hand passed it. I picked up that one instead and handed it to Stephen, whose face broke out into a grin.

"All right," he said. "I believe you a bit more now. Not enough to stake my life on it, but you've definitely got a touch of something."

He set the yellow-stringed bag aside and dumped out the red one I'd almost chosen. Dozens of small, rectangular pieces of wood piled onto the table. The cedar had been lacquered, so the runes shone in the light from the window, and each one bore a different symbol.

"Do they have to be wood?" I asked.

"No, that's all just personal preference. Some people like to cast with wood. Some like crystal. Some people think the only thing that matters is that you made the runes yourself."

"Did you make these?"

"Yep. Go ahead, touch them. It won't hurt anything."

I picked up a rune and ran my thumb over the smooth surface. The symbols looked old and sharp. I couldn't see any curved lines in the pile; the shapes were all composed of straight lines, and some almost looked like letters.

"These are Elder Futhark runes," he explained. "I made this set myself when I was first starting out. I wanted to burn the runes into the wood while meditating on their meanings."

"Do you have to make your own for them to be effective?"

"Nope."

He gently pushed the cedar rectangles aside and grabbed the bag with the green string. When he tossed it onto the table, a random assortment of objects flew out: an old soda can top, a seashell, the thimble piece from a Monopoly game, a St. Christopher's medal, and a gold wedding ring. I raised an eyebrow at Stephen, and he laughed.

"This is my favorite bag. You should see the looks on people's faces when I cast these during a reading. But the funny thing is: it's usually my most accurate set."

"What are they?" I poked at the St. Christopher's medal. I'd worn one in elementary school and didn't see how a Christian symbol factored into an occult practice.

"Curios. Little things that mean something to me. It's like letting life design your runes for you. When I find something that feels right, I add it to the set. Maybe a curio replaces another object or maybe the set grows." He pointed to the pile. "The medal was a gift from my mother before I left Ireland. To me, it signifies travel or movement. I found that seashell on a cruise right before I got awful food poisoning, so it's an omen of bad tidings."

"And this?" I held up the wedding ring.

A wicked grin spread over his face. "That's a fairly recent addition. My wife left me last year. As soon as we finalized the divorce, I won a mint in the state lotto. She didn't get a dime, and I got enough to move here and be a full-time weirdo."

"So, does it mean 'luck'?"

"Almost. It means change. If it's far away from that seashell, it usually means the change will lead to a favorable outcome. Thing about runes is, the symbols don't really matter. As long as the caster knows what they mean, anyway. You could have a set of popsicle sticks with emojis painted on them, and as long as you've got a connection to them, you can get a good reading."

He gathered his curios into a pile and put them beside the wooden runes.

"This next set," he explained while opening the blue-stringed bag, "is the one that got me into all this stuff. They're why I call myself a 'caster.' Did you know that some people call reading runes 'casting the bones'?"

I shook my head. A sinking feeling in my stomach warned me I wouldn't like what was in that bag, and I was right. Thirteen small bones clattered across the tabletop, and I cringed at the sound they made.

"I got these from a voodoo priest in New Orleans when I was about your age. He read my future, told me life would never be dull if I followed the bones. I bought that very set, and my life has been interesting ever since. Not always the good kind of interest-ing, but you can't have it all." He pushed the bones toward me. "They use a different set of symbols than the Futhark, see?"

Fighting to keep a frown off my face, I leaned forward to examine them. Unlike the straight, abstract symbols burned into the wooden runes, these were more complex and had been painted, rather than carved, onto the bone. One of the bones with a wide, flat piece had a blue eye painted on it. The wishbone was covered with a pattern of black and red dots.

"What kind of animal is... er, was this?" I asked, leaning back and away from the table. The bones made me uncomfortable, and not just because I didn't love the idea of them once having been a living creature. They put off a strange energy.

"Chicken. Pretty standard." He gathered the bones and put them back into the velvet bag. "Most people are a little put off by the bones, and that's okay. Now, think about everything I just told you. Do you believe me? That I've the gift?"

We were back to this. He was going to make me decide if he was lying or not. I thought about it, tilting my head and narrowing my eyes as I considered the smiling Irishman in front of me. He'd seemed genuine while we were talking. And there was some-thing... *off* about that set of chicken bones.

"I do," I told him honestly.

"Okay. Now, you're new to all of this, right? I heard you discovered your powers while the Soul Searchers were filming you."

"Yeah… I mean, I saw things when I was little. Ghosts my mom called 'The Travelers.' But I didn't know what they were." I frowned unhappily. "My mom kept all this stuff from me."

"Well, try to imagine we were having this conversation a year ago. Back before you knew the things you know now. Imagine you're at a farmer's market, and for a laugh, you stop in at my booth to have me tell your fortune."

It was an unlikely scenario. For one thing, farmer's markets were way too early in the day. I'd never been to one in my life. But for the sake of whatever it was he was trying to tell me, I humored him with a nod.

"Imagine I just showed you my runes and told you their histories. Would you have believed me?"

A wry smile tugged at the corners of my mouth. "No. But I'd have been too polite to tell you."

Stephen grinned again. "How very kind."

"Was any of it true? Or were you lying?"

"Well, I didn't win the lottery. I made that part up. But the rest of it's true." He winked. "Here's the point: the more we believe, the more we're apt to believe. And there are people who can—and do—take advantage of that. So, like I said, keep a healthy amount of skepticism. Not a Raziel amount. A healthy amount."

He scooped up the three sets of runes he'd shown me and slid them back into their bags. Then, with a flourish, he scooped up the final sack and loosened the yellow string. "Since you chose these, I'll use them for your reading."

I straightened up in my chair and leaned forward. I hadn't expected to see him work so soon. And I'd never had my fortune told, not even as a child.

"Do you have a particular question or problem you'd like to address?" he asked.

That was easy. *Who really killed Raziel Santos?* But little as I knew about runes and fortune-telling, I knew they couldn't answer a question like that.

"We can do a general reading," Stephen suggested.

"Yeah, let's go with that."

"Okay." He bounced the bag in one hand a few times, gazing in my direction with unfocused eyes before tossing it gently onto the table. Five small stones spilled out. One of them skittered all the way across the table and landed outside the circle, near my arm. Three others clustered around the center, where the two lines in the cloth's design crossed. The fifth had barely cleared the edge of the bag at Stephen's side of the table.

Leaning closer to study them, I realized they weren't polished stones like I'd initially thought. Each the size of a nickel but twice as thick, they'd been carved out of clay and covered with a shining black glaze. The runes themselves were an earthy green and stretched from edge to edge. I reached out to pick one up, but Stephen stopped me.

"How they lay on the table plays an important role in their interpretation," he explained.

"They're beautiful. Did you make them?"

"They were a gift from a certain good-looking young sculptor who wanted to welcome me to town." He cupped his chin in one hand. "You two have quite the connection. I've seen it, when you're together. Either you felt his energy through that bag, or we've got one hell of a coincidence on our hands."

I remembered the way the bag with the yellow string had called to me at the last moment, and the usual Graham-related flush rushed into my cheeks. I hurried to change the subject. "What are these symbols? Are they Elder-whatever, too?"

Like the wooden runes, the symbols carved into Graham's

ceramics were somewhat abstract and composed entirely of straight lines. One of them reminded me of tick marks someone might use for counting in fives, except the four perpendicular lines were slanted and the crossbar was straight.

"They're based on an ancient alphabet from Ireland, called Ogham. He's a thoughtful man, your Graham. Now"—he rubbed his hands together—"let's see what these gorgeous stones have to say."

As he studied the way the runes had landed, I studied his face. He was intent, but that meant nothing. Maybe he was really seeing something in those runes, or maybe he was thinking about the things he knew about me and trying to come up with something that would make me happy enough to leave a fat tip on the table.

But there was a sincerity in his eyes. If I had to decide, right now, based entirely on a gut feeling... I trusted him.

"Hmmm. Well, there's a clear message here, a message of change. You've set something in motion, jostled the threads of the web that connects us all. Something big will happen soon, something that will define the rest of your life."

"In a good way, I hope?"

He pursed his lips. "I'm not sure. There'll be an important lesson learned, and, well... knowledge is never easy to come by."

"Great, that's encouraging. Any idea what *kind* of change?"

"This Straith rune"—he pointed to the one with four slanted lines crossed by a fifth straight one—"points to an impending journey. Your plans may be altered or even destroyed completely."

"If you're trying to make me nervous, mission accomplished."

"Well, there's nothing especially negative here. It's like the Death card in Tarot. It looks ominous, but it really just means, 'Don't get too comfortable.' But there is..." He frowned at the runes.

"What?"

"There's an external force at play here. Something's moving in the background, influencing events from behind the scenes. Whatever 'journey' is coming…" He looked up at me, his brows tilting upward in a pained expression. "It won't be your choice to take it."

CHAPTER SEVENTEEN

B axter's engine shuddered and complained at a stop sign on Main Street. If I turned right here, I could park on the street behind the inn and sneak in through the back. I'd be able to avoid the press and—assuming Penelope was open to the idea—spend some time in Raziel's room. There was no better place in town to contact him, and yet… I hesitated.

I'd been so eager that morning, but now I wondered about the wisdom of that plan. Deputy Wallace might understand the need to call out to Raziel's spirit in the place it'd left his body, but anyone else would probably chalk it up that inexplicable need of the guilty to return to the scene of the crime.

For two days now, it'd been my only idea, but my conversation with Stephen had given me another one. So there I sat, debating whether to stick to my original plan or follow this new thread. I chewed my lip. Would it be better to add to the list of reasons the sheriff thought I'd killed Raziel, or to look for answers via a slower route?

Anxiety pricked my nerves. I hungered for a clear direction, some kind of clue I could pass on to Wallace. On top of my desire to stop being a "person of interest," I wanted them to quit wasting time. The more they looked into me, the less they were looking into whoever really killed Raziel.

The inn pulled to me. I knew, deep in my soul, I needed to reach out to Raziel. But when I'd tried to go there before, I'd been drawn in a different direction and ended up at The Enclave instead. That had to mean something. I could at least investigate the possibility of finding answers without further implicating myself before barreling back to the place he'd been murdered.

My decision made, I threw Baxter into gear. The car lurched and complained all the way up the hill for which the town had been named. The incline steepened as we left the commercial center of Donn's Hill behind, and just before the road ended at an old stone chapel, I turned right into the ritzy Estates at Hillside.

"How are you today, ma'am?" the guard at the community's entrance asked.

I claimed to be fine and handed him my driver's license. He scanned it and noted who I was there to see before opening the large, wrought-iron gate that protected the most lavish homes in Donn's Hill.

It was my second time visiting the ritzy neighborhood, but I still marveled at the difference between the antique, aging feel of downtown and the modern, ostentatious feel of these homes. Tall hedges protected most of the enormous houses from view of the street, and there was no activity on any of the sidewalks. The few other cars I passed had shining Mercedes and Jaguar ornaments protruding from their hoods, and I felt conspicuously out of place in my borrowed Geo.

"What do all these people do for a living?" I wondered aloud.

Many residents of Donn's Hill did what Graham called "moonlighting" outside of festival season to make ends meet. I'd heard that some early residents had made fortunes in lumber and mining, but I couldn't imagine what kept this many families living in so much luxury. The curving street went on for miles, wrapping around the backside of the hill and affording the many dozens of tiny mansions with views of the surrounding farmland.

A miniature brick-and-stucco castle and a giant shaker-style home with six garage doors flanked Nick and Daphne's rustic-looking log home. It was a fraction less oversized than the surrounding homes but still big enough to swallow Primrose House whole.

Nick answered the door with bloodshot eyes, and a thick growth of stubble covered his face. Being day-drunk appeared to be the latest fashion among the local psychic community.

"You here to see Daphne? She's… uh…" He narrowed his eyes and glanced over his shoulder, down the dark hallway behind him. "She's not here."

"That's okay. I came to see you."

"Oh. Well… Come in then, I guess." He turned away from me and trudged slowly down the hallway to the kitchen at the back of the house. I took that as an invitation to follow.

"Coffee?" he asked, throwing himself into a chair at his dining room table.

It was the same room where Yuri and I had convinced Nick and Daphne to take part in the cabin séance. Back then, I'd been envious of the level of cleanliness that hinted at a recent visit by a maid service. Now, the kitchen counters were barely visible under piles of dirty dishes, and the garbage overflowed with takeout containers. A moldy, rotten smell wafted lazily from the kitchen sink. I declined his offer, taking a seat on the side of the table nearest the open windows.

"Suit yourself." Nick took a slug from a can of beer and glared at me. "So. You here to ream me out? 'Cause your boss already gave me an earful."

"Yuri was here?"

Nick nodded. "He dropped by yesterday and trampled me with his high horse."

That didn't sound like Yuri. He approached everything from a place of compassion. I couldn't picture him talking down to someone.

"Does that mean it's true?" I didn't bother to specify what I was asking about. Raziel's accusation filled the room like the proverbial elephant.

Another slug of beer. Another nod.

"Oh."

I didn't know what I'd been expecting. A fiery denial maybe? An offer to prove that he really had psychic powers? Anything but this sad, colorless admission.

"Why?" I asked.

"Seemed like a good idea at the time." He drained his beer, stood, and collected a new can from the near-empty refrigerator. He tilted it toward me and I shrugged, so he grabbed a second. At least it was almost lunchtime.

I cracked open my can as Nick sank down into his chair with a deep sigh. I tried to remember what he'd looked like when he was happy.

"You know what's the worst thing about getting older?" he asked, gazing out the back windows. "It's not the way your body ages. It's your mind. When you're young, consequences don't matter. Not really. But now, consequences are all I think about. I can't take one step forward without worrying I'm walking into a trap."

"I'm sorry," I said. "I didn't want Raziel at the cabin. I hope you know I didn't invite him."

Nick said nothing for a few moments but ran the rim of his beer can back and forth on his upper lip and considered me with narrowed eyes. "So," he said at last. "You didn't come here to see Daphne, and you look like a kid who just got caught stealing gum from the corner store. Just ask me whatever you want to ask me and get it over with."

I nodded and took a deep breath. "Raziel said he knew you were tricking people because that's what he did too."

Nick's eyes were flat. Again, his lack of denial or protest unnerved me.

"I want to know how to trick people," I said.

He raised an eyebrow. "Daphne said you're the real deal."

"I am." I straightened my shoulders. "I don't want to know so *I* can trick people. I want to spot it when someone else is lying."

"She's the real deal, too, you know."

"I know." I'd seen the look on Daphne's face when the red-eyed spirit had appeared at our séance. She'd seen him. Nobody else in the room had. Certainly not Raziel.

"I'll tell you right now, Mac. You don't want to know what's behind most of the curtains in this town."

"It can't be 'most.' The frauds have to be the minority here."

His lips twisted into a smile, but there was no joy in his eyes. "I like you, Mac. Your enthusiasm. Your naïveté. I don't want to be the person who takes those things away from you."

"I'm not naïve. And it's not like I'm excited about finding out which psychics around here are conning their customers."

"Then why do it?"

I paused. I wasn't proud the sheriff thought I'd killed Raziel. I considered lying so I wouldn't have to admit someone thought I could take a life. But what other reason was there? If I wasn't trying to clear my name, would it really matter if there were some pretenders mixed in with the true psychics? Not everyone who came to town for the Afterlife Festival was looking for meaningful answers or a deep connection to the other side. It was kitschy and unique, and some people came just for a good story to tell. They were tourists, and who cared if tourists saw the real thing or a flimsy imitation?

My neck tightened at the thought of people like my mother coming here and getting scammed. It did matter that the psychics here were real. It mattered a lot. In a place where the lines between life and death blurred so easily, there was nothing more important than sincerity.

"I think whoever killed Raziel was probably afraid he would expose them for being a fake." I flinched, remembering who I was talking to. "Um... no offense."

Nick shrugged. "None taken. I didn't kill the bastard. But I still don't get it. His manager will probably continue his smear campaign. Why not just leave it to her to figure out who's who around here?"

"Because..." I fiddled with my beer, twisting the tab around the top of the can in circles, unable to look Nick in the eye. "Because Sheriff Harris thinks I did it."

He was silent. I peeked up at him and was surprised to see a smile quirking the edge of his lips. It soon spread across his face. His eyes widened, and he tossed his head back and roared with laughter. I watched in uncomfortable silence, wishing I could join in on the joke, but I couldn't see anything funny about my situation.

After a full minute of laughing at me, Nick finally calmed down, wiping tears from his cheeks. "Oh, boy. I needed that. It's been a hell of a week. Thanks, Mac."

"No problem," I muttered out of reflex.

"They can't really think you did it."

"Well, they pulled me in for questioning yesterday."

"Did they arrest you?"

I shook my head.

He shrugged again. "They're just covering all their bases. Don't let it bother you."

My eyebrows shot into my hairline, and I opened my mouth to tell him exactly how impossible that would be, but he cut me off.

"I know, I know. How can it not bother you? But I mean it. You have nothing to worry about. Sure, you tried to clock the guy.

But who can blame you?" He drained the rest of his beer, stood, and shook the empty can at me. "Refill?"

"No, thanks." I'd cracked mine open but barely taken a sip.

Laughter overcame my host again as he crossed the room with a fresh beer in his hand, and he waved the can at me apologetically. "I'm sorry. I'm just picturing you trying to charm your way into Raziel's room so you can strangle him."

I stared at him. The Sheriff's Department still hadn't released the details of Raziel's death to the press. "How did you know how he died?"

"Everyone's talking about it—Stephen, that little weenie Fang, everybody. It's a small town. But they're also all talking about who killed him. And spoiler alert: it wasn't you."

"Hilarious."

He chuckled and leaned forward to pat my knee. "Lighten up, Mac."

"I'll lighten up when the Sheriff's Department stops telling me things like 'don't leave town.'"

"I told you, you've got nothing to worry about. Everybody knows Raziel got in over his head with some girl. He was a total womanizer, and he didn't concern himself with strictures like monogamy or the legal age. Know what I mean? Either a girlfriend got jealous of another girl in his life, or someone's husband or dad decided enough was enough. So unless you were sleeping with him…" He raised an eyebrow. "Were you?"

"No!"

"See? You're fine."

I leveled my gaze at him, unable to share his confidence. "So I guess that's a 'no,' then?"

He belched. "No to what?"

"Teaching me how to spot a fraud."

"Waste of your time. And mine. Just do your thing. Make your show. It's a good show, by the way. Keep being you, and let the cops figure out which part of Raziel's love life did him in, okay?" He yawned and stood up. "Man, I am beat."

I took the hint and left the house, leaving my nearly full beer on the table, but my head was swimming with so many thoughts, I didn't think to start the car. Instead I sat there, looking out over Donn's Hill. From up here, the town looked so different from what I saw out my little turret window.

Drumming my fingers on Baxter's steering wheel, I took stock of my options. Not only was Nick unwilling to help me, he didn't even see the point. Maybe he was right; maybe I had nothing to worry about.

As I considered letting everything go and just heading back to Primrose House to while away the afternoon with Striker, Sheriff Harris' mustached face loomed in my mind. He hadn't seemed like he was just covering his bases, like Nick thought. He'd been deadly serious and downright hostile.

I sighed. My bright idea had been a bust. It was time to stop procrastinating. I'd known from the beginning what I needed to do. Kicking the clutch to the floor and gunning the engine, I pulled out of Nick's swanky neighborhood and headed back down Main Street.

I had a spirit to summon.

CHAPTER EIGHTEEN

Penelope waved me into her office when I knocked on the open doorframe. The room sat off the kitchen at the back of the house and was as organized as I imagined her closet to be, with binders, photos, and storage boxes arranged neatly on built-in shelves along all four walls. The space was a study in neutral colors, accented only by Penelope's bold, lime green sweater.

Her face registered zero surprise when I asked to rent the attic suite for the night. In answer, she opened a desk drawer, revealing a collection of dried sage bundles wrapped in Gabrielle's trademark red string.

"They're from the hidden compartments on the second floor." She handed one to me. "I suspected they might be useful someday."

"You're sure you don't mind me using the room?" I turned the bundle between my fingertips. "Nobody's reserved it?"

"Not yet, but I expect there to be a certain level of ghoulish curiosity about the room once the facts about his murder become public." She sighed. "I already need to redecorate. We can't have curtains with cords in any of the rooms. It'll be too morbid."

"I'm guessing we'll see the details on the news tonight,

regardless of when Sheriff Harris wanted the public to know," I said. "Everyone in town is already talking about it."

She nodded. "They were planning to hold off on the official announcement until after the funeral, but the press won't wait. I expect plenty of people will want to stay in the room where the deed happened. We've pushed the supernatural history of this house from the beginning, and his murder will increase that draw." She frowned. "Violence isn't what I wanted us to be known for."

The last hotel she'd been associated with had—through no fault of her own—developed an unsavory reputation. I felt a sudden surge of affection for this woman who worked so hard to increase tourism to Donn's Hill. She might not be psychic, but she had even more invested in the continued success of the Afterlife Festival than any of the intuitives here, especially any of the fake ones.

"Don't worry," I told her. "You've done an incredible job with this place. It'll be a draw for anyone, not just ghost hunters and Raziel nuts."

"Thank you, Mac. Now, I want to be sure future guests can sleep soundly in that attic." She handed me an ornate, old-fashioned bronze key. "I liked Raziel, but I don't want his spirit lingering here. If you can make sure the room is clear, your stay tonight will be on the house."

"Will do." I stood and shouldered my bag.

"Are you headed up now?"

"No, I need to grab a few things from home."

"Park on First Street and sneak in through the yard when you come back."

That was exactly what I'd done before coming to see her, but I didn't mention it. "Okay. Any particular reason?"

"News of Raziel's strangling isn't the only gossip swirling

around town. Several people have asked me if I know why Sheriff Harris brought you in for questioning."

I imagined the people of Donn's Hill, many of them strangers, thinking I was capable of murder. Whispering about me behind closed doors. Pulling their children closer as I passed, just in case I snapped.

The thought crushed me. I sank back down into the chair beside me and momentarily forgot to breathe.

"Are you all right?" Penelope asked.

My reply was a near-whisper. "What did you tell them?"

"That you're a well-known psychic who's consulted on murder cases before, and that's why you were at the station." She folded her hands beneath her chin, her gray eyes boring into mine. "And I tell them, and anyone else who will listen, that you're a kind and wonderful person and it's preposterous to imagine you could harm anyone."

Any attempt my brain made to form a reply was immediately choked off by my heart, which ballooned in my chest to the point of pain. I could only stare at her through rapidly pooling tears and hope she knew how much her words meant to me.

After a few moments, I cleared my throat. "Thanks, Penelope. I'll do my best upstairs."

Then, resisting the urge to run around her desk and give her a hug, I left the inn and drove Baxter back to Primrose House. I had the sage I'd grabbed that morning, plus the bundle from Penelope, but I decided I needed a black candle. Raziel had called those "stage setting," and I planned to use the memory of that argument to connect with his spirit. Anger, after all, was the strongest emotion I'd felt when I'd been around him.

To my surprise, Striker jumped onto the driver's seat as soon as I stepped out of the car in front of Graham's garage.

I raised an eyebrow at her. "Now you're on board?"

"Brrllll." She rubbed her face against the steering wheel.

It dawned on me that she'd refused to join me on my earlier outing, which had resulted in not one, but two time-consuming detours. Her meaning was clear: *Next time, let me drive.*

THE SUN HAD ALREADY BEGUN to set by the time I closed myself in Raziel's former suite, casting the sky in an orange glow that filtered into the room through the curtainless dormer windows on both sides. I shivered, wishing I hadn't let myself get so distracted earlier. This would have been a hell of a lot less creepy in the middle of the afternoon.

As soon as I shut the door, Striker leapt out of my arms and rolled around the bearskin rug so vigorously that I second-guessed my initial assessment about it being fake. I lifted the corner to check the tag. The rug claimed to be made of polyester, but that didn't stop my cat from gleefully pouncing from edge to edge and burying her nose in the soft piling.

I left her to her one-sided game of tag, trusting her not to scratch any of the furniture, and checked the suite for anything unexpected, like a murderer hiding behind the shower curtain. On impulse, I checked behind the folding screen by the wardrobe, half expecting to see Raziel's prone body again. Thankfully, no part of him remained.

A familiar sadness filled me as I gazed around the space. Those walls should have been dark and covered with heavy, embroidered tapestries. This room felt classy but cold without them, and I hated it. Then I hated hating it. Would I ever be able to think of Gabrielle without being overcome by this crippling cocktail of sorrow and shame garnished with a hint of anger? Yet again, I felt the urge to write her a letter. But I didn't know what I'd say, and I had even less of an idea what I'd want to hear back.

Shaking my head, I got down to business. The coffee table in the middle of the room felt like the best fit for me to work from. Shaped like a scalene triangle with each side a different length, it reminded me vaguely of a planchette from a Ouija board. I placed a black candle atop a laminated room service menu to protect the table's polished wood top and lit the wick.

Once the flame was burning steadily, I set the bundle of sage from Penelope's office beside the candle. It was there, ready for the moment I might need to clear this space. I'd also brought bundles of my own from home, ones I'd wrapped myself, but it seemed right to use one of those Gabrielle had secreted away in the house. One Penelope had saved for me. Penelope, who had owned the motel where I'd first encountered the ghost of her husband and rediscovered my psychic abilities. I felt connected to the history of this place, tied to it by an invisible, red string that stretched to every corner of Donn's Hill.

I watched a white tendril curl away from the candle's flame and let a love for this town fill me like smoke fills a jar. Striker climbed into my lap, and I stroked her back, allowing the rhythm to sync up with my heartbeat. My body was rooted to the floor, bound by my connection to this room, this house, this town. But my spirit was free, free to reach out and touch the flimsy curtain that separates our world from the next.

"Raziel Santos," I called in a clear voice. "If your spirit lingers here, please give me a sign."

The room was still. The candle's flame burned straight upward, undisturbed by any movement.

I tried again. "Raziel, this is Mackenzie Clair. Can you hear me?"

To my left, a floorboard creaked. I jerked my head to the side, startled, and saw nothing. Striker purred gently in my lap. I glanced down; her eyes were wide, and she stared toward the closed attic door. The candlelight reflected off her huge pupils, making them glow in the gloom.

"Raziel, if you're here, I just want to talk."

Another creak sounded to my right. I whipped my head around, but nothing moved in the bathroom. All was calm.

"I'm here," a voice whispered beside my left ear.

I jumped. Striker leapt onto the table with a low growl. Beside her, the candle sputtered.

"Raziel?" I asked.

I don't know why I bothered; I knew in my gut the voice didn't belong to him.

In answer, the flame went out, plunging the room into darkness.

CHAPTER NINETEEN

A pair of red eyes burned at me through the blackness. My hands went clammy; this was too close to my dream for comfort. I pinched my arm in case I'd fallen asleep, but the red eyes remained.

Slowly, my vision adjusted to the darkness. From her hissing, I identified the blob in front of me as Striker, who had landed on the coffee table and puffed out to twice her normal size. Beyond her, lines coalesced around the pair of eyes to form a wide face below a smashed top hat.

There was no mistaking it. The spirit from the cabin stood before me once again.

Immediately, I tried to break off contact, centering myself and focusing on slamming mental barriers in place between my mind and the spirit world. My mind fuzzed. The connection refused to break. The spirit wanted to keep it open, and he was stronger than me.

Much stronger.

The more I tried to close myself off, the cloudier my mind became. I shook my head and scratched at my scalp, desperate to be back in the light and away from this apparition. Striker growled but didn't move from her spot atop the table.

"Don't fight me, Mackenzie. Relaxsssssss..." He dragged out the last syllable into a long hiss, and his red eyes dimmed to a deep black.

Slowly, my mind cleared. My arms dropped to my sides, hands tingling. It reminded me of the feeling after pushing myself too hard in gym class and hyperventilating. I sucked in deep breaths through my nose and let the air escape out my mouth. Hands shaking, I leaned forward, struck a match, and re-lit the candle. The room filled with a soft, flickering glow, and the spirit smiled, revealing a mouthful of shining, narrow teeth.

"See? It's so much easier when we just get along." He stood just behind the opposite couch, his arms wrapped around his torso. His long, thin fingers gripped his shoulders, and his pale, pointed fingernails caught the candlelight. Like at the cabin, he wore a dark cloak, only now he'd pushed it back like a cape.

My body shivered, but the logical part of my brain stepped in before fear could take over. I reminded myself that this was nothing more than a ghost. It just wasn't the one I'd been trying to reach out to. The important thing to figure out was the *type* of spirit I was dealing with. I'd encountered two since discovering my psychic abilities: peaceful ones and poltergeists.

The peaceful ones, like the girl I'd encountered at the library during my first investigation with the *Soul Searchers*, had been so solid and looked so alive that I'd been convinced she was a library patron. She hadn't done me—or anyone else—any harm.

The poltergeists I'd known had a tendency to make themselves heard before allowing themselves to be seen. Neither of them had been great conversationalists, either. Odds were, I was dealing with a peaceful spirit here.

I hadn't been a medium for long, but I drew comfort on falling into the routine I'd established while working with my team. With the bundle of sage in my hand, I asked, "Who are you?"

"My name is Horace," he said. Then he repeated his words from the last time he'd appeared. "I've been looking for you."

"You found me at the cabin, didn't you?"

He grinned, flashing his teeth again. "I did. You were reaching out with such strength that you pulled me from here."

"From here?"

He flickered in time with the candlelight, like an old movie playing on an ancient projector. "I'm bound to this house, but on rare occasions I'm able to... piggyback, you might say, through a powerful medium."

"You can do that? How?"

"I've had many, many years to practice."

"Did you..." I'd been about to ask if he'd died here before remembering not all spirits are even aware they're dead. I changed course halfway through the sentence. "... live here?"

"No. I was visiting a cousin and had the unfortunate luck to die here. But you didn't call out tonight to speak with me. You were trying to reach another. The man who was murdered here." They weren't questions. Just like the power in the room, he had all the answers.

"Did you see it?"

He nodded. "I see everything that happens in this place."

"Then you can tell me—"

"Certainly," he interrupted. "But the dead are not generous. Even we have a price." He flashed that Bible-salesman smile again.

"What can the living do for the dead?" I asked.

"Many things. Remember us, honor us. But in my particular case, I have need of a more specific type of assistance."

I glanced down at Striker, who stared back at me with wide

eyes. Her little body tensed, and every strand of fur stood on end, but she huddled immobile on the coffee table.

My body mimicked hers. Tense. Unmoving. Graham's concerns about me attempting another summoning rang in my memory, but I didn't have any mental space to feel guilty for doing exactly what he'd been worried I would do. My mind was wholly occupied by the task of processing this spirit's words. He spoke to me far more clearly than any ghost I'd ever encountered, and the tingle in my spine warned me that wasn't a good thing.

"There's a reason I've been trapped in this house for so long," Horace said. "I tried to move on but found it impossible. I believe unfinished business is keeping me here. Once I rectify my last mistake, I hope to leave."

Good. He wanted to move on. That seemed easier than trying to force a spirit like Richard Franklin to leave this world behind against his will. "What was the mistake?"

"Before I died, I stole something precious from my cousin: his mother's jewelry box. It was so beautiful, carved from a single piece of alder, and contained her wedding ring. I traded it to a lumberjack at Cambion's Camp." His form flickered again. "In return, he gave me the gin that killed me."

The pieces clicked together in my mind. He'd stolen something, and his guilt over the theft tied him to this plane of existence. I immediately knew what had to be done. "The box needs to be returned, so you can make things right."

"If I have any hope of seeing the next world, yes."

"How long ago was this?" I wasn't sure how long it took wood to decompose, but I suspected it was about the same amount of time it took top hats and cloaks to go firmly out of style. "And do you know where the lumberjack left it?"

"Time moves strangely when you're dead. I don't know how long it's been, but I do know the box is still at Cambion's Camp. I feel it always, pulling at me. Never letting me forget what I did."

His pupils, which I'd thought were at their maximum size already, grew larger in his wide eyes. "Will you help me?"

I hesitated. It seemed like a wild goose chase. I didn't even know where this Cambion place was, and a jewelry box felt like a very small thing to survive the decades that must have passed since Horace stole it.

"Mackenzie." Horace frowned. "Help me, and I will help you."

His voice was louder inside my mind than outside it, and my head swam. The physical sensation of my fingernails digging into my palms was suddenly muted by the oppressive, powerful energy that rolled off Horace in unending waves. The pricks of pain were present but muffled, and that same feeling spread to my brain as well. My thoughts became sluggish. What was he saying? He was offering me information, but at a price.

"Do you understand my terms?" he asked.

"I think so." The words were slow to work their way out of my mouth. Even my breathing felt hampered by his presence. "I'll bring the jewelry box back here, and you'll tell me who really killed Raziel Santos."

"I'd be deeply indebted to you."

"And if I refuse?"

He flickered again. "My incarceration here will continue *ad infinitum*, and you'll never be able to clear your name."

The pressure in the room increased. I wondered if this is how deep-sea divers felt—oppressed, suffocated, and desperate to be free. The air thickened around me. Penelope's tasteful decor swirled. I had no time to wonder if his words were true or to reassure myself that there were other ways to prove my innocence. Time seemed to slip away from me along with my breath. He promised answers. He promised relief.

"I'll find the box," I gasped.

A grin spread across Horace's face. "I'll be watching."

He vanished, and the pressure let up immediately. I tumbled off the couch and onto the faux fur rug, clutching my stomach and wheezing. I hadn't felt this winded since running a mile and a half in high school, and if I closed my eyes for more than a blink, the darkness spun around me like I'd had too much to drink.

Striker jumped off the table and huddled beside my face, her body low to the floor. A deep rumble came from her chest, half purr, half growl. I realized she'd probably felt as squashed and suffocated as I had throughout Horace's visitation, trapped on that coffee table and unable to move.

It took a long time to recover my breath, and still longer to light the sage and cleanse the area to clear it of any remnants of the heaviness Horace had left behind when he'd disappeared. Circling the room and focusing on making space for positive energy helped me clear my mind and make sense of everything that'd just happened. Horace might not be a poltergeist, but he was a negative presence in this house. How long had Gabrielle had to deal with him while she'd lived here? Had he appeared at her séances? Had she ever tried to banish him? These were questions to which only she would know the answers, and I realized I had two important decisions to make.

Exhausted but in no mood to sleep in the bed Raziel had slept in or to rest in a space now firmly associated with a bully of a ghost, I gathered my things and retreated to the first floor of the inn. It was after midnight, but light spilled into the lobby from the kitchen. Penelope's office door stood open, and I knocked at the doorframe again.

"Any luck?" she asked.

"Not with reaching Raziel." I handed her back the key to the attic suite. "But there's someone else up there, a spirit named Horace. He's strong." I bit my lip. "And he's not happy. I'm worried he could harm your guests."

Penelope's eyes widened with alarm, and her face paled. "Can we get rid of him?"

"I'll try." That was the easier of the two decisions. Horace was desperate to move on to the next life, and just as anger fueled a poltergeist's ability to affect the living world, his desperation appeared to have made Horace powerful enough to scare me.

Penelope looked as afraid as I felt, and she pressed the bronze key back into my hand. "I won't put any guests in the attic until you give me the all-clear. It's your jurisdiction now. Any time you think you can banish him, I want you to try."

My trembling fingers curled around the key. I didn't know if I was strong enough to force Horace out if he wasn't willing to go. Not alone. And when I realized who I needed to call on for help, my second decision was made.

At my request, Penelope gave me a folded slip of paper with an address written on it. Then, with only the barest fumes of energy left to carry me home, I climbed into bed and shut off my alarms. I needed as much sleep as possible to face the tasks ahead.

CHAPTER TWENTY

The next morning, armed with another weak cup of instant coffee and a toaster pastry, I stared down at a blank sheet of notebook paper. My countertop was littered with a dozen crumpled attempts to write to Gabrielle, and more had been abandoned all over the apartment where Striker left them. She preferred live prey, but a fresh ball of paper was an acceptable substitute on rainy days like this one. And once she'd soaked the paper through with kitty saliva, it was "dead" and she needed a fresh one.

She sat on the stool next to me, assessing her prey. One of the rejected letters called to her, and she darted out a paw, hooking the ball with a single claw. She flung it onto the floor behind us and leapt after it with so much force that her barstool rocked back and forth, tapping against the cupboards. Leaving chaos in her wake, she tore after the ball of paper, batting it this way and that until it found the edge of the large square rug that covered most of our floor.

That's when she took her game to Expert Mode. Sitting on the rug, she lifted a corner with one paw and batted the ball of paper beneath it with the other. Then, she shot under the bed. Her yellow eyes appeared seconds later, watching the lump she'd made in the rug for any sign of movement. Apparently, she saw something, because she exploded out from beneath the bed and dove under the carpet to retrieve her prize.

Not for the first time, I wished I was a cat. Striker was well-fed, spoiled rotten, and always entertained. She didn't have any major decisions to make or people depending on her.

"Well, that's not true," I told her. "I don't know what I'd do without you."

In response, she rolled over and cleaned her backside in a manner that somehow managed to be smug. She'd recovered better than I had from our encounter with Horace the night before. I felt a constant weight on my mind, the lingering remnants of his display of power.

With a sigh, I forced myself to turn my attention back to my notebook. I needed to tell Gabrielle what'd happened in the attic, because I needed to know more about Horace's history. But I hadn't written her before and, like the worst kind of friend, I was only reaching out now because I needed something. Guilt over the timing of my letter convinced me to write it by hand instead of typing out the letter on my laptop and borrowing Graham's printer, and shame prevented me from having anything to show for the last half-hour of trying to get something on paper.

The hardest part was the beginning. My rejected efforts had included several unsatisfactory starts, like:

Dear Gabrielle,

On a scale of "Orange is the New Black" to "The Rock," what's jail like?

Or more contrite openings:

Dear Gabrielle,

Sorry I got you arrested. I was wondering if you'd do me a favor...

"This is stupid," I muttered. There were no perfect words. No matter what I said, part of it would be wrong. And even if I didn't think it was wrong, she could interpret the wrong mood or meaning. That was the trick of the written word. The important thing, I decided, was honesty.

Chewing the end of my pen, I tried again.

Dear Gabrielle,

I'm sorry I didn't write you sooner. I wasn't sure if you'd want to hear from me. If you tore up this letter as soon as you saw who it was from, I wouldn't blame you. But I hope you read it.

I can't imagine what things are like for you, but if you want to write me back and tell me, I'd like to hear about what's going on.

I'm also hoping you can help me with something...

I detailed the events in the attic the night before, explaining that Horace had appeared to me twice now when I'd been trying to make contact with another spirit. I described the way his energy had overpowered me as best I could and included the request he'd made that I retrieve the stolen jewelry box and return it to the Oracle Inn.

I'll try to find it, I wrote. *I'm honestly afraid of what will*

happen in that house if I can't help him move on. Enough
people have been hurt because of spirits I've left untended. I
won't be able to forgive myself if one of Pene-lope's guests is
injured... or worse.

Writing the words made my fears more real than I'd wanted,
and I picked up the letter to crumple it up.

"Brrrllll," Striker scolded me from the floor.

"What, don't you want a fresh ball?"

She glared at me then went back to her bath.

Not wanting to start over yet again, I put the paper back down
and finished the letter by asking Gabrielle if Horace had ever
shown up while she was having one of her famous séances in the
attic and if she had any advice for helping spirits move on to the
other side. If Horace's idea didn't pan out, it'd be nice to have a
backup plan in place. One way or another, I was determined to get
him out of the inn.

As soon as I signed my name, I folded up the letter and
stuffed it into an envelope. Then, to make sure I couldn't talk
myself out of sending it, I marched down to the foyer and slid it
into the outgoing mail slot.

A wave of panic slammed into me the instant the envelope left
my fingers. The letter was all wrong; I hadn't been apologetic or
kind enough. Or had I been too syrupy? So over-the-top she'd be
insulted? I had to get into that box to retrieve the letter. Graham
had to have a key somewhere in his apartment, or I could just wait
here until the mail carrier came.

The knob on the front door rattled, making me jump. *The mail
lady!* my brain shouted illogically. But it was only Kit, dripping
with sweat through distinctly un-Kit-like clothes: jogging shorts,
running shoes, and a neon yellow t-shirt.

She raised an eyebrow at me. "You look like one of those

dogs who just got caught eating the Thanksgiving turkey. Why do you have 'guilty' tattooed on your forehead?"

"You look like one of those people who runs for fun," I retorted. "Who are you, and what have you done with Kit Dyedov?"

Not bothering to respond, she pushed past me to retrieve a glass of water from the kitchen sink, panting slightly between gulps as she drank.

"Seriously," I said. "When did you take up running?"

"Today."

"Okay…. Why?"

She shrugged. "Just felt like it."

In all the time I'd known her, Kit had never once worked out. She claimed hauling equipment cases to and from her van was equivalent to lifting weights for half an hour a day, and her version of cardio was dashing around like a puppy when she was excited. Now she stood before me, the beads of perspiration on her forehead proof that she'd been pushing her body.

Before I could point out the obvious, that her sudden interest in fitness had developed just when she'd started seeing someone, she ducked into Amari's apartment. She returned a minute later with a freshly washed face and slid onto a stool with a sigh, wrapping her hands around another glass of water.

I smirked. "Keeping your toiletries at her place, huh?"

"No." She glared at me. "I just like her face wash better than mine, that's all."

"Right. Face wash she didn't bother to take with her to Reno. I bet you fifty bucks if I go into her bathroom I'll find your toothbrush."

She leapt off her stool, intercepting me before I could make good on my threat. "Hey! Respect her personal space!"

"Don't you mean *your* personal space?" I pushed her shoulder with a single finger. "Why don't you just bite the bullet and move in there already?"

"I might. My lease is up next month. I'll talk to Graham about switching when he gets back."

"And Amari will take your old place, huh?"

"No." Kit folded her arms. "She'd just stay with me downstairs."

"O-ho! Look who's combining apartments now!"

Kit rolled her eyes, but a red flush spread across her face. A murmured "shut up" was the best response she could muster, which counted as a victory for me. As I am a gracious winner, I didn't twist the knife.

"Are you busy today?" I asked.

"I've got to make a few calls, fill in a couple gaps in our production schedule. Why?"

"How would you feel about a field trip?"

"Field trip?" She frowned. "I thought you're not supposed to leave town."

"It's not far. And it'd be for work. They can't stop me from doing my job."

She grinned. "Atta girl. What do you have in mind?"

"Have you ever heard of Cambion's Camp? I checked, and…" I trailed off as Kit started squealing.

She covered her mouth with two balled-up fists, and her eyes glowed like crystal balls. She reminded me of the kids in amusement park ads, right after their parents show them the tickets. "Cambion's Camp?"

"Yeah. You've heard of it?"

"Heard of it?" She shrieked, then clapped a hand over her mouth and took a deep breath through her fingers. When she'd recovered herself, she grabbed me by the shoulders. "Tell me everything!"

I caught her up on what'd happened during my attempt to

reach Raziel, treading gently to avoid reminding her that Amari and I had colluded to keep the *Soul Searchers* from filming me while I reached out to him.

When I got to the part about the spirit from the cabin interrupting me again, Kit exploded. "Are you kidding me?"

"His name is Horace. He asked me to find a jewelry box he stole while he was alive." I related the rest of Horace's story, relieved to be telling it to someone I trusted instead of laying it out on a piece of paper I wasn't confident the recipient would read. "He claims he saw who really killed Raziel. He'll only tell me if I bring the box back to him."

Kit's excitement faded. "Wait, what? This ghost is, like, extorting you?"

I hesitated then nodded. "That's how I see it too. I wrote to Gabrielle to see if she's encountered him before, but in the meantime, I kind of want to see if we can find what he's looking for. I feel like if I don't do everything I can to clear my name..." I trailed off, unable to vocalize my fears of ending up in prison like Gabrielle. "Is that stupid?"

She stared at me for a few silent moments before answering. "No. You're right, we have to do whatever we can to make sure you don't take the fall for someone else. Count me in. I know Dad and Mark will be on board too."

"Good. Since the cabin cleansing didn't go the way we wanted, I thought we could use this for another episode."

The grin returned to her face, and Kit whooped and punched the air. "Do you know how long I've wanted to film something at Cambion's Camp?"

"Why haven't you?"

"Well, it's not like the cabin. Nobody has ever reported a ghost sighting there, and Dad doesn't like 'fishing expeditions' where investigators just go somewhere with a generic, spooky reputation and wait for something unexplainable to happen. He likes to look into a genuine claim of paranormal activity. But that's kind of hard because nobody goes there. Like, ever."

"Why not?"

Her eyes glowed. "Because everyone around here knows: Cambion's Camp is cursed."

CHAPTER TWENTY-ONE

K it and I easily persuaded the rest of our team that an excursion of Cambion's Camp was worthy of filming. Mark's freelancing schedule meant we had to squeeze the trip in that Saturday, and for two full days Kit roamed Primrose House restlessly, continuously making and re-making supply lists and hitting the grocery store again and again to buy enough "snacks for the road" to last us a week.

"It's a three-hour drive," I'd reminded her when she brought her fourth set of grocery bags into the house.

"Anything we don't eat on the way, I'll eat while I edit the footage."

When Saturday finally arrived, Kit's speed nearly matched Striker's as she zoomed up and down the stairs to pack the van with our equipment, plus four large tote bags filled with fruit snacks and potato chips.

Striker climbed into one of the sacks, crushing a bag of Doritos.

"Sorry, sweetie." I lifted her out of the bag, a simple task made difficult when ten razor-sharp claws hooked into the canvas. I eventually coaxed her claws out of the material and deposited her onto the floor, where she glared at me with narrowed, yellow eyes. "Stay here and protect the house from dragons."

Before we left Donn's Hill, Yuri insisted we film the account of my conversation with Horace where it had happened. Kit parked the van in an employee space behind the inn since all other spaces were once more taken up by news vehicles. True to Penelope's prediction, the crews had returned as soon as the gruesome details of Raziel's strangulation reached the press, and cameras swarmed the front lawn.

Inside, two Oracle Inn employees tried to stop us from going upstairs, telling us only guests were allowed farther than the lobby. They eyed Mark's camera bag and folded their arms; I could tell it was a conversation they'd had to have a lot today.

"I'm a guest." I flashed the key to the attic suite, and they let us climb the stairs.

We passed a crew from a security company who were installing surveillance cameras in the hallways and on the staircase. I glared at them, wishing they'd finished their work a week earlier so I wouldn't have to be trading favors with a ghost to find out who'd killed Raziel.

On the second-floor landing, a skinny, intimidatingly tall guy about my age did a double-take upon seeing me, nudging the shorter, stouter man he was with and whispering in his ear. I avoided their gaze. They didn't seem to recognize Yuri, which could only mean one thing. They weren't fans of the show. They'd heard the other rumor Penelope had been worried about: the one about me killing Raziel. Their eyes bored into the back of my skull as we made our way up the final flight of stairs to the room where he'd died.

I stopped in the doorway to the suite, watching Kit and Mark set up their equipment but not crossing the threshold. A lump of fear had formed in my throat, and it took me awhile to swallow it down. I'd had time to process my conversation with Horace, but it still made little sense to me. How was he able to communicate with me so clearly? Why couldn't I cut off our connection? What made him so powerful?

Kit, heedless of any hesitation on my part, focused on whipping everyone into a frenzy. "Come on, come on!" she barked, clipping a mic to my collar. "Let's finish this and get on the road!"

Yuri and Mark seemed as eager as she was to reach the camp, and within ten minutes, I was mic'd, lit, and on camera. Yuri sat beside Mark, giving me someone to look at and talk to. From the audience's perspective, I'd be looking just to their left instead of directly into the lens. I went through the events two nights before in more detail than I'd given either Kit or Gabrielle, trusting that Kit would cut out anything boring.

My team's faces paled as I described the way Horace had filled the room with spiritual pressure, nearly suffocating me until I agreed to help him. Their reaction made me stutter, stop, and have to find my place in the tale again. Half my mind stayed focused on relating my story, but the other half reeled in terror. My assessment had been correct. There was something different about Horace.

We finished filming, and I bolted from the suite, choosing to wait on the stairs while Kit and Mark packed our gear. Happily, the pair of men who'd been eyeing me were nowhere in sight. No other guests ogled us as we left the inn, and we snuck out the back of the building and piled into Kit's van to avoid any questions from the press.

"I don't mean to second-guess you," I told Yuri when we were finally on the road. "But couldn't we have filmed that part afterward?"

"If we'd had no other choice, yes. But you'd already told your story to Kit. Each time we tell a story, certain details start to feel more important than others. I wanted to get your account on film before you'd had too much time to overthink things or begin downplaying anything in your mind." He smiled. "And obviously, I prefer to hear the background before leaving on a journey like this."

Journey. I remembered Stephen's reading, which felt like ancient history considering what'd happened since. Cambion's Camp was three hours away, on the other side of Moyard. It was the longest journey than I'd taken since moving to Donn's Hill.

But you don't have to be here, I reminded myself. Stephen had said the journey wouldn't be one I chose. I'd decided to come here. I could have ignored Horace's request and not bothered with any of this.

Deep in my heart, I knew that wasn't strictly true. Nobody had a gun to my head, but there was no way I could pass up an opportunity to clear my name. And the thought of leaving a spirit like Horace in a place like the Oracle Inn... Well, what would my father have said to that?

As we passed Moyard, I searched for the hospital in the city's skyline without finding it. Somewhere in that sprawl, Connor Miles lay in a hospital bed, still recovering from the injuries he'd received at Richard Franklin's spectral hand. I wondered again how Horace might be connected to the cabin. It still nagged at me that Franklin hadn't appeared when I'd tried to summon him— and that Horace had. Where had Franklin gone? Was that another riddle Horace could help me solve?

Moyard's outskirts thinned into suburbs and eventually farmland. This was the farthest west I'd travelled since the bus ride I'd taken from Salt Lake City in the spring. Soon we turned off the four-lane highway onto a narrower country road that cut a straight path through massive fields and pastures. Soon we passed line of trees that marked the boundary between the farmland and the forest. A few miles after entering the woods, we slowed and turned down an unpaved lane. The van's tires bounced on ruts and crunched over small branches. This wasn't a road that saw much use.

"Have you ever been here?" I asked Yuri.

He shook his head. "Despite its infamy, I haven't had the time."

"What do you know about it?"

Yuri taught history at Donn's Hill High School, which was a steadier income than conducting televised paranormal investigations. His two careers dovetailed nicely, though, as he handled the lion's share of the historical research needed for the show.

"Hang on." Mark unzipped his camera case. "Get your lavs on."

Yuri and I obediently retrieved the sound equipment from a milk crate and pinned lavalier microphones to our shirts. Only when the audio levels looked good and the red light on Mark's camera was glowing did Yuri continue.

"There's not much documented history about the place. We know it was a small lumber camp, founded in 1857. But near the end of its first season, a lumberjack arrived in Moyard, claiming a foul illness had taken over the camp. He collapsed into a coma and later died, but his report prompted a Moyard physician named Caldwell Perkins to visit the camp. Upon arrival, he found the road empty and the animals silent.

"He eventually found a half-dozen lumberjacks huddled in the cookhouse with a supply of food and water. They warned him not to go into any of the other buildings. They said he would risk the 'curse' following him home. He ignored their warning."

I realized I'd been so absorbed in his story I'd forgotten to breathe. "What did he find?"

"Bodies," Kit chimed in from the driver's seat. "Sooooooo many bodies."

Yuri shot her a disapproving glance over the rim of his glasses. "Katarina, please. It's true, he found the remains of the rest of the lumberjacks. The bunks were full of men who appeared to be sleeping, except their skin was dry and wrinkled and hard to the touch. Strangely, their eyes were missing."

"*Missing?*" My skin crawled. They sounded like mummies I'd seen at an exhibit with my father. I'd known their organs had been removed, but at least you couldn't see the evidence.

"He found the same thing in the foreman's cabin," Yuri continued. "The foreman and his family were dead in their beds. But most oddly, when he returned to the cookhouse, the remaining lumberjacks had vanished. Perkins rode back for Moyard at once, returning the next day with a dozen men to help him deal with the dead. They found only the smoking remains of the log buildings. The entire camp had burned to the ground during the night."

Kit shivered with delight. "So freaky."

"Of course, most of his story couldn't be corroborated. The men who accompanied him on his return only saw the aftermath of a fire. Perkins could have made up the rest, written it down like a horror story, or he could have been suffering from delusions."

"Has anything weird happened there since?" I asked.

"Nothing that's been documented. Whether the physician's account was real or imagined, it kindled a deep superstition about the area. There was no attempt to rebuild. The camp is today as it was over 150 years ago."

I stared between Kit and Mark's shoulders, watching the trees roll by at a leisurely pace. Kit carefully navigated the overgrown lane while Mark turned his camera to face the windshield. I recognized the collection of B-roll footage Kit could use as cutaways to make long stretches of Yuri's storytelling more visually interesting.

Kit turned up the music and bounced up and down in the driver's seat. Black Sabbath's *War Pigs* pounded out of the speakers at a volume that made Yuri cringe, but Kit winked at me in the rearview mirror while she sang along. Her spirits were higher than I'd seen them in weeks.

"We're close. We should be able to see the camp soon," Yuri shouted above the song.

Despite the autumn sun shining high above us, the surrounding woods grew darker. Everyone except Ozzy Osbourne grew silent, and a feeling of unease wrapped around my chest.

The van lurched to the right. Kit swore.

"Easy," Mark said.

"It wasn't me. The wheel—"

The van lurched again with enough violence to slam Kit's head into her window. I opened my mouth to ask if she was okay and the steering wheel spun beneath her hands, sending us careening off the road and into the trees. Time slowed as the van accelerated. An enormous oak tree loomed on the other side of the windshield.

Then: impact.

The van slammed into the tree with a massive *BOOM!* I flew forward an inch before the seatbelt stopped me, digging into my chest and belly. The back of the van bucked into the air, sending the crates and equipment cases flying, and all I saw was white.

CHAPTER TWENTY-TWO

Hissing filled my ears. Unsure if it was coming from my brain or the engine, I rushed to get out of the van.

Something pinned me to the seat—*I'm stuck!*—and I remembered I still wore my seatbelt. After fumbling with the buckle, I was free.

Yuri was already on his feet, standing in front of me to bend over Kit. Russian words poured out of his mouth as he inspected her, touching her forehead and holding her wrist between his fingers.

"*Yav poryadke, yav poryadke*," she protested, un-clicking her own seatbelt and pushing against the inflated airbag to slide out the driver's side door.

I followed suit, pulling open the sliding door and dropping to the uneven ground beneath us. The hissing sound was definitely coming from the engine; white steam wafted up into the cool air above the crumpled front of the van. The tree tilted backward but otherwise looked no worse for the wear. Meanwhile, cracks spider-webbed across the entire windshield, which had thankfully stayed in place. Kit's window, on the other hand, had shattered completely.

Mark grabbed my elbow and led me away from the van, back toward the dirt road we'd been heading down. Yuri had an arm around his daughter, whose face was sprinkled with small gashes. Mark ignored a rivulet of blood running down his left temple, shouldering his camera and turning it on the wreckage.

"Is everyone okay?" Yuri asked.

Miraculously, we'd all escaped with minor injuries. Even the van didn't look too damaged. I patted myself down, checking for tender spots, but found nothing apart from the stripe of pain across my chest. I gingerly poked at my sternum, vowing to never complain about any bruise the seatbelt left while saving my life.

Kit rubbed the back of her neck. "I'm so sorry, you guys. I don't know what happened."

"These are some deep ruts." Mark kicked at a ridges of dried mud that ran the length of the road. "We must've hit one just right. Or wrong, I guess."

I traced the tracks of mud with my eyes. Deep gouges marked the place where the van had careened off the road and into the trees. More tracks continued north, where the road turned sharply to the right and disappeared into the trees. Cambion's Camp lay right around the corner; I could feel it, the same way I could feel someone's eyes on the back of my head in a crowded restaurant. And if I closed my eyes and concentrated, I even thought I could feel tendrils of Horace's energy somewhere nearby. The jewelry box was close, waiting for me to find it.

"Mac, where are you going?" Kit called from behind me.

I opened my eyes and turned toward her voice. She, Mark, and Yuri stood a hundred feet away from me. They were walking back to the highway—wait, no. They were still level with the van. I'd been the one who moved. My feet had carried me down the dirt road, toward the turn. I rubbed my temples to clear the fog from my brain and walked back to my team. I hadn't hit my head in the crash, but my mind apparently thought otherwise.

As I returned to the group, Yuri slipped his cell phone back into his pocket.

"Penelope is on her way with the city tow truck," he said. "They'll be here in a few hours."

My gaze returned to the bend in the road. "A few hours would be long enough for us to poke around the camp and come back, right?"

"Yes." Kit's answer was immediate and emphatic. "I didn't come all this way and wreck our van just to stand in the dirt all day."

But Yuri looked doubtful. "We rushed out here and look what happened. We shouldn't rush into any other decisions."

"We already made this decision," his daughter argued. "We're just finishing what we started."

He stared at her. She met his gaze and stared back, unblinking. Unspoken words seemed to flow between them, and I wondered if Yuri lost arguments to Kit as often as I did.

Finally, he sighed. "Fine. But we tend to your wounds first."

Once the steaming from the engine subsided, I ferried the gear we'd need from the van to the road while Yuri dabbed at Kit's face with antiseptic from our medical kit. Mark managed to avoid carrying anything by keeping his hands busy with the camera.

"Tilt your head to the left," he told Kit as Yuri placed small bandages over the cuts on her face. "You'll catch the light better. There you go."

Once Yuri was satisfied Kit's injuries were only skin deep, we continued down the road on foot. Yuri took the lead, his shoulders high and tense. Mark filmed us from behind. I walked beside Kit, whose bright eyes were a strange contrast to her bandaged face.

We held our parade in silence. No sounds emanated from the dense forest; no birdsongs or animal cries filled the air. Only the soft clump of our feet on the hard-packed dirt broke the stillness in the air.

The adrenaline that'd filled my body in the crash wore off, leaving the sour feeling of disquiet I'd had earlier with nothing to hide behind. My apprehension grew as we approached the turn, and I imagined we'd turn the corner to see the camp exactly as it'd been in the 1800s. I followed Yuri around the bend, and the woods opened to a small clearing.

We paused at the edge of the space, but there wasn't much to see. Over a hundred and fifty years had passed since Caldwell Perkins had visited this place, and whatever remained of the buildings after the fire had been reclaimed by encroaching trees and grasses. From where I stood, it was impossible to tell where the cookhouse or barn had been. It looked like a little meadow, a peaceful pocket of openness in the woods.

Kit deflated. "This is it?"

I contemplated the clearing with narrowed eyes. Ideal as it looked for a picnic, something in the air set off alarm bells in my gut. It felt like something or someone was watching us from the edge of the trees, and the unnatural quiet hung over us like a suffocating blanket.

Whatever I was feeling, the others seemed unaffected. Kit and Yuri walked the perimeter of the clearing, their eyes fixed on the ground. Reluctantly, I headed toward them, but as I crossed the midpoint of the open space, a wall of nausea brought me to a halt.

Kit hurried over. "What is it? Do you feel something?"

"Yeah." I looked down at my feet, then called to Yuri, "What would've been here?"

"It's hard to say." He joined us, kneeling to brush his hand through the long grass. "I'm not sure where any of the buildings were. I suspect the forest has retaken them. But if we assume they lay outside the perimeter, this would have been a landing where they loaded the logs onto sleds for transport."

"There's something here. Buried, I think." I spoke my

thoughts aloud, a habit I'd developed after months of Kit barking at me that our viewers couldn't read my mind. "Do we have a shovel?"

Kit and I returned to the van while Mark filmed Yuri explaining the buildings he thought would have been at the original camp and where they might have stood. The van's roadside emergency kit didn't include a shovel, but we found a short black pole with a jagged end under the driver's seat.

"Aha!" Kit held it above her head in triumph. "I wondered where this thing went."

"What is it?"

"Broken boom arm, for holding a microphone over people's heads. It snapped a couple years ago—Dad was pissed, the mic hit him right in the face—and after that I used it to jab Mark when he was being annoying."

I laughed. "I can't picture Mark doing anything obnoxious. He hardly ever talks."

"That's what's so annoying!"

Armed with our makeshift digging stick, we hustled back to the clearing and got to work. The dry earth came away easily, especially once Kit straddled the hole and started yanking dirt toward her stomach with her hands. Her antics made me laugh and offset the nervous cloud hanging over my head. I focused on the task at hand, pushing any other thoughts aside and jabbing at the more stubborn edges of the hole with my stick. Soon our pit was deep and wide enough for me to stand in up to my knees.

"How deep do you think we need to go?" Kit asked as I stood in our accomplishment with my hands on my hips.

"No clue. I feel like we're getting closer, but…" I focused, trying to feel the energy beneath my feet. It was hazy. Nebulous.

Yuri sat on an upturned equipment crate a few feet away, his long legs stretching toward us. "If someone buried something here while the lumber camp was still in use, the woods have had over a century to cover the spot with dirt and overgrowth. Something that was two feet down back then could be twice that today, or more."

Kit and I glanced at each other then continued digging in earnest. Something drove me to find whatever was tugging at me before Penelope and the tow truck arrived. I felt certain that if we didn't find it in that three-hour window, we never would, though I couldn't say why. With dirt packed into our fingernails, we scooped and stabbed at the ground. I glared at the equipment crates, wishing they were solid plastic. I was desperate for something more shovel-like than my own cupped hands.

After a while, Kit took a break, stretching out beside the hole on her back.

"You should rest, too," Yuri told me. "Come out of there and have some water."

I shook my head and kept working. "In a minute."

Sweat rolled down my back despite the cooling temperatures. The sun burned straight above us, robbing us of any shade, but didn't seem to penetrate the canopy of the surrounding woods. Whatever silent birds or animals who lived in the trees watched us from the darkness, their eyes boring into the back of my head as I leaned in and out of the hole, bringing up handful after handful of earth.

Just when I was thinking I'd have to crouch in the hole to dig any deeper, my fingers brushed against something harder than the surrounding dirt. The nervous tension in my belly tightened and a low buzzing filled the air.

"Here!" I called.

Kit and Yuri leapt to their feet. Mark brought the camera closer to me as I lifted our prize out of its resting place. It was a wooden box, about the size of a Rubik's cube and very light in my hand. As I got to my feet, the buzzing grew louder, drowning out the sound of Kit's applause.

"Do you hear that?" I shouted.

Before they could answer, my nausea crescendoed. Bile filled my mouth, and I collapsed to the ground.

CHAPTER TWENTY-THREE

"Drink," Penelope ordered, passing me a water bottle from the driver's seat of her Lexus.

With shaking hands, I struggled to do as she commanded. My body didn't want to swallow, and when I finally convinced it to, the cold water slid painfully down my burning throat. I moaned and slid down in the car's passenger seat, willing myself to keep the water down. Penelope had thrown the words "emergency room" and "IV fluids" around when she'd first arrived and found me vomiting into the hole I'd spent so long digging. She'd shepherded me to her car, drowning out my weak protests with a series of orders to sit down and put my head between my knees.

Through her windshield, I watched a city employee use a tow truck's hydraulic arm to hoist one end of the Soul Searcher's van into the air. The front of the vehicle crunched inward where it'd slammed into the tree. I winced, thinking about what could have happened to Kit and Mark's legs if the crash had been any more serious.

"We should take her to the ER in Moyard. It's the closest one," Penelope told Yuri.

He stood by the driver's side door, arms folded across his

chest. "I don't think it's heatstroke. Her pulse is steady and—feel her forehead—her temperature seems normal."

She rested a cool hand above my brow for a moment and grunted. "But she's been vomiting and her shirt is soaked through."

My annoyance at being talked about as though I wasn't there was dwarfed by the layer of exhaustion that pressed down on every muscle in my body. I wasn't even sure I'd be able to raise my voice above the beeping of the tow truck, so I stayed silent. I'd save that energy in case I needed to revive my protests against being taken to the hospital, where there would surely be needles involved.

"I've seen this before," Yuri said. "Her abilities are extremely powerful. If this place is truly as 'cursed' as they say, she could be feeling that force so strongly that she's manifesting symptoms in response to it. We should get her home and see how she does."

There was no further argument from Penelope. Once the van was securely hoisted, the rest of the Soul Searchers piled into the backseat of her car, and we followed the tow truck up the dirt road. I glared suspiciously at the trees as we passed them, sure we would crash again. It wasn't until we were cruising down the paved backcountry road toward the highway that I realized I'd been bracing my feet against an imaginary brake pedal under the dashboard.

I hoped Yuri was right and I'd start feeling better the farther we got from Cambion's Camp. There were improvements. We stopped at a gas station off the highway for some soda to settle my stomach and some antacids to calm the burning in my throat, but I couldn't shake the feeling that something was following us from the clearing. No matter how far we drove, a faint buzzing tugged at my mind, teasing the back of my skull. I imagined something trying to get inside my brain and shuddered.

"Are you okay?" Penelope asked.

"Fine," I said, not trusting myself to string multiple words together. The more I opened my mouth, the greater the risk I'd need to use the gas station grocery sack Penelope had pointedly left at my side.

"Try to get some rest," she suggested. "We have a long way to go."

I took her advice, dozing lightly for the rest of the drive. Every few minutes, a bump in the road or a snatch of conversation from the back seat jolted me awake, but I slept enough that the journey passed quickly. Soon, we passed the painted wooden sign that welcomed visitors to Donn's Hill, and a flash of guilt burned in my chest.

Something was tracking us, and we'd led it straight to our home.

GRAHAM'S FATHER'S truck and trailer were parked in the Primrose House parking lot when we returned. Tears welled up in my eyes at the sight, pouring down my face when his tall figure burst out the back door of the house and he jogged to Penelope's car.

"Mac!" He threw open the passenger door and gathered me into a hug before I'd even unbuckled my seatbelt. "Are you okay?"

"I'm fine." My words were muffled against his shoulder, but I meant them. I immediately felt better with him there. Even the buzzing against my brain was more muted, as though Graham provided a physical shield between me and the thing that'd followed us here.

"Striker's waiting for you," he said. "She's been screaming at me since I got home."

He helped me out of the car, and I threw an apologetic glance at my team. They had to deal with unloading the equipment from

Penelope's trunk and ferrying it up to Kit's apartment. Some of it was already stacked on the lawn, and—

Something I'd seen registered in my mind, and I whipped my head back toward the pile of equipment so fast I heard a pop in my neck. On top of our microphone case sat the small, wooden jewelry box from the clearing.

I sagged against Graham. "That's been in the trunk this whole time?"

"What?" He followed my pointing finger with his eyes. "The wooden thing?"

It *had* been following me. I'd assumed something from the clearing had been trailing us under its own power, but we'd given it a lift. It'd been ten feet behind me the entire ride home, poking and scratching at my mind from the trunk. Nausea welled up inside me once more, and I vomited clear soda onto the lawn.

"It's okay." Graham stroked my back. "You'll be okay."

I shook my head, panting between dry heaves. "Don't let them... bring that... inside."

"Bring what?"

"Box." I wagged a hand in the pile's direction. "Wooden box."

"Here, sit down." He led me to the back steps before disappearing into the house. He returned a minute later with a glass of water. "Sip this slowly."

The back door opened again and Amari joined us on the steps, crouching down beside me. "Mac! Are you okay?"

With a few dozen yards of lawn separating me from the box, I was able to honestly nod. At this distance, I could still sense the box. I felt it strongly enough that I was sure I could point to it even if they blindfolded me and spun me around a few times, Pin-the-Tail-on-the-Donkey-style. But my head was clear, and the nausea was fading.

"That box... it's like it's radioactive," I croaked. My nausea might have dissipated, but my throat still needed to recover from the most recent dose of bile.

"What box?" Amari asked.

Graham saved me from having to strain my voice any further. "I think it's something they brought back from their investigation. I was about to go ask Kit about it."

"You stay here with Mac. I'll see."

As she walked across the grass, Graham settled onto the steps and put an arm around me. I leaned into him and watched Primrose House's newest resident sneak up on my best friend. Kit was distracted, pulling cases out of the car, and Amari was able to get right behind her and jab her in the kidneys.

Kit spun around, and her annoyed expression immediately brightened. She shrieked in delight, yanking Amari into a hug. Amari pulled backward, cupped Kit's face in her hands, and demanded to know what'd caused the spatter of cuts and scratches.

"I didn't realize Amari would be back today," I said.

"She wanted to surprise Kit." Graham smiled. "She was a little cranky when she showed up this afternoon and you were all gone."

"Do you think she'll stay in Donn's Hill long?"

"I hope she will. It's nice to see Kit so happy."

Kit was relating the story of the van crashing into the trees with an oddly elated expression, gesturing dramatically. I couldn't help but laugh as she grabbed the broken boom arm out of Penelope's trunk and reenacted our labors in the clearing. She used the stick to point to the little wooden jewelry box, explaining to Amari that the box matched the description Horace had given me.

Amari picked up the box, turning it over between her fingers. Squinting, she scratched at one of the sides. Her eyes widened, and she threw the box to the ground and crossed herself.

"Hey!" Kit moved to pick up the box, but Amari threw out an arm and stopped her.

"Leave it." Her sharp voice carried across the yard. "This box must not come inside this house, or any other."

"Why not?" Yuri demanded. "What is it?"

"It's a Dybbuk Box," Amari said. "If you keep it, you will die."

CHAPTER TWENTY-FOUR

F ive of us crammed in and around the window seat in the
turret of my apartment. It was physically the farthest we
could be away from the box in the backyard without leaving
Primrose House, and I was too tired to go anywhere else. Cool air
breezed through the open windows, carrying in the chirps and
whistles of nearby birds.

I leaned against Graham on one half of the bench, and Yuri
lay on his side across from us. Kit and Amari had carried up two
bungee chairs from Kit's apartment that looked like dream catch-
ers; Amari sunk into hers gingerly but declared it to be more
comfortable than it looked. Mark had gone home to get ready for
his freelance job the next day, and I was envious that he was all
the way across town, physically and mentally away from the thing
we'd brought back with us.

Striker took possession of my lap the instant I'd sat down. My
stomach already burned from the abuse of her claws; for whatever
reason, she seemed to think the best remedy for stress and anxiety
was for her to knead her paws into my belly again and again for
hours.

As she worked at my stomach, I tried to resist mentally

feeling for the box. We'd left it on the lawn where Yuri covered it with a white handkerchief embroidered with a small, gold Orthodox cross. He'd explained his uncle, who'd been a priest in Russia, had blessed it.

"I'll admit," he said to Amari. "I'm surprised to hear you mention a Dybbuk box. Such cursed objects are considered 'urban myths' by most people, even within the paranormal community."

"But not by you," she said.

"No, not by me. But then, I grew up in a place where there was no such thing as superstitions. There were only traditions."

She smiled. "Yes, I understand that completely."

"Can we back up?" I asked. "What *is* a Dybbuk box?"

"A Dybbuk is an angry spirit from Jewish mythology," Yuri explained. "Someone sold a wine box said to contain a Dybbuk on eBay and the legend spiraled from there. The term went viral and has become a catch-all with any kind of container that supposedly contains a malevolent entity."

"In recent years, the idea went viral," Amari said. "Many copycats and fakes have popped up online. You can find dozens of videos of so-called Dybbuk boxes, or haunted containers, but I've only seen one true instance in all my travels."

Kit pulled out her phone and showed me the screen. Amari was right; there were videos with titles like, "We opened the box: you won't believe what happened next!"

"They're clickbait," Kit said. "We've never been contacted by anyone claiming to own one, and we've never reached out to them either. We figured they were a hoax."

"You're right about most of them," Amari said.

"Okay, assuming these things are real, can these ghosts get out of the boxes?" I asked.

Amari nodded. "Opening the box releases the spirit back into the world. It may still be tied to the box, following that object around, but the spell containing the spirit's power is broken when the box is opened."

I eyed her levelly. She'd just said two things I wondered if she'd ever talked about in front of Raziel: *'spell'* and an admission of the existence of spirits.

"And you've seen one," I said flatly.

She nodded. "I know what you're thinking. I told you the other day: I believe in the spiritual world. I've seen magic—*real* magic, not stage illusions like those Raziel performed."

"Magic like... witches?"

"Yes." Her eyes narrowed as she watched me process her answer. "You don't seem surprised."

"My friend Gabrielle told me witches who were burned at the stake were sometimes psychics whose gifts were misunderstood. But I didn't think there were witches left."

"Neither do many people, but there are thousands of witches in the United States alone, practicing in a variety of ways. Herbalism, hedge craft, et cetera. There are even more around the world, working their craft in peace. But there are also some who practice arts you might describe as medieval."

"Such as?"

She paused and glanced at Kit. "I don't want any of this to make it into a Soul Searchers episode."

I expected Kit to argue, but she said, "I understand."

Amari nodded then turned back to me to explain. "There are things we call 'superstitions' that other people call 'medicine.' Witch doctors all over the world kidnap and kill people with conditions like albinism, believing their skin or organs contain magical properties. I believe many of these crimes are carried out by individuals who don't even believe in the power of these poultices and magic pouches. They do what they do for profit alone. Body parts can sell on the black market for tens of thousands of dollars, because the people buying them believe in their power."

Something clicked in my mind. "That's why you don't want a story like that to air on our show. People might take away the wrong message."

She nodded. "People need to know this is still going on, but it has to be presented the right way. That's why I leapt at the chance to join Raziel's team and help him grow his audience."

"But wait—you said you've seen a box like this before. Raziel's show... He said there are no such things as psychics and mediums and ghosts."

"We disagreed about how firm a line to draw in the sand. But I stood by his goals, and I plan to continue to work toward them."

"Did he see what you saw?"

"No, this was before I met him. I was traveling with"—Amari glanced at Kit—"a friend. We'd gone to Romania to look into reports of a poltergeist. In a village near the southern border, an elderly woman's house would light up at night, and her neighbors witnessed her furniture moving around on its own through the brightly lit windows."

"Sounds like a poltergeist." I'd had more personal experience with those than I'd have liked.

"Yes, and that's what we thought it was. Then she developed lesions on her skin and inside her mouth. We wanted to visit her, but the villagers forbade us from entering the house."

"Why?" I asked.

Amari paused for a moment, considering her next words. "Did you know that in some cultures, there are no such things as ghosts? Any kind of supernatural activity is blamed on demons. If the spirit looks like someone who died, it's because the demon is playing a trick on us. Letting outsiders see such a demon would be considered very dangerous."

"But you saw her anyway," Kit guessed, elbowing her.

"You know me too well." Amari elbowed her back. "Yes, we went into the house. I saw the disturbances with my own eyes, and my friend attempted to treat the woman's injuries. The woman begged us to take a large, wooden hatbox with us. She claimed it would heal her faster than anything my friend could do. I attempted to open the box, and she screamed so loudly...." Amari shuddered. "I'll never forget that scream. The village priest rushed into the house and chased us out. Then, he brought the box into her garden. He ordered it to be buried deep in the forest, away from anywhere the villagers hunted or fished.

"We left the village three days later. The woman's lesions had completely healed, and there'd been no further disturbances in her home."

I stroked Striker's back and thought about Amari's story. Apart from the lesions, it sounded exactly like a poltergeist. Objects moving by themselves, flashing lights, and a haunting that wasn't tied to a specific location. But none of those things seemed related to what we'd experienced at Cambion's Camp, unless we counted the van smashing itself into a tree.

"What makes you think Horace's jewelry box is like that hatbox?"

Amari folded her legs beneath her and crossed her arms in front of her chest. "There are a few things that bother me about that box. First, it had the Seal of Solomon engraved on the bottom."

Before I could ask what that was, Graham drew one on my palm with the tip of his finger. The shape was invisible, but I could see it in my mind: a six-pointed star, surrounded by a circle.

"A Star of David?" I asked.

"Slightly different and a little older," Amari said. "Imagine two triangles interlaced with one another, impossible to pull apart. The Seal of Solomon was said to give the ancient king power over demons, who would be drawn in by the beauty and simplicity of the symbol and get trapped by the never-ending pattern."

"Okay, so they both have the same symbol on them. But that could just be a coincidence. Religious symbols are everywhere."

"That's true," Graham said. "I get asked to put the Seal of Solomon on a few sculptures every year. I doubt they're being used to trap evil spirits."

Amari nodded, conceding the point. "You're right. It'd be impossible to prove there's a malevolent presence in that box unless we opened it. But I think it's better to be cautious, don't you?"

I wanted to leap to my feet and start cheering. *Yes, let's be cautious. Cautious enough to throw the box into a fire and be done with it.*

"However, that's not the only thing that bothers me. Yuri, what did you think about the age of the box?"

"Hmm." He stroked his chin. "Yes, it seemed too new to belong to Mac's ghost. If it had truly been buried for over a hundred years, I would have expected far more decay in the wood. Every corner is still perfectly sharp. You can even still see the shine of varnish. That should have worn off decades ago."

"But it matches his description exactly," I protested. "What are the odds of there being two wooden boxes, both the same shape and the same size, buried in the same abandoned lumber camp?"

"That's another thing," Yuri said. "It was too easy to dig out. The earth was loose and soft, as though it'd recently been moved."

Kit stared at him. "You mean somebody buried the box recently? How long ago?"

"Even one winter would have hardened the earth more than that."

The implications of his words were staggering. "Wait... If we assume there *weren't* two boxes, and this was the one Horace told me about, that means it's some kind of magic box that resists decaying and is always easy to dig up. Or he was lying to me."

Yuri nodded.

"Have you ever known a spirit to lie before?" Graham asked.

"I've never had the gift of speaking to spirits as clearly as Gabrielle," Yuri said.

"Neither have I." As I said it, the truth of the words hit me. Every ghost I'd encountered before had been mute, either unwilling or unable to speak directly to me. The exception was the spirit I'd seen talk through Gabrielle, using her as a megaphone to amplify his own voice. She'd promised to teach me how to do the same thing. Then she'd been arrested, and that promise had evaporated.

With or without her, my abilities had been growing. I felt my strength increasing every time I used my gift. Now I was strong enough to speak to Horace and understand his replies. Was that normal? Or was it the abnormal side effect of being somewhere like Donn's Hill?

I looked around my little circle of companions and again felt the pang of loss. None of them would know the answer. Gabrielle might. Maybe my mother would have too. Neither of them were easily accessible to me. One of them was in jail, and I prayed the other had moved on.

"There's one thing that bothers me most of all," Yuri said. "Let's assume the simplest solution is the correct one. That would mean Horace not only lied to you about the provenance of that box, but he also knew something had been buried there recently. How would a spirit know that? Especially one supposedly tied to the Oracle Inn?"

Amari ran a hand over her shaved head. "And if there's a demon trapped in that box, what does Horace want with it?"

CHAPTER TWENTY-FIVE

I stayed up late after everyone left, researching the recent surge in supposed "haunted box" phenomena that'd spread across the internet. It was impossible to know if any of the stories were genuine, but there were a few details that synced up with tales of other cursed objects that made my stomach hurt. The stories confirmed the suspicion I'd had that bringing the jewelry box back with us was a mistake, because everyone who encountered objects like these suffered terrible misfortunes. I read about a chair that doomed those who sat in it to an early death, a painting that appeared to survive house fires caused by its very presence, and a mirror that gave its owners odd skin conditions. Where the objects went, tragedy followed.

The sources of the so-called Dybbuk Box hauntings were never clearly identified in the stories I found online, which struck me as odd. There was plenty of lore about malicious spirits called Dybbuks, but they'd historically clung to people the way Thomas Bishop had followed me around. Like poltergeists, they haunted people instead of locations. But in all the recent stories, the spirits attached to an object—the box—rather than a particular person or even a particular place.

That begged the question: was there something special about the spirits themselves... or about the boxes they haunted?

I kept reading deep into the night. Guilt nibbled at my consciousness, growing stronger with every anecdote and article. I'd felt something wrong in that clearing, but I'd still brought something back. I blinked at the screen, forcing myself to stay awake, hoping I'd find a story that included details about how to stop a curse from taking hold once some foolish psychic let it follow her home.

Eventually sleep won out. My eyelids slid closed, opening again in my mother's backyard. The New Mexico heat warmed my back as I faced the house. As a child, that house had been everything. Home, sanctuary, magic castle. Looking at it now, I realized how much time had passed since I'd been inside. How many years had gone by since the day a neighbor had helped me pack my things to go live with a father I'd never met?

The small, single-story bungalow was a common sight in the Albuquerque suburbs. Back then, the house had seemed enormous. Now, compared to the overlarge structure of Primrose House, my childhood home stood small but proud. My mother had taken good care of this place, tending the gardens and learning how to make small repairs from *This Old House* reruns on TV.

She'd watched me play in the backyard from the window above our kitchen sink in the evenings after dinner. In the disconnected way of dreams, her figure appeared there now, shimmering and indistinct. I didn't need to see her face to recognize her, and I started up the steps, excited to sit down and catch up with her.

Before my hand touched the knob, the buzzing in the back of my mind spiked intensely. I winced and rubbed the back of my head, but it was useless trying to massage it away from the outside. I glanced up at the window, expecting to see my mother's worried face, but two glowing, red eyes watched me instead.

Horace stood at the window, one arm outstretched so his palm rested on the glass. A sudden wave of déjà vu disoriented me, and I stumbled backward off the steps, careening across the patio. Instead of landing on the grass, I floated upward, enjoying the sensation of flying. It was something I wouldn't be able to do when I woke, and I savored the feeling of weightlessness that buoyed my limbs.

Up I went, over the roof and into the front yard. I'd never played out here; there was no lawn to tumble across, no patio to draw on with my chalk. There were just bark chips and stones and succulents. I wondered if it'd been that way when she moved in or if my mother had engineered things that way so I would stay where she could see me from the kitchen window.

My feet touched down on the asphalt in front of the house and I started walking. I had no destination in mind, but I wanted to be away from the house while Horace was there. I traveled faster than I could while awake, and soon I was outside the city. There, the desert stretched away from the highway until the edges shimmered in the sunlight. Magic, my mother had called it. I knew now they were optical illusions, and I thought of Raziel. He'd make a distinction about the difference between magic and tricks of the eye. I didn't feel such a thing was important.

I stepped off the road and kept walking toward that shimmering nothingness. A figure waited for me there. She was my height, and her skirt billowed in the wind. She pushed her dark hair behind her ears with both hands at once, and for the first time, my mother's face came into clear view, so similar to my own—large blue eyes and a narrow bone structure, framed by waves of brown hair.

Tears spilled down my cheeks when I saw her smile. I'd never expected to see it again. I wanted to run to her, but my feet refused to quicken their pace. Fear stabbed my heart; I was certain she'd fade before I reached her.

But she didn't fade. Not this time. Only her smile melted away. Her lips parted until her mouth fell open in a silent scream. Eyes wide with terror, she raised a hand and pointed behind me. A shadow approached from the road, his top hat visible even through the heat lines rising from the earth. His red eyes glowed, illuminating a wide, toothy smile.

My mother grabbed me from behind and yanked me backward into her arms. Cradling me, she whispered in my ear, "He lies."

His shadow descended upon us, and I woke up gasping for air. My laptop slid off my legs and onto the window seat beneath me. Above me, moonlight shone down through the windows. I slipped off the bench and into my kitchen, wishing I had a privacy screen or some blinds to give me more privacy. I couldn't get the memory of those burning red eyes out of my mind, and the sensation of someone watching me followed me around the room.

My arm ached where my mother had grabbed me in the dream, and I realized I'd been squeezing my biceps in my sleep. It took a full glass of water and several long minutes of reminding myself I was in Donn's Hill—not New Mexico—to shake the buzzing from my mind and the tingling from my skin.

While most of the dream faded into echoes and vague memories, my mother's warning rang in my mind. Whether it had truly come from her, or if my brain had just used her image to tell me something important, that was something I wasn't sure I'd ever truly know. Regardless of the source, I felt the truth in her words.

Horace lies.

Questions churned in my mind as I climbed into my bed and hid my head beneath the covers. Why would a spirit lie? What did he have to gain?

CHAPTER TWENTY-SIX

"Do you ever get tired of change?" I asked Graham the next morning as I leaned against the kitchen counter with my second cup of coffee in my hands. The first had disappeared in a quick series of scalding gulps but still hadn't chased away the lingering unease my dream had left behind.

"You mean, like there suddenly being such a thing as cursed boxes?"

The jewelry box in question was gone. Yuri had taken it with him when he'd left the night before, promising not to bring it into anyone's home. He didn't say what he'd do with it, and I thought that might be for the best.

"It seems like every day since I've come to Donn's Hill, I've found out that something I assumed kids made up to scare each other actually exists. But I mean bigger change." I sighed. "This past year has felt like walking through a minefield. There's no time to adjust to the status quo before life throws something new at me."

"Not all new things are bad, though." He put an arm around me and kissed the top of my forehead. "I'm glad my life changed when you got here."

I smiled up at him. "I never asked you how the exhibition was."

"Not bad."

"Yeah?"

He grinned. "Come see."

I followed him out to the back where he'd parked his father's cargo trailer beside the garage. He drummed his fingers on the trailer's white siding for a few moments while simultaneously making a drumroll sound with his mouth.

"Exciting enough for two drumrolls, huh?" I teased.

"You don't even know."

He pulled open the back door to the trailer, revealing an all but empty space. A few scraps of bubble wrap littered the floor, but not a single sculpture remained.

"You sold out?" I stared at the barren trailer. "Really?"

"Really!" He grabbed me and spun us around in a circle for a few dizzying moments. We whooped and cheered in the backyard, and I wished we'd taken the time to create a special high-five in anticipation of this moment. I wished I'd been in the right mindset to celebrate with him the night before instead of letting the supernatural hijack our evening.

I told him as much, adding, "I knew this would happen."

"You didn't, but I appreciate your confidence in me." He closed the door on the empty space and folded his lanky arms behind his head. "And you were right about Raziel. He put some photos of my sculptures online after the cocktail party, and a ton of people already knew who I was before I even got to the exhibition."

"Holy cow. That's awesome."

"Yeah. And yesterday, Amari asked me to sculpt a bust of Raziel for his gravesite in the same style I used for the Donn statue. She said he genuinely loved my work."

For a moment, I forgot how much Raziel had hated me and

every other psychic in town. He could have rubbed my name in mud for ten years, and I would have forgiven him the moment I saw this look in Graham's eyes. For once, there was no self-doubt clouding the victory. There was no fear that nepotism or cronyism had played too large a role, and no sense of imposter syndrome. There were only pride and joy, and I felt the same emotions threatening to burst out of every pore on my body.

"We have to celebrate," I said. "Brunch?"

"Deal." He grabbed my hand, leading me into the kitchen where his car keys hung on a hook above the coffeemaker. "Hey, next time I go to one of these things, I want you and Striker to come with me. It wasn't the same without my sidekicks."

"*Your* sidekicks? I thought you two were *my* sidekicks."

"Let's be honest. We're Striker's." He chuckled. "I realized how much I cater to her when I unpacked my cashbox in Chicago and found a bag of kitty treats under the money tray."

Hearing the magic "T" word, Striker limped into the kitchen. She favored her left hind leg, barely picking up that foot as she took each step forward at a pitifully slow pace.

I raced forward to scoop her up, but when I touched her back, she growled.

"Whoa, what's wrong?" I kept my voice low and calm, but inside, I was screaming. Had she fallen off the banister and landed wrong in the foyer? Been too reckless when jumping from my open windows to the trees outside? Hesitantly, I reached out a hand to stroke her back, and she swatted at me with full claws.

I threw a panicked glance at Graham as he raced out of the room. He returned a few minutes later with the hard-sided cat carrier we'd used to take her to the Franklin cabin. He put it in front of Striker, and I dreaded what was sure to happen next. She would refuse to get in, we'd try to lure or force her, and by the end she'd be howling with pain and we'd be covered in scratches.

Oddly, as soon as he opened the little metal door, she limped inside and settled down.

I stared at Graham. "Did she go that easily when you loaded her up for the cabin?"

"Nope. But that should tell us how much pain she's in. Come on, let's get her to the vet."

Striker howled in the car all the way up Main Street. The sound twisted the muscles in my back, and I hugged the carrier to my chest. When we pulled up to the Donn's Hill Animal Hospital, a red CLOSED sign hung in the window.

I swore. "Of course. It's Sunday."

"What do we do?" Graham asked.

I racked my mind for a solution. There might have been an emergency vet in Moyard, but that was an hour away. In desperation, I pulled out my cell phone and dialed a former housemate.

"Mackenzie!" Phillip Lee's familiar, dramatic voice poured out of the phone at top volume. "What a pleasure to hear from you!"

"Hey, Phillip. How's New York?"

"Delightful. The energy here cannot be beat, and I've been spoiling myself with tickets to all the best shows. Come visit! You'll love it, and you can stay in my guest room."

I rolled my eyes at Graham, who smothered a laugh with his sleeve. He'd been sad when Phillip had left Primrose House to join a prestigious financial firm in Manhattan, but I hadn't missed the constant invitations to brunch or late-hour cocktails in the butler's pantry, always accompanied by hyperactive eyebrow raises.

"Thanks for the invitation, Phillip. I have a question for you— does your sister do emergency appointments on Sundays?"

Phillip's sister, Dr. Lee, was Striker's veterinarian. The two of them shared the same upbeat energy, but she'd funneled her outgoing nature into a thriving animal practice instead of general-ized lechery.

"No, on Sundays she does her on-site visits to farms with her equine partner. Why, what's the matter?"

I filled him in on Striker's behavior, and he clucked into the phone.

"Poor little minx," he said. "I do miss her knocking bits of garbage under my apartment door. I'm sure the good doctor would see her first thing tomorrow morning. In the meantime, you might try my friend Elizabeth Monk."

"Is she another vet?"

"No, but she's the closest thing you'll find in Donn's Hill on short notice. She does furrapy out of her shop in The Enclave."

"She does what?"

"*Furrapy.* Pet massage. She works with animals all the time and might be able to tell you if this is urgent enough to warrant a trip to Moyard."

Striker's yowl from the carrier in my lap convinced me anything was worth a shot. I checked my watch; it was after eleven, so the shops in the little occult district would be open. Graham drove us there and parked the Geo in the same spot I'd used when taking Stephen home the week before, and we carried a howling tortoiseshell cat through the cobblestoned neighbor-hood, looking for Elizabeth Monk's shop.

Halfway down the block, a wooden sign hanging from the eaves of a building advertised reiki, massage, and furrapy. I remembered seeing the strange word the last time I'd been in The Enclave and hurried toward the building's door, holding it open for Graham and Striker.

We passed the darkened door of Daphne's tarot shop as we headed up the narrow stairs to the second floor. At the top, a glass door greeted us. The design etched onto the clear surface featured animals and humans in various postures, all of them active:

running, jumping, doing a cartwheel, and in the case of a large dog, chasing its own tail.

An electric doorbell sounded when we entered, and a tall, broad-shouldered woman emerged from behind a curtain made from strings of wooden beads. A network of fine lines criss-crossed her tanned skin, and deep crows' feet ringed her heavily shadowed eyes. Her snowy hair was pulled back from her face in a long, loose braid that cascaded over her left shoulder. Dozens of short, black crystals hung from silver bracelets around each of her wrists, jangling pleasantly.

"Can I help you?" The question was polite, but her voice was deep and gruff, and when she finished speaking, her mouth settled into a deep frown.

"Phillip Lee referred us here—" I began.

"Phillip?" She grunted. "That old scoundrel. Haven't seen him in months."

"He moved to New York," Graham put in.

"Well, that'd explain it, wouldn't it? You'd better not be after the kinds of things he'd ask me for."

I snorted. "I doubt we are."

Graham lifted the carrier to the countertop, and Striker mewed pitifully. "Our cat is limping. The vet's closed, and we're hoping your—uh—furrapy can help?"

Elizabeth scowled. "Depends what's wrong. Come on back. Let's have a look."

She led us behind the curtain and down a short hallway. A small room at the end held a large, cushioned table covered with a vinyl sheet and a wooden bench that looked like it'd be more at home in a mausoleum than a massage parlor. Soft, new-age music tinkled out of speakers mounted in the ceiling corners, and hand-painted wooden signs advised the benefits of deep tissue massage, aromatherapy, and reiki. As we settled ourselves on the bench, she misted the room with a floral scent.

"What is that?" Graham asked.

"Lavender and Frankincense, my own blend," she explained. "Helps cats relax."

He raised his eyebrows and nodded. "Makes sense. Could we use it at home?"

"Surely can," she said. "Cats are anxious little critters. Let her out of that contraption. Best if she runs around here a bit, gets used to the room."

Elizabeth left the three of us alone, and I released the latch on Striker's carrier. The cat poked her nose out, sniffed the air, and promptly yanked her head back into the darkness.

"Should I pull her out?" I didn't want to risk hurting her leg, but this was all uncharted territory. I'd only just gotten used to taking an animal to a veterinarian where everything was fast and clinical. This place, with its relaxing yoga-studio vibe, somehow put me on edge.

"Let her chill out in there for now," Graham said. "She'll come out when she's ready."

We sat on the bench in silence. Guilt gnawed at me. Striker had been fine the morning before. Only one thing had changed in the last twenty-four hours: we'd brought that blasted jewelry box home. Now, just as Amari warned, misfortune had followed.

I stared glumly at the floor, mentally kicking myself. If Striker had some incurable disease…. I couldn't even think about it.

A tear rolled down my cheek, and Striker emerged from the safety of her plastic cocoon with a soft meow. She stared at me from the floor for a few moments, measuring the distance between us with her bright yellow eyes. When she jumped, her back legs failed slightly, and she nearly fell short, landing on the bench in an awkward huddle. After a quick shake, she stumbled onto my lap and rubbed her face against my chin.

Alarmed, I gathered her up into my arms and cradled her against my chest. "Easy, kiddo. Don't push yourself."

Never one to listen to reason, she squirmed out of my grasp and slid down my jeans to the floor. There, she stalked around the room, still babying her left hind leg as she sniffed the table's legs, rubbed her chin on every surface, and finally settled down on the floor between Graham's feet.

Elizabeth came back a few minutes later. I expected Striker to bolt back into her carrier at the sight of an unfamiliar person. But she stayed put, purring loudly and staring at the masseuse with wide, yellow eyes.

"There's a nervous purr if I ever heard one." Elizabeth's voice was softer than it'd been at the counter. She cooed to Striker and held out a hand for inspection. When Striker didn't flee or scratch, Elizabeth picked her up and placed her gently on the table.

Elizabeth's hands were large and strong, and she swiftly examined Striker's legs, gently pulling them outward and testing the muscles with practiced fingers. Striker endured the indignity with more grace than I'd expected, purring throatily all the while.

Elizabeth frowned. "When'd the limp start?"

"We just noticed it this morning," Graham said.

"Ever done it before?"

I shook my head. "Not while I've known her."

"Could be arthritis." Elizabeth scratched Striker under the chin. "How old is she?"

"Dr. Lee thinks she's about ten. Isn't that young for something like arthritis?"

"Age don't matter. Had a kitten once, jumped out of the hayloft in the barn, landed right on her feet the way cats do. Impact jarred her bones somethin' awful. She was just a year old. Had arthritis after that, but you'd never know it the way she carried on." She ran a hand down Striker's back as she spoke. "Could be that. Or, could be tender from jumpin' off somethin' she shouldn't have. Let's do a bit of massage today, tide her over 'til you can get her into the vet."

I agreed, and Elizabeth got to work. For the most part, it looked like she was just petting Striker with short, fluid motions. Her bracelets tinkled as she worked, the black crystals clanking against each other with each stroke. Striker rolled her head backwards to squint happily at me.

"How long have you been doing this?" I asked Elizabeth.

The older woman shrugged and kept massaging. "For people, goin' on thirty years. For animals, 'bout five."

"Which one do you enjoy better?"

For the first time, a smile appeared on her lined face. "You know the answer, sure as I do. Animals can't tell me where they hurt, but they make their appreciation known more than most."

I nodded toward the hand-painted sign on the wall. "And reiki?"

"Been doin' that before I even knew what it was. My gran taught me energy work when I was a little girl." She continued the repetitive strokes, moving down Striker's back. "Things were different then. People 'round here were proud to call themselves hedge witches, and they charged fair prices for fair work. We didn't have all these new folk comin' here and stirrin' up trouble."

Intrigued by the matter-of-fact way she discussed the town's psychic community, I leaned forward, resting my forearms on my knees. "What kind of trouble?"

"All these outsiders, movin' here from big cities and settin' up their shops. Half of 'em don't practice the arts the way they should. They're after money, and when they don't find it, they go lookin' for other things." She scowled again. "This way don't lead to riches, but it'll lead you right, if you let it. These new folk... they're more interested in climbin' into each other's beds than helpin' the people who come to 'em."

She continued complaining about the way of the today's world, lecturing us about the wickedness of dishonesty and infidelity as she massaged Striker into a state of total bliss and relaxation.

I envied the cat; I couldn't remember ever feeling so stressed in my life. The faint buzzing in the back of my mind had started up again halfway through the treatment, and by the time my feet hit the little square entryway separating Daphne's shop from Elizabeth's stairs, it had matured into a full-grown tension headache.

Striker, meanwhile, was limp as a noodle in the carrier in Graham's arms. I poked a finger through the slats to stroke her forehead and she purred quietly.

"You'll be fine," I told her, more for my benefit than hers. My voice hitched in my throat and I willed the tears to stay away, hating how easily I cried these days.

Graham was staring at me with more concern in his eyes than I felt I deserved just then. He rested a hand on my arm. "What's wrong?"

I shook my head. "I feel awful about all this. She was fine yesterday, and then I brought back that box…"

"Hey." He pulled me into a one-armed hug. "This has nothing to do with that. Elizabeth didn't seem concerned, and Striker already seems better. Let's pick up some lavender oil on the way home, like the stuff Elizabeth had. We can spray it around your apartment and help Striker relax."

"Yeah." I sniffed. "That's a good idea."

He pulled open the heavy door to the street and stepped outside, but my feet stayed rooted where they were. I couldn't shake the feeling that something was following me like a dark cloud. Paranoia tickled the back of my mind, and I remembered the way the van had crashed itself into a tree. Was it even safe for me to ride in a car with other people? Just how contagious was this curse?

"Go on without me," I told him. "I have to… um…" I looked

around the small space and glimpsed Daphne sitting inside her empty shop. "I need to talk to Daphne."

He looked doubtful but nodded. "Do what you need to do. I'll take Striker home. We can get the oil later. You sure you're okay to walk?"

"I'm sure, thanks."

He left me alone after a quick kiss, but I didn't reach for Daphne's doorknob. Instead, I hid my face in the corner of the entryway, pretending to read the instructions on the fire alarm that hung there. I could feel someone's eyes on my back, but I didn't care. If I couldn't see them, they couldn't see the tears rolling down my face.

CHAPTER TWENTY-SEVEN

Daphne's shop, Visions, had a similar layout to Elizabeth's upstairs. Customers entered the large sitting room at the front, which she'd furnished with wood-trimmed chairs and couches that looked like they belonged in a stately home in England. A beaded curtain separated the sitting room from the other spaces in the back, but unlike the space above us, there was no counter or computer terminal in the corner. The only sign we were in a business establishment came from the shop's logo, applied to the window in gold leaf.

She leapt up from her seat when I entered, concern etched across her round eyes. "Mac! What's wrong?"

I let the door swing closed behind me and shook my head. "I'm sorry. It's been a rough morning."

"I've been there. Sit down. I'll make some tea."

She disappeared behind the curtain and returned a few minutes later with a tall, silver teapot, a pair of teacups, and a bottle of light brown whiskey. She handled the teapot with the grace of someone who did this a dozen times a day.

"Do you serve tea to your customers?" I asked.

She nodded. "It's sort of my ritual. It helps me get into the right mindset, and my clients seem to find it relaxing."

"Whiskey too?"

"Nope. That's just for friends who've been crying on my doorstep." She poured a healthy slug of whiskey into my tea, added twice as much to her own, then picked up her cup and clinked it gently against mine. "*Sláinte.*"

Grateful for something a little stronger than Earl Grey to chase the buzzing from the back of my mind, I sipped the beverage in silence for a few minutes. Soon the pounding in my head subsided and a gentle warmth spread through my body. I relaxed into the antique sofa and stretched my limbs out in front of me with a sigh.

"Want to talk about it?" Daphne asked, eyeing me over her teacup.

"I feel bad taking up your time." On the other side of the gilded window, people streamed up the walkway toward the pub. "I'm sure you'll have some customers soon."

She laughed. "It's barely noon. On Sundays, the tourists come in for the day or the weekend, and the Ace of Cups is their first stop. Brunch lasts for hours, and we don't get much business until after two. But you won't hear me complaining. Their two-dollar mimosas are the reason Sunday is our best day."

"Well, I'll take off if someone else comes in." I sipped the whiskey-laden tea again, wincing slightly at the sting of the alcohol. "Never mind. You have a heavy hand. I'll hide in the back."

"Deal. There's a bed back there. It's all yours."

We sat in companionable silence for a while at her window, watching tourists parade up the road toward the pub. Neighboring practitioners brought out sandwich boards that advertised their services. Stephen waved at us from across the way, where he was rinsing off his stoop with a garden hose.

"I haven't been sleeping well," I said at last. "Not since the cabin."

She flinched at the c-word. "Me neither, to be honest."

"I'm sorry. It was my fault we were all there."

"Don't beat yourself up. We knew the risks. And terrified as I was in the moment, I've always wanted to see a ghost."

"What do you know about them?" I asked.

She shrugged, and one side of her embroidered shawl slipped off her shoulder. "I've picked up a few things from watching Nick."

She delivered her words in such a matter-of-fact way that I wasn't sure if she was serious or just sarcastic. In case it was the former, I said nothing and waited for her to continue.

"I think it's safe to say you're the expert here," she said. "Why do you ask?"

"I don't know." I took a deep breath, then laughed. "Raziel got into my head. I feel stupid talking about this stuff now, like I'm some kind of fake."

"I've seen what you can do. You're no fraud."

Coming from a woman who was married to an admitted charlatan, her words carried extra weight. Even so, self-doubt lingered in my mind.

"Every time I try to reach someone, I can't," I said. "And I don't just fail. Horace barges in and—"

"Horace?"

"That's his name. The spirit who showed up at the cabin."

"You saw him again?" Daphne's voice was sharp.

"Earlier this week." For the fifth time in as many days, I related the events in Raziel's hotel room and Horace's request that we retrieve the jewelry box from Cambion's Camp.

"I drove past there a few months ago," she said. "Well, past the dirt road leading to it, anyway. I thought about poking around, just to see if the stories were true, but couldn't stand being in the area. There's something wrong with those woods."

"I think we brought it back with us." I rubbed the back of my head, where the ever-present buzzing remained despite the muting effects of the alcohol. "Do you know Amari Botha?"

Daphne gave me a terse nod, her lips pressed together tightly.

"Oh, right." Between my headache and the stress of reliving the visit to Cambion's Camp, I'd momentarily forgotten that Amari and Raziel were probably frequent topics of bitter conversation around the Martin house. "Well, she thinks we brought back a haunted box, like a cursed object. And this will sound crazy, but... I think whatever is in that box is following me around."

She frowned but didn't look as frightened at the idea as I felt. Instead, she gazed out her front window for a few silent moments. I twisted in my seat, trying to see what she was looking at, but it looked the same as it had a few minutes before. Brunchers trooped toward the Ace of Cups, and a few speedy eaters meandered back down the walkway, looking at the New Age and occult goods in shop windows as they passed.

Still watching the activity outside, she spoke at last. "Nick told me you want to know how to tell when someone is conning you."

"Yeah. He wasn't interested in teaching me."

"I told him he should." She looked at me and smiled, but her eyes were sad. "You're new to this life. It hasn't even been a year since you started seeing spirits again, right?"

Something about her tone made me feel uncomfortable, like she was bracing me for a blow. "Yeah."

"I think there's a period of naïveté we all go through. Years and years ago, when I learned I'm an Empath and started using the cards to channel that energy, I took every other claim of psychic ability at face value. I knew what I was experiencing was genuine. Why would anyone else lie?"

I fiddled with my teacup. That's exactly how I'd felt since coming to Donn's Hill.

"I didn't want to believe it the first time I realized a friend of mine was duping her customers. This was back in Chicago, before we moved here. Nick told me she was full of it, but I didn't want to listen. It's like a bubble bursting. Nothing's the same once you know not everyone in your community is who they pretend to be."

"When did you find out Nick was a fraud?" The question flew out of my mouth before I could stop it, and I clapped a hand over my lips.

Daphne grimaced, but didn't get angry. "Not until last year. I've been naïve longer than I'd like to admit. And you're naïve, too."

"Stephen told me the same thing."

"I'll ask Nick to help you again. You're too suggestible, Mac. Don't believe everything you hear." She leaned back and cradled her teacup between her hands. "Especially if it comes from Amari."

CHAPTER TWENTY-EIGHT

By the time I'd walked back to Primrose House, my bottom lip was raw and bleeding from being chewed so vigorously. Daphne made it sound like I couldn't trust anyone. I hated the idea that more people in Donn's Hill were faking their abilities. It was bad enough that spirits could lie. I had to trust *someone.*

I took comfort in the knowledge that not everyone in the paranormal community was a scam artist. People like Kit, Yuri, and Mark were true believers, and they used their show to help people. It was noble, not shady. It certainly wasn't making a ton of money for any of us. In a way, it was insane that we did it at all, especially when so many of the places our work took us ended up being dangerous.

Had it only been two weeks since Kit and I had parked outside the Franklin cabin to plan the séance? She'd been so convinced Raziel was out to destroy the *Soul Searchers* and everything else in Donn's Hill. I wanted to laugh at the irony that he'd been the one in danger, but I didn't have enough emotional energy left to summon so much as a smile.

Exhausted, I trudged up the front steps of Primrose House and leaned against the front door for a few minutes, resting my forehead against the rough grain of the wood. I felt no closer to clearing my name, and every time I went searching for answers, I just found more questions. Were the sheriff and his deputies experiencing the same phenomenon?

Probably not, I decided. *They already have their answer. They're just looking for enough evidence to nail me to the wall.*

Dismal as the thought was, it propelled me forward. I couldn't stop looking for the truth, no matter how tired I might feel. With a sigh, I pushed open the door and stepped into the house.

A small, wooden jewelry box sat on the braided rug, dead center in the middle of the foyer. I didn't have to pick it up to check for the Seal of Solomon on the bottom. The sharp hum that pressed against my head and face from all sides was enough to confirm that this was the same box I'd dug up in Cambion's Camp.

Warily, I circled the box from a distance of a few feet, skirting my way around the foyer until I could get to the stairs. Every instinct in my body told me to run, but I didn't dare turn my back on the box. I didn't even dare to take my eyes off the thing. Instead, I backed slowly up to the second floor, one step at a time, not blinking and scarcely breathing.

An agonizing eternity later, I reached Graham's door and knocked without facing it. I pressed my body against the wood, trying to put as much distance between me and the box as possible. When the door opened, I tumbled backward into Graham's arms.

"It's back," I whispered, pointing down the stairs.

"What's back?"

"The box."

His eyes flared with recognition at those two words. Another time, I'd have laughed. How could something so simple scare us so much?

Proving himself to be braver—or perhaps more foolhardy—

than I am, Graham went downstairs and investigated on my behalf.

"Don't open it!" I reminded him from my position of safety on the second-floor landing.

Tipping the box backward with the end of an umbrella, Graham confirmed it bore the symbol Amari had noticed. He left it where it was and came back upstairs to stand beside me. "It's the same one. I don't get it. Yuri told me he buried it back at the lumber camp."

"He went *back?*" A wave of dizziness set my head spinning. "When?"

"Right after he left here the other night."

He'd gone back. I couldn't imagine doing the same thing; there'd been something so obviously wrong with that place. I imagined a greedy presence being so desperate for our arrival that it yanked our van off the road, like it was trying to take us on a shortcut through the trees.

"Is he okay?" I asked.

"I think so." Graham gestured for me to follow him through the open door to his apartment. "Come on, sit down. I'll call him."

"I'm not letting that thing out of my sight."

"Fine. I'll be right back."

While Graham disappeared into his apartment, I settled onto the floor of the landing and leaned my head against a pair of balusters to watch the box below for any sign of movement. Striker sauntered out of Graham's living room looking relaxed. She still limped a little, but it was nowhere near as pronounced as it'd been that morning.

"Come here, sweetheart." I patted my vacant lap.

Her yellow eyes sparkled with interest. She started toward me but stopped partway across the landing and turned her head toward the stairs, glaring at the box on the floor below us. A loud, low growl rumbled forth from her chest and her ears swept backward. The growl crescendoed into a shriek, and she bolted down the stairs on a collision course with the box.

I leapt to my feet. "Striker! No!"

She launched off the bottom step, sailing above the box with her claws extended. When she landed on the floor on the other side, she snarled and spun around. But she wasn't looking at the box; she was looking *above* the box.

Something cold and wet ran down my back, dampening my t-shirt. "Striker!" I whisper-shouted. "Get away from there!"

Tail puffed, she circled the box, growling continuously. When she came back around to the stairs, she darted up them and hunched beside me. I reached down to pick her up, and she hissed, swiping at me.

"Fine!" I folded my arms across my chest. "You're okay."

"Who's okay?" Graham asked from behind me.

Striker answered for herself, growling and muttering at the box below us.

"Whoa, she's huge." Graham reached out to stroke her back, but I stopped his hand.

"She's super agitated," I said. "I wouldn't touch her."

He nodded and filled me in on his conversation with Yuri, who verified he'd returned to Cambion's Camp and re-buried the box there in exactly the same place we'd found it. He'd had no trouble getting there or back, and he'd gone alone.

"Kit wouldn't have gone to get it, right?" I asked when Graham hung up. "To mess with me?"

As soon as the question was out of my mouth, I knew it was an unfair one. All this thinking about fake mediums and scammy "psychics" was making me paranoid. Maybe some of those people would do something like retrieve the box to manufacture some kind of supernatural event, but that wasn't Kit. She'd never even used a Ouija board out of respect for the paranormal. No way would she bring something like this box back into her own house.

"Yuri only told me where he was taking it in case he ran into car trouble and needed a rescue," Graham said. "He didn't tell anyone else where he was going, not even Kit or Penelope."

That left one other possibility, and it was too outrageous to consider. Objects didn't travel on their own. Someone—or something—had to move them.

Gazing down at the small, innocent-looking box laying on the rug at the bottom of the stairs, I wondered if Horace knew I'd brought the box back to Donn's Hill but hadn't taken it to the inn. He'd said he could see everything that happened in that house. What if Yuri had talked to Penelope in her office, and Horace put the pieces together? Would that make him angry enough to transition into a poltergeist state so he could act on the living world? Was the force in Cambion's Camp strong enough to pull Horace from the inn so he could retrieve the box?

Even if the answers to those last two questions were "yes," why would Horace have left the box at Primrose House instead of returning it to the inn to finish his business?

To send a message.

The ache in the back of my skull spread forward until it felt like two giant hands were pressing against my face. I rubbed my temples and groaned.

"Headache?" Graham asked.

"I've had once since the accident, mostly at the back of my head. And there's been this buzzing sound…" I shuddered. "Sometimes it's so loud. Now I feel like there's a vise on my skull squeezing my sinuses."

"Sounds like a migraine. My mom gets them. Yuri is on his way—why don't you go lay down for a while?"

I shook my head. "I won't be able to relax with that thing in the house."

"Well, sit back down at least. I'll get you an ice pack."

Sitting cross-legged and using my forehead to pin a cold pack to the balusters, I glared at the box in the foyer. Beside me, Striker did the same. Her tension was contagious, and I felt knots forming in the space between my shoulders as my head continued to pound. Together we sat, keeping vigil over whatever thing called the jewelry box home.

There had to be a way to cleanse the box, clear it of any negative presence, then return it to the inn so Horace could move on. Two ghosts, one stone.

Upon his arrival, Yuri agreed with me. "I don't know offhand how to do it, but we'll find a way. In the meantime…"

He produced a wooden crate the size of a small microwave. Light poured out of it when he lifted the lid, and I realized he'd lined it with mirrors.

"An old superstition," he said. "The mirrors trap a spirit within. I thought it couldn't hurt."

After the performance Striker had given me, I was all in favor of taking any and all precautions. From my position of safety behind the second-floor railing, I watched Yuri pick up the box with the same embroidered altar cloth he'd used to cover it before. He placed it with care in the mirror-lined box, flipped down the metal clasp on top, and fed a padlock through the mechanism.

"Overkill?" he asked.

I shook my head. "I don't think there's any such thing with this stupid box. What are you going to do with it now?"

"Well, driving it back to Cambion's Camp didn't work, for whatever reason." Yuri spoke in his usual calm, comforting way, but the alarm in his eyes was visible through his glasses. "I think we find somewhere closer to keep it while we investigate how to deal with it."

"We can keep it in my workshop," Graham suggested. "I'll lock it up in a cupboard."

"Are you sure?" Yuri asked.

Graham nodded.

"I don't want you working out there while that thing is in the garage," I said.

"I could use a vacation, anyway." He reached down and squeezed my hand. "Don't worry."

His suggestion was impossible to follow. Worry seemed to be my new default state. It was all I did while I watched Graham carry the box outside, and all I did until he came back into the house. He joined me on the landing again and pulled me into a tight hug.

"It's going to be okay," he mumbled into my hair.

Like millions of other comforting promises spoken throughout time, his words were soon proven to be utterly false.

CHAPTER TWENTY-NINE

My headache failed to get better after a solid night's sleep, and a morning visit to the veterinarian didn't help. Dr. Lee quickly came to the same conclusion Elizabeth Monk had, and a quick x-ray confirmed their shared hypothesis.

"I have mild bad news, but good news to go with it." Dr. Lee tucked her blond hair behind her ears and shot me a reassuring smile. "Striker has arthritis in her hips, which is very common for a kitty her age. The good news is: it's treatable. We'll get her started on a series of injections to help prevent further deterioration of the joints, and between that, a nice heated bed, and more furrapy sessions with Elizabeth Monk, she'll get back to her old tricks."

Dr. Lee sent us home with a sample of a special joint-care cat food, and Striker zoomed up and down the stairs at Primrose House for a while to convince us she'd be okay. Despite the good news and Striker's high spirits, my head throbbed. If I closed my eyes, I could picture a monkey sitting on top of my skull, screeching while it squeezed my forehead and the back of my skull with its paws.

I left Striker in Graham's care and walked to the grocery store where I was immediately overwhelmed by a shelf of essential oils. Graham's mom said diffusing lavender oil relieved her migraine symptoms, and Elizabeth had recommended lavender and Frankincense to help Striker relax. The latter was something I'd assumed only existed in Christmas songs, which I hummed as I tried to decide which version of four identical-looking bottles of lavender was probably best.

Eventually, I grabbed the mid-priced option. As I turned to hurry away from the sweet-smelling section and back to the comfortable aisles of cereal boxes and peanut butter, I slammed into Nick Martin.

"Easy." He steadied me by my shoulders, and the annoyance in his eyes dissipated when they met mine. "Oh. Sorry."

"It's okay." Rubbing my left temple with one hand, I squinted up at him. "How's it going, Nick?"

"It's good. Uh…" He shifted uncomfortably and cleared his throat. "Listen, I've been meaning to call you. I'm really sorry about the way I brushed you off at my house last week."

I remembered Daphne's promise to talk to Nick for me and smiled. She must've put some serious pressure on him to result in an apology like this.

"It's okay, really," I repeated, trying to put him at ease. "I've been a little preoccupied. Plus, Stephen gave me some tips for evaluating if someone is really drawing on a gift, so—"

"Stephen? Stephen Hastain?" Nick's face clouded with anger. "That hack doesn't know anything."

I frowned, irked by the insult. "Hey, he's a friend of mine."

Nick snorted. "He doesn't know the meaning of the word. If you think that guy is on your side, you better watch your back."

Startled by the vitriol in his voice, I took an involuntary step backward. "You can think what you want about people, but I'm not interested in listening to you insult my friend."

"Oh, I'll do more than talk. I'll show you. If you really want to know how to spot a fake, let's go."

"Now?" I looked down at the bottle of lavender oil in my hands. "I'm shopping."

He snatched the bottle away from me, marched over to the cashier, and slapped a twenty onto the conveyor belt along with the oil. "There. You're done."

He stalked out of the grocery store, throwing a furious glare over his shoulder at me. I stood in the checkout line a few moments longer, staring after him in indecision until the cashier handed me the change.

I should keep it. That would teach him to be so demanding. But then I'd miss out on seeing whatever it was Nick was suddenly so interested in showing me. And I'd feel guilty about having someone else's money in my pocket. Curiosity overrode my irritation at the way he'd ended my shopping trip, and I followed him out of the store. He waited for me beside a sleek black Mercedes.

I handed him his money. "Where are we going?"

"The Enclave."

"Why?"

He opened the passenger door and motioned for me to get in. "Because there are more fakes there than you think."

Nick said nothing on the drive. Happily, we didn't have to sit in awkward silence too long before arriving at The Enclave. He parked across the street, glaring out the driver's side window for a few moments before turning off the ignition.

"I hate this place," he said at last.

"Really? I thought Daphne liked having a shop here."

"Oh, *she* loves it. But what does she know." He got out of the car, slammed the door closed behind him, and marched across the street without waiting for me.

I sprinted to catch up and followed him down the footpath. He kept his head facing straight forward, not even looking at Daphne's shop, where a flashing neon OPEN sign beckoned. Instead, he led us toward the lime-green building next to Stephen's shop. A rectangular wooden sign hung above the door displaying a hand with an eye emblazoned on the palm. Nick pushed open the door and beckoned me to follow him inside.

It was a stuffy space, crowded with pillows and sagging furniture. The air was heavy with incense to the point where it was difficult to see across the room through the haze.

The same sleepy kid who'd spared Stephen from being locked out of his shop stepped out from behind a curtain. Today, he wore a floor-length robe embroidered with a paisley pattern, and his long, black hair fell down on either side of his bony face. Like Raziel, he had a heavy hand with the eyeliner pencil.

"Welcome," he said. "Ah, Nick. It's a pleasure to see you again."

Nick sneered. "Mac, this is Fang."

"Mac, is it?" Fang glided forward on bare feet and held out a hand.

I raised mine to shake his, but he flipped it over and pawed at it with light fingers.

"Lovely lines," he murmured. "Are you here for a reading?"

"She is," Nick said.

"And you as well?" Fang spoke with a light accent that would've been at home announcing a yacht regatta in the northeast, but his sense of style felt like a knock-off of Raziel's distinctive Las Vegas aesthetic.

"No, I'm just here to watch," Nick said. "Evaluate, you might say. Pretend I'm not here. Do everything exactly as you normally would."

Fang's eyes widened a fraction of an inch, then he cleared his throat and his features relaxed. "Yes, of course. Please, relax in the parlor." He gestured toward a cluster of overstuffed, low-backed armchairs near the front window and turned to me. "I find it's most conducive for positive energy if we settle the payment before the reading. As you're a friend of Nick's, I'll give you a discount. Forty dollars."

Forty dollars? I shot a glare at Nick, who'd already settled into the chair facing the window. If I'd known this lesson—or whatever it was—would cost me forty bucks, I might have skipped it. But I couldn't think of a way to get out of paying that wouldn't seem rude, so I dug out my credit card, regretting giving Nick the change from the grocery store.

"I'll just be a moment." Fang disappeared behind a curtain, and I heard his footsteps growing lighter down the hallway.

I waved an encroaching cloud of incense smoke away from my face and made to sit down in the chair facing the door. Nick snapped his fingers and pointed me toward the chair with its back to the window.

"Watch him constantly," he murmured.

"What was all that about 'evaluating' him?" I followed Nick's lead, keeping my voice low. "Is that something you do?"

"Only recently. You may have heard Daphne is putting together a traveling *cirque de l'étrange*."

"What on earth is that?"

Nick glanced in the direction Fang had disappeared in and leaned closer to me, lowering his voice even further. "In the old days, they would've called it a freak show. She'll have contortionists, intuitives, fire-eaters—it'll be a hit. She has twelve cities lined up already."

He kept saying "she," with no mention of his own involvement.

"Are you part of it?" I asked.

His gaze hardened. "No."

"Why not?"

"Focus on the task at hand, Mac. Don't worry about me."

Something about the way he dug his nails into the upholstered armrests at his sides convinced me it wasn't worth pressing the issue. I looked back at the curtain Fang had ducked behind and leaned back into my seat. "So is this like... an audition?"

"Good Lord, you're even more naïve than I thought. That's what I want him to think, but Daphne wouldn't let this guy buy a ticket, let alone perform with her." He wrinkled his nose, like he smelled something foul. "He's the worst kind of fraud. He assumes he's the smartest person in the room, so he doesn't bother with subtlety. He's the perfect case study for you."

I shifted uncomfortably in my chair, hating being called naïve. The worst part was, he was right. Even though Nick had brought me here, even though this guy chose to be known professionally by a name I'd expect a child to give a dog, I didn't want to believe Fang was a fraud. I wanted him to have a true psychic ability.

"Okay, let's test your instincts," Nick said, voice still hushed. "Were you expecting to pay up front?"

"I wasn't expecting to pay anything at all," I said pointedly. "Ten minutes ago, I didn't even expect to be here."

He cracked a smile. "Fair enough. I'll reimburse you. But humor me. When you get your hair done, do you pay in advance?"

"No, I pay at the end."

"Right. So, think like Fang. Why ask your customers to pay before the reading?"

I shook my head. "I don't know. To make sure they don't stiff me?"

"No. You were glaring at me when you got out your wallet, so you didn't see him clock your driver's license when you opened it up. I'll give him credit, he's got a quick eye. But you gave him even more. You forked over your credit card, with your name stamped along the bottom. Don't you think it's taking a while for him to run the charge?"

He was right. Fang had been gone several minutes. The reason dawned on me at once.

"He's back there, looking me up?"

Nick nodded. "If he can find one or two details about you, it'll be just enough to convince you he's got the gift. He can make up the rest and you'll eat it up like chocolate pie."

I chewed my lip. It sounded exactly like what Raziel had accused Nick's team of doing when someone bought a ticket to his shows online. Nick hadn't denied the truth of Raziel's accusations when I asked him about them, and I didn't understand why his eyes burned with anger as he explained the way the technique worked to me now.

At that moment, Fang reappeared from behind the curtains with a flourish and bowed to me as he returned my credit card. I ran my thumb down the raised MACKENZIE CLAIR, wondering what he'd found in those few minutes alone with his search engine.

He took a seat in the chair across from me, so we flanked Nick, who steepled his fingers in front of his mouth and narrowed his eyes. Fang flicked a glance in Nick's direction, and Nick nodded as though giving the younger man permission to begin.

"Your hands, please." Fang smiled warmly at me. "Palms up."

I rested my hands on the table between us, which was tall enough to support my elbows without pitching me forward. Fang stroked my palms again, coaxing my fingers into an open and relaxed state.

"Is there anything in particular you're concerned about today?"

"Not especially," I lied, not wanting to feed him any more clues about myself than I already had.

"Hmmm." He traced the three most obvious lines on my right hand with a fingertip, clucking and tsk'ing as he went. "You've had a tumultuous life. Do you see the way your lifeline splits here? It speaks to your roving nature. You'll call many places 'home' over the years."

Despite my efforts to control my face, my eyebrow quirked upward. If Nick hadn't warned me, would the accuracy of Fang's words have hooked me right there?

He continued, commenting on the length of my fingers compared to the size of my palms. He pronounced that the break in the ring around my thumb meant that I had multiple families, whether bonded by blood or not. At one point, he covered his mouth with one hand and quickly compared my left palm to my right, then shook his head and smiled at me.

"Your restless nature could be problematic, but your fate line shows you'll have great prosperity in your chosen career. A word of caution: don't forget to lean on the people around you for help when you need it." After a few more minutes of doling out generic advice and finding compliments hidden in the way the lines on my palms crossed or failed to cross each other, he clasped my hands together with both of his and squeezed them gently. "I hope you found that as enlightening as I did."

I was trying to formulate a polite response when Nick made a sound of disgust and slapped Fang's hands away from mine. Fang's eyes filled with a sudden fear, and he drew backward.

"God, you're pathetic," Nick snarled. "You don't even *try* to hide what you're really doing."

He stood up, and Fang did the same, tripping backward over his own bare feet in his haste to back away from Nick's hulking form. But Nick didn't give him time to escape down the back hallway. He grabbed Fang by the front of his robe and shoved him against the wall with enough force to make the framed photos above them jiggle on their hooks. I sat in stunned silence, my mouth hanging open as I watched Nick's fury boiling over onto our host. His anger seeped out in every direction, rolling off him in an invisible black cloud that filled the room.

"I—I—" Fang stammered.

"Cut the shit, Kevin." Nick twisted Fang's—or Kevin's—robes in his hands, hoisting the younger man off his feet. "You and I both know you're the fakest guy in town. At least lie with some dignity."

"Help!" Fang screamed. "Help me!"

His shout unfroze me, and I jumped to my feet, shouting, "Nick! Let him go!"

Neither my voice nor Fang's did anything to stop Nick from unraveling. He raised one hand to Fang's throat, squeezing his fingers. Fang gasped, and I ran forward, tugging futilely at Nick's arm.

"Stop!" I yelled. "You'll kill him!"

The door behind us burst open and Stephen barreled into the room, smashing into Nick with one lowered shoulder and knocking him to the ground.

"You!" Nick scrambled to his feet, eyes ablaze. He balled his hands into fists but didn't move toward Stephen.

"Jesus, Nick!" Stephen moved in front of Fang, panting as he protected the younger man with his body. "What's the matter with you?"

"What's the matter with me? With *me*?" Nick lifted a shaking hand to point a finger at the rune caster. "You have the balls to ask me that when you're sleeping with my wife?"

Stephen paled.

Triumph lit up Nick's crimson face. "Didn't think she'd tell me, huh? Well, you were wrong. See, that's how strong our connection is. She tells me everything."

"Strong?" Stephen said. "Don't make me laugh. She's left you, in case you haven't noticed."

At that, Nick lunged forward. On pure, insane instinct, I dove between them.

"Stop!" I shouted, raising my arms at my sides to keep them apart.

If Nick had been serious about hurting Stephen, I'm sure he could have batted me aside as easily as wafting away incense. But he backed away, the color slowly draining from his face.

"Get out," Fang croaked, struggling to his feet. "Before I call the cops."

"You're not serious." Stephen stared at him. "Call them no matter what."

The younger man rubbed his neck with one hand, eyeing Nick. "I'll keep quiet about this if you make sure I'm part of the show."

Stephen shook his head. "I wash my hands of this. Mac, you're okay?"

"Yeah, I'm fine."

"Good." He backed away from Nick and pulled open the door. "You need a ride home or anything?"

"She's with me," Nick growled.

"No, actually, I'll walk," I said.

He pursed his lips then strode for the door, blowing past me and knocking his shoulder against Stephen's, growling, "Watch your back."

"You watch yours," the Irishman countered.

Before he stepped out the door, Nick turned his cold eyes on me. "You wanted to know. Don't say I didn't warn you."

CHAPTER THIRTY

"And then he just lost it," I said.

Graham and I were having lunch at the new deli on Main Street. The space had previously been home to the best coffee shop in the world but sat empty for months following the owner's passing. The leafy green murals of forest animals on the walls had been painted over with a clouded honey gold, but the new owner had kept the same square, scrubbed tables that Donn's Hill gossips had loved to crowd around any time anything interesting happened.

The informal news network had moved its headquarters to the lobby café at the Oracle Inn, but I had no desire to return to that house. I felt sure Horace would manifest the instant my feet crossed the threshold. Thinking about seeing him again made my stomach twist like a wringing washcloth.

My second choice would've been the Ace of Cups, but I was no more eager to return to The Enclave than the inn. Over deli sandwiches and deliciously salty house-made potato chips, I filled Graham in on Nick's implosion at the palm reader.

Graham's ears darkened to crimson as I described the way Nick had unexpectedly turned violent. He absently crumpled his sandwich wrapper into a tiny ball in one hand. "You could've been hurt."

"I don't think he would have done anything to me." I didn't have any evidence to back that up, and not even my gut agreed with the words that'd just come out of my mouth.

Graham's eyes were doubtful, but he didn't challenge me. "I never really liked Nick, but I didn't think he was capable of something like that."

"Me neither. It was so weird. He was unrecognizable in that shop."

"The palm reader kid isn't pressing charges?"

I shook my head. "He didn't even call the cops."

"Weird."

Strange as I thought it was to let Nick off the hook on the vague promise of being included in Daphne's traveling circus, I was relieved not to have to face Deputy Wallace again. Every day that went by without a knock on my door made me feel like I was cheating time. I hadn't gotten any answers out of Horace, and after Nick's "lesson" about the dishonesty that ran rampant in Donn's Hill's psychic community, I felt no closer to discovering anyone with a stronger motive for killing Raziel than the police thought I had.

The box is in Graham's garage. It'd be so easy to take it to Horace.

The thought snuck up on me, popping into my mind as though from somewhere outside it. The idea of retrieving the jewelry box, handling it and carrying it to the inn, sent a shiver of dread down my entire body. But if I did it… could Horace give me the answers I needed?

No. No, it wasn't worth the risk of unleashing whatever was inside that box or exposing myself to Horace again. I'd only go that route if—and hopefully not when—I ran out of options.

"You okay?" Graham asked, pulling me back into the moment.

"Yeah," I lied. "Sorry. What were we talking about?"

As we finished the rest of my chips and debated whether Nick's fame would have gotten him out of an assault charge with no jail time, a familiar redhead walked into the deli.

"Mark!" I waved him over to our table. "What's up?"

My cameraman's default facial expression—a deep scowl—shifted to a guilty cringe at the sight of us. He slowly made his way over to our table and nodded at Graham. He glanced at me then focused his attention on the stack of napkins at the edge of our table. "Hey, Mac. How are you feeling?"

"Better, thanks. How about you?"

"Oh... you know..." Mark cast his gaze around the deli. "Keeping busy."

"How'd your freelance job go? You were in Moyard the last couple days, right?"

"Yeah. It was okay."

I frowned. Mark was never exactly loquacious, but this was awkward even compared to his normal standards. I stretched my neck, trying to make eye contact with him, but he seemed determined to avoid meeting my eyes.

"Is something wrong?" I asked.

His eyes finally flicked up to mine, and he sighed, pulling out the chair beside me and lowering himself into it. After rubbing the back of his neck with one hand for a few silent moments, he dropped his bombshell.

"I'm leaving the *Soul Searchers*."

"What?" I stared at him, unable to process his words. "Why?"

"I got an offer to join a documentary film crew that shoots internationally."

Silence mounted as I waited for him to add a "just kidding" or to laugh. Eventually, my contact lenses started drying out, and I had to remind myself to blink.

"You're serious," I said.

He nodded, frowning down at his lap.

"Uh, congratulations," Graham said. "When do you start?"

"Next week. I'm packing up a truck on Sunday and heading out to Los Angeles." He glanced up at me again. "I'm sorry, Mac."

"I—" I fished around for words, but found few. "I don't understand."

"I can't pass up this chance," he said. "It's my dream job."

"You said your dream changed when you started working with Yuri. What about helping people? Can you do that on a travel show?"

"I'll still get to help people. It's not a travel doc. It's more like investigative journalism. We'll be showing both the good and bad sides of the paranormal community around the world. Real hauntings, but also the kinds of inhumane travesties that happen under the radar."

His words were familiar. Too familiar. I knew at once how he'd suddenly found a gig like this.

"Amari recruited you, didn't she?"

Mark's face flushed. "Yes."

"When?"

"At the cocktail party. She and Raziel both said they wanted to hire me for their show."

"That's why they loaned you that sound equipment—to give you a taste of what working with them would be like."

He didn't answer. He didn't have to. Whatever their strategy had been, it'd worked.

"I'm sorry," he said.

Inside, my brain screamed that this was sure to spell the end of the *Soul Searchers*. How dare Mark screw us over? What kind of selfish jerk would do something like this?

But my memory whispered that it'd been Mark who talked me into joining the crew in the first place. He'd been my friend when I'd been finding dead bodies on every shoot, and he'd never asked for anything in return. His leaving wasn't selfish, but me trying to keep him from living his dream would be.

Besides, as long as the show had Kit and Yuri, it would survive. It was their baby. Truth be told, Mark and I were just appendages.

"I'm happy for you," I said. "I mean it."

He sagged like a marionette who'd just lost its strings. "Thank you."

"Kit and Yuri already know?"

"Yeah, I told them yesterday."

"Are you having a going away party or anything?"

It was a foolish question. Mark wasn't the type to celebrate anything he did. He'd never invite a bunch of people over to his house for a nightlong, awkward goodbye. The look of horror on his face at the suggestion confirmed it.

"Well, what time do you leave on Sunday?" I asked.

"Early. It's a long drive."

"Don't do it all at once," Graham warned. "Break it up over a few days."

"That's the plan." Mark stood and ran a hand through his mop of red curls. "Well, I better go. I've got a lot of packing to do."

I stood and gave him a tight hug, promising we'd come by on Saturday to say a proper goodbye. He extricated himself, got a sandwich to go, and we followed him out the door on our way home.

"That's a bummer," Graham said as we walked down the residential back streets toward Primrose House.

It was the understatement of the day. Mark had been one of

the first friends I'd made in Donn's Hill. His presence was part of the fabric of this place. I couldn't imagine life without him, and I certainly couldn't picture being on an investigation without seeing his red hair behind the camera.

"Shirley will be furious," Graham went on. "Mark's her favorite nephew."

Mark's great-aunt Shirley was the on again, off again organist at Hillside Chapel atop Main Street. I'd had the pleasure of meeting the little old lady at a séance and the displeasure of being deafened when she'd played the organ at a funeral. Mark seemed to be the only person who could convince her to turn the volume down.

"The congregants at Hillside will never forgive him for leaving town," I said.

We joked and laughed all the way home, parting ways in the back driveway. Graham was driving to Stephen's place to make sure he was doing okay after the previous night's altercation. For a moment, I was tempted to join him, just to be in his company a little longer. But it was still too soon. The Enclave had become a sour place in my mind. Instead, I sought out Kit to see how Mark's departure would affect our production schedule.

I didn't have to look far; she was in the shared kitchen, rinsing plates and glasses at the sink. It was a mundane task, but her grim expression and pale face put me on instant alert.

"What's wrong?" I asked.

"Nothing," she said. "Just, uh… you know. Thinking about the future."

I settled on a barstool and grabbed an apple from the fruit bowl. "Mark just gave me the news. Where are we going to find another cameraman?"

She turned away from me to load the rinsed dishes into the washer. "ScreamTV can help with that. They've got a whole network of freelancers and stuff. It'll be okay."

"You're less upset about this than I expected you to be." I'd figured the angry voice inside Kit's head would have beaten her rational, supportive voice to death, and then done the same thing to Mark. She was fiercely protective of her father's show. Then I realized if Mark was leaving this weekend, Amari would probably head back to L.A. around the same time. Compared to saying goodbye to her girlfriend, losing a cameraman was nothing. "When does Amari leave?"

"Next Wednesday."

"I'm sorry. That must be hard. Will you be able to go visit her soon?"

She finished loading the dishwasher and turned back around to face me. Her lower lip was trembling.

"Oh, no." I slid off my stool and rushed around the counter to squeeze her shoulder. Amari must have broken things off. "What happened?"

Kit shook her head. "I'm so sorry, Mac."

"For what?"

She brushed my hand from her shoulder and took a deep breath. "Ugh, this is so hard." She balled her hands into fists a couple times, shook them out, and then looked me dead in the eyes. "Amari asked me to help on her new show."

I gulped. "And you said…?"

"I haven't answered her yet."

"Are you leaning one way or the other?"

"Honestly… I'm not sure. I know this is crazy. We haven't been dating long—"

That was one hell of an understatement, but I didn't interrupt her.

"And the thought of leaving Dad to produce the show on his own scares me, and the thought of leaving Donn's Hill scares me even more. But when I'm with Amari… I don't know." She bit her lip. "I'm crazy about her. I've never felt this way about anybody. And thinking about her going back to L.A. without me and not seeing her every day, that scares me more than anything else."

For some reason, I burst out laughing.

"What?" she demanded.

My laughter rose to a shriek and I doubled over, gripping the counter for support. Every time I came close to settling down, the stupidity of the situation struck me again, and I let out another squeal of panicked mirth.

Finally, my laughter subsided, and I brushed the tears from my cheeks.

"I don't get the joke," Kit said.

"Neither do I." I wiped my eyes and sighed. "It's just so typical of my life right now. Everything feels weird, my head hurts, Mark quit, and now you might follow him. It's just perfect in the worst way, you know?"

Her cheeks reddened. "I haven't decided yet or anything."

"That's the funniest part. You're so conflicted and just completely tortured by this decision, I can't even be mad at you." I grinned at her. "Honestly, I feel cheated."

The flush in her face dissipated, and she sagged against the dishwasher in relief. "You're not mad?"

I shook my head, and she sighed.

"Good," she said. "Look, I won't do anything rash. I just wanted to give you a head's up."

"I appreciate it. Keep me posted, okay?"

She nodded, and I fled the kitchen, racing up the stairs to my apartment against the ticking time bomb in my chest. The burst of laughter couldn't have come at a better time; I'd been on the verge of tears when it came.

I wanted to be angry that she was considering leaving, but there wasn't any room for anger. My heart was too busy breaking to feel anything else. I was sure she'd leave with Amari. And even if—*if*—the show somehow survived her departure, where would that leave me? What was I supposed to do without my best friend?

My bed was a comfortable place to cry; I'd shed many tears here since moving to Donn's Hill. But I never thought I'd be crying about Kit leaving me behind.

Striker emerged from beneath the mattress with a ball of paper in her jaws. She leapt onto the bed and dropped it beside my face like a gift, trilling softly.

"That better not be a letter of resignation," I told her. "If Amari tries to hire you as their mascot or something, you say *no*."

When Graham returned a few hours later, I was too terrified of bursting into tears again to tell him Kit was considering leaving Donn's Hill. He fell asleep quickly, unburdened by the knowledge that my life was on the verge of imploding. As he dozed beside me, I reflected on the many ways Raziel had ruined everything.

First, he'd derailed the cabin cleansing. It was clear now; things would have gone better if he hadn't crashed the séance. I didn't know how, exactly, but I certainly wouldn't have tried to punch anybody that night if he hadn't been there.

Then, he'd been killed. And while that part wasn't technically his fault, if he hadn't goaded me into lunging at him, Sheriff Harris wouldn't think I was some unhinged, violent murder suspect.

Now, from beyond the grave, he was tearing apart the *Soul Searchers* team. I gathered up the blanket into my fists, twisting and squeezing at the fabric as I imagined Kit telling me she'd told Amari "yes."

She'd been so sure Raziel posed a threat to the show. I'd thought she was being dramatic, but she'd proven herself right.

There was a strong chance the death of the Soul Searchers was another part of the curse brought on by that damn haunted jewelry box. But even that could be laid at Raziel's feet; if he hadn't come to Donn's Hill, if he hadn't stayed in the Oracle Inn and been killed there, I'd have never held a séance in that attic. Horace would never have appeared to me, and I wouldn't have had any reason to agree to help him, so I would never have dug that cursed thing up from its resting place in the clearing.

Every time I thought about the box, my headache grew more painful. This had all started with Raziel, but everything had gotten worse since I'd gone to Cambion's Camp. And it wasn't just my life the box impacted; even Striker had gotten hurt. Who would be next?

Beside me, Graham's chest rose and fell in time with his gentle snores. He was the only person left who hadn't suffered some kind of misfortune. If I did nothing, it was only a matter of time before the box got him too.

I didn't have time to find a way to banish whatever haunted the jewelry box. And I felt a nagging suspicion that Horace knew more about the spirit than he'd told me. Wild theories sprung into my mind—Horace could be haunting the attic and the box at the same time, he could have buried that box in the clearing himself for someone to eventually find, or the spirit trapped in the box could be his aunt, furious for decades about the theft of her wedding rings—but none of them rang true enough to take hold.

Horace would know the answers, I could feel it. And he claimed to know who'd really murdered Raziel in that attic. If I did as he'd asked, if I took him that box, I could fix everything all at once.

And if I went right now, while everyone around me still slept, I wouldn't have to put anyone else at risk.

Acting before I could talk myself out of it, I grabbed Graham's keys from the bowl in his living room and crept down the stairs. Feeling eyes on the back of my head, I whipped around halfway down to the foyer.

A tiny tortoiseshell cat limped behind me on silent paws.

"Striker!"

Her whiskers bristled and surprise flooded her round, yellow eyes.

I thought about picking her up and locking her back in Graham's apartment but didn't want to risk making any more noise in the house than necessary. Besides, the box had already gotten to Striker. I felt like that made her immune to further misfortune, at least for a while.

"Okay," I told her. "You can come. Probably best if you're with me, anyway."

Together we slipped through the kitchen and into the back-yard. Above us, thick clouds covered the moon and the stars. Only the light from the streetlamp at the end of the driveway lit our way. I strode toward the garage with a straight spine, projecting a confidence I didn't yet feel.

Once inside, I flipped on the fluorescent overhead lights, illuminating the near-empty tables and shelves that waited for Graham to refill them. At the back of the space, a bank of utility cupboards lined the wall. This was where Graham stored his supplies, including a locked cabinet for his cashbox.

I didn't need his keys. The cupboard was unlocked, and— apart from the small metal cashbox—it was empty.

The jewelry box had disappeared.

CHAPTER THIRTY-ONE

A deputy from the Driscoll County Sheriff's Department stood in front of the garage with us, taking our statements about the robbery in the misty light of dawn. I was glad Deputy Wallace wasn't with him. I still didn't know where I stood with her, but I trusted her enough that I wouldn't have been able to resist sounding like I'd lost my mind. She was normally receptive to my supernaturally charged theories, but given my current status as a "person of interest" in Raziel's case, I didn't think she'd want to hear me tell her the box had stolen itself.

To this stony-faced deputy, it was easier to stick to the mundane. I didn't color my account with any details about the ghost who'd been wreaking havoc on my life from inside the tiny jewelry box or the nonstop headache and the sensation of being watched. Instead, I claimed I'd been awakened by an odd noise and had gone outside to investigate. Concerned about Graham's cashbox, I'd checked the garage to make sure it was still there.

"But the cashbox wasn't taken, correct?" The deputy flipped backward through his small notebook to check something. "All four-hundred and thirty-seven dollars are intact?"

"That's right." Graham stood beside me and looked straight ahead, watching the deputy.

Striker watched the exchange from atop the tall toolbox with its many drawers, one of which often held her favorite brand of kitty treats. She hunched uncomfortably on the cold, hard metal; her hips poked sharply away from her body like fins as she eyed the uniformed stranger in her territory.

The deputy made a mark in his notebook. "All that was taken was the wooden crate which contained some kind of antique jewelry box?"

"Correct," Graham confirmed.

"Okay." The deputy flipped his notebook closed and jerked a thumb toward the posters on the back wall of the ceramic studio. "Let's see the video."

"Video?" I whispered to Graham as we led the deputy into the kitchen. "Since when have you had a camera in the garage?"

"Since always." He was doing an even better job averting my gaze than Mark had done and kept his eyes fixed on the back door. "Insurance is cheaper with a security system."

In all my time in the garage, I'd never noticed a camera. "Where is it?"

"Behind the wall clock."

Inside the house, Graham accessed his security system's cloud storage from a laptop on the kitchen counter. There were hundreds of video clips on the first page alone, all date and time stamped within the last week. Graham clicked on the clips from that night, and we watched in silence as the black-and-white night vision footage played through at a multiplied speed.

The view of the garage was from the side, and the fisheye angle captured the overhead doors on the left and the bank of storage shelves and cupboards on the right. The long tables of sculptures filled the space in between. Just after the timestamp flipped past midnight, a crack of light flared from the garage's side door. The crack widened, and two men stepped inside.

One was so tall he needed to bend down to get through the door. The other was shorter and, despite his rotund build, moved smoothly across the frame like a cat. Both wore dark ski masks that covered their faces, and I watched in horror as they rummaged through the cupboards. They carefully set any object they moved back in its original place without speaking. Eventually, they huddled around the single locked door and broke it open. Ignoring the cashbox, they retrieved the wooden crate and fled the garage.

"Recognize either of them?" the deputy asked.

Something about them was vaguely familiar, but I couldn't figure out why. It was an occurrence that'd been happening frustratingly often lately. Graham and I both shook our heads. The video played on, and not five minutes later, it showed me walk into the garage and flip on the lights. A muscle in Graham's cheek twitched.

The deputy had Graham send him links to the videos and gave us each his card. "We'll do what we can to recover your property. In the meantime, let me know if anything else comes to mind."

After the deputy left, I collapsed into a chair at the kitchen table and stared out the window. My mind churned. Striker prowled restlessly across the kitchen floor hunting for mice or spiders along the baseboards. Graham lowered himself slowly into the chair across from me and I glanced up, surprised he didn't have mugs of coffee or cocoa in his hands. His normal reaction to a stressful situation was to make something hot to drink.

I was on the verge of making a joke about it when his expression finally registered in my brain. His jaw was set, and his features were hard and closed off. He still didn't look at me. He just glared at the wall a few feet to the side of my head.

"Are you okay?" I finally asked.

"Honestly?" He blinked and shifted his cold eyes to mine. "No."

"What's wrong?"

A humorless smile twitched at the corner of his mouth for an instant, replaced immediately by his stony-but-neutral expression. "You mean apart from burglars invading my studio? Oh, and the fact that you heard something in the backyard and instead of waking me up"—his voice rose—"you went outside *alone?*"

I stared at him, unable to do anything more than state the obvious. "You're angry."

His reaction surprised me. He was usually Mr. Placid, always calm and quiet. Now, two pink spots burned in his cheeks and a vein of tension protruded above the nose of his glasses. His arms were folded across his chest so tightly it looked like he might snap himself in half.

"Of course I'm angry. I'm pissed. What if those guys had still been in the garage when you went out there? You could've been killed! Or taken! All while I slept upstairs like an idiot." He flexed a fist against his bicep. "When I saw them on the video, all I could think about was what it would've been like come downstairs in the morning and find you hurt—or worse—on the studio floor."

"I'm sorry," I whispered, hating to see him this way. "If it makes you feel any better, I didn't wake you because I didn't actually hear anything outside. I sort of lied to the deputy."

He stared at me with wide eyes. "Great. About what, exactly? And why?"

"I don't know." I really didn't. When asked why I'd been in the garage, the lie about hearing a noise had come easily to me and had oozed out of my mouth without my help. "I wasn't thinking. I was in shock, I guess. But I didn't hear anything in the yard, okay? I didn't realize there was something going on."

"Then why were you outside in the middle of the night?"

"I was going to take the box." I shifted my weight, sliding my hands beneath my backside to punish them for the theft they'd almost committed. "I was going to take it to Horace."

Graham's incredulous gaze pierced into me for several long, silent minutes. When he finally spoke again, his voice was quieter but somehow angrier than before. "Even though you told Yuri you weren't going to."

I looked down at the napkin holder on the table and nodded.

"You were going to take the box and then go over to the inn in the dead of night and present it to that lunatic ghost like an offering?"

"I don't know," I said again, rubbing the aching spot at the back of my skull. "I just… I don't know. I've been so tired."

"You scare me sometimes, you know that? What if, somehow, the sheriff figures out you lied to that deputy just now?"

"I don't know how—"

He didn't let me finish. "If they catch you in one lie, even about something stupid, they'll assume you're lying about every-thing else. And if the box had been in the cabinet, you would've gone back to the scene of the crime, by yourself, in the middle of the night?" He stared at me for a few moments. "It's been over a week since they brought you in for questioning. Obviously, there's no evidence for them to find that can tie you to the murder, so for a minute there, I stupidly thought you would be okay. But I should've known you'd do what you always do."

"Oh, yeah?" Despite my desperate desire to de-escalate this conversation, I found myself glaring at him across the table. "And what's that?"

"Recklessly dive into things all by yourself, like you don't care about your own safety."

"I *do* care."

"You don't act like it." He pointed to the scar on my neck. "Didn't you learn anything from that?"

Heat flooded my face. I hated being treated like a child. Was it my fault I'd nearly been killed the spring before? Was I supposed to stay locked in my apartment, never going anywhere or doing anything for fear that someone might jump out of the shadows and attack me?

I asked Graham, since he clearly thought he was smarter than me. "What do you want from me here? I said I was sorry for scaring you. What else can I do?"

"I want you to stop acting like you're alone in everything. I want you to talk to me, or Kit, or *someone* when you decide to go out in the middle of the night or try to summon a spirit." A brief flicker of sadness touched his eyes. "I want you to trust me."

The implication that I didn't already trust him was more than I could take. I stood and pushed my chair beneath the table, gripping its back with my hands. "I do trust you. The real problem is that you don't trust me. But I'm too exhausted to fight about this anymore, so I'm going to bed."

He and Striker followed me out of the kitchen and up the stairs. When I continued past the second-floor landing toward the third, he asked, "Where are you going?"

"I think I'll sleep at my place."

He sighed. "Do whatever you want, Mac. Like always."

I expected him to storm into his apartment, but he just folded his arms and stared at me. Striker sat beside his feet, and together they watched as I climbed the stairs to the third floor. Only when I opened the door to Number 8 did Graham finally turn around and walk into his apartment.

Striker's yellow eyes burned at me a moment longer before she slowly turned her back on me too.

CHAPTER THIRTY-TWO

The last few hours of the night passed slowly as I lay awake —and alone—in my apartment. Striker's decision to stay with Graham was clearly a message. She was as angry with me as he was, and that was just fine. If they wanted to be pissed at me, they could deal with me being pissed at them. I pulled the covers up to my chin and fumed silently at the dark ceiling until the first rays of sunlight crept into the apartment. Only then did I slip into a fitful rest, not sleeping deeply enough to dream or recharge.

The chime of a text message on my phone woke me just after noon. *Going to Moyard for clay*, Graham wrote. *Be back tonight.*

An involuntary snort escaped my nose as I tossed the phone unceremoniously to the foot of my bed. Part of me was relieved we couldn't continue our argument from the night before. Another part of me felt cheated. I hadn't gotten a chance to win. Plus, we'd left things unresolved, and the world seemed out of balance. Right this second, Graham's Geo was carrying him farther and farther away from me. I hoped the physical distance didn't correlate with an emotional one. Hurt as I'd been the night before, the thought of Graham and I drifting apart was too painful to dwell on.

I lay in bed until my bladder convinced me it would be prudent to get up and then slumped down the stairs to the kitchen. The house was thankfully empty. No other residents were lunching at home, and it occurred to me that the ones with regular jobs were probably at work. As I chewed a piece of toast, I reflected that I'd probably have to get a day job soon myself. Despite Kit's assurances that *she* hadn't made a decision, I predicted she'd leave, and the Soul Searchers would die a quick death by the New Year. I glared at the closed door to the butler's pantry. Amari's show would probably take off, fueled by Raziel's loyal fanbase, while *we* faded into obscurity.

My restless mind infected the rest of my body, and I absently dug my fingers into the skin between my shoulders and my neck, rubbing the sore muscles there. What I needed, I decided, was a massage. Putting my feelings about The Enclave aside, I looked up Elizabeth Monk's number. She was one of three people in that neighborhood I was certain wasn't lying to her customers, so I called to set up an appointment. I was in luck; she could squeeze me in early that evening.

That left me with several hours to kill, and I made the mistake of searching through the classified ads for jobs nearby or ones I could do online from home. The listings reminded me I'd lucked into my position as a professional medium in the first place, and the advertised jobs all held zero appeal compared to the thrill of making a TV show with my friends. By the time I left for my appointment, my shoulders rode at ear level.

I headed for The Enclave on foot since both Graham and Kit's vehicles were missing from their spaces in the long carport. Crisp autumn air filled my lungs as I made my way across town, and I marveled at the length of all four seasons in Donn's Hill. I was used to the short shoulder seasons and long summers and winters of the Rockies, where you begged for winter by the end of summer and vice versa. Here, we'd already had weeks of stunning fall foliage and there were still many more to go before we had to worry about the first snowstorm.

A dull ache filled my chest as The Enclave came into view. The reality I had to embrace was that the city I thought I knew had changed. It wasn't the same one I'd discovered six months before. The feeling of betrayal lingered whenever Nick or Fang's face popped into my head. Gabrielle might have helped rob her clients, but at least she hadn't lied to them about seeing their dead loved ones.

The street was quieter than it'd been on Sunday, as few out-of-towners bothered to make the trip to Donn's Hill in the middle of the week. The faces I passed on my way to Elizabeth's parlor were locals grabbing dinner at the pub or ducking into one of the quirky little occult stores to do some shopping.

Elizabeth's face lit up with recognition when I entered the little lobby at the top of the stairs. "Didn't recognize your name on the phone," she said. "How's the little puff?"

"Her limp is much better, and she's her usual active self. We've got her on some injections, and we're going to keep bringing her in for regular massages."

"Good. Come on back."

She led me back to a different room than the one where she'd treated Striker. This one was dimly lit by a large pink salt lamp in the corner, and the only piece of furniture was a tall, narrow table with a donut-shaped pillow protruding from one end. String music over a background of rain sounds played softly from speakers in the ceiling, and a soothing, earthy aroma filled the air.

"Smells good," I said. "More of your oils?"

Elizabeth nodded. "Ylang ylang."

She left me alone to undress and position myself on the table, and I sighed as the heated blanket beneath me warmed my muscles. In the strange, pinkish light, the lines between the slats of the hardwood floor looked like a puzzle to solve, and I searched for patterns and pictures in the wood grains.

A soft tap sounded at the door and Elizabeth let herself back in. "What's troublin' you today?"

"Well, I feel like a bunch of pretzels have replaced my neck muscles," I said. "So pretty much that."

Her feet appeared beneath my face, clad in comfortable-looking tennis shoes. She started working on my back, and I almost giggled as I pictured myself looking like Striker had on the little table in the other room. My eyes closed as she massaged my muscles, and her words about holding stress in my shoulders registered strangely, a few moments after she said them. For the first time in weeks, I felt myself relaxing.

I need to do this more often.

The little crystals hanging from her bracelets tickled my back, and I imagined them leaving behind trails of white light as they passed over my skin. The image soothed me.

A bell chimed from the lobby and Elizabeth apologized. "I usually have a girl mindin' the desk, but she's been sick. Be right back."

The door clicked shut behind her, leaving me alone in the room. I didn't mind. The table was warm, my muscles were untangling, and my mind was quiet. No thoughts or regrets or plans hopped around in there. I just relaxed. My eyes closed, and I sighed contentedly.

The peace lasted a mere thirty seconds before the floor creaked and the hair on the back of my neck stood at attention.

"Elizabeth?" I called, not expecting a response. I hadn't heard the door open.

The feeling of unease crept down my back. A sudden stab of fear in my stomach made the case that it'd be better to keep my eyes closed. But I'd spent too much time with a cat and picked up her bad habits. I couldn't be content without knowing what was wrong in the room. Against my better instincts, I looked.

Red eyes stared back at me from the floor beneath the table.

The woodgrain pattern behind the eyes was just visible through Horace's semi-translucent form, but his presence was all too real. I inhaled sharply and my breath caught. His jagged grin and low top hat hung in the air two feet from my face, so close I thought I could smell him.

Ghosts don't smell, my brain reminded me. But that knowledge didn't stop the faint tendrils of a bitter, sage-like scent from lingering in my nose. I pushed myself up off the table and gathered the sheets around my body. The insane worry that he could grab my feet kept me off the ground, and I wished the table had been pushed up against the wall instead of the middle of the room. I'd never felt so exposed.

I blinked, and Horace stood before me, blocking the door.

"I've missed you, Mackenzie." His voice was a low purr. "Why haven't you come to call?"

I couldn't answer right away. My lungs still refused to do anything with that last gasp of air I'd sucked in, and my brain struggled to process what was going on. Had I been trying to reach him? Had I been trying to reach *anyone*? I'd just been lying here, relaxing and allowing my mind to be blank. How could he be in this room?

"Something the matter?" he asked. "No need to be shy."

Experimentally, I tried to close myself off to spiritual energy again. I imagined shields made of white light slamming up around me, protecting me and keeping me firmly rooted in the living world. Just as before, the shields did nothing. Horace remained in front of me, his red eyes slowly fading to black.

Breathe, I told myself. *Keep breathing.*

Finally able to speak again, I told him, "I don't have the jewelry box."

"I know. It was taken from you."

My eyes narrowed. "How did you already know?"

"I told you before." He flashed his teeth at me again. "I see everything."

"You said you saw everything that happens *in the inn*. The box wasn't stolen from there."

"And I also told you I can ride the energy of psychics like you to escape that prison, however temporarily. Your energy…" He closed his eyes and inhaled. "I've been waiting to find something like it for a very long time."

"I want to help you move on," I said, ignoring the feeling of rising bile in my throat. Everything about this spirit made me feel like my skin was on inside out. "I don't know if we'll ever get the jewelry box back, but we might be able to help you find peace otherwise."

His black eyes bored into me, and he registered no reaction to my offer to help him reach the next life. He tilted his head to one side and asked, "Could you feel it?"

"Feel what?"

"The spirit in the jewelry box."

I struggled to keep my face neutral. Something deep inside me warned that it'd be dangerous for him to see how easily he threw me off balance. Not trusting my voice to remain steady, I simply nodded.

He licked his lips. "I thought you would. There's something special about you, Mackenzie. Your power… It's greater than anything I've encountered in many, many years."

"Tell me about the spirit," I said. "The one in the box."

"I'll explain everything the next time I see you."

An involuntary shudder shook me. I didn't want there to be a next time. Though he was far less violent than Richard Franklin, he terrified me more deeply. I tried to stop myself from asking the next question, but the treacherous words spilled out of my mouth anyway. "When will that be?"

His form flickered, fading into the door behind him. His answer was a hiss in the air. "Sssssssoooooooon."

Okay, we're done. My hair tried to leap off my scalp to find safety elsewhere. I tried to follow its lead, but my legs were unco-operative. They carried me off the table just fine, but collapsed beneath me, leaving me a crumpled heap on the floor.

I gripped the table with both hands and pulled myself back to my feet. Panting from the exertion, I pulled on my clothes and tried to wrestle my breathing back under control. I wished Striker were with me. She had a knack for slinking out from wherever she'd been hiding just when I needed comfort, and her throaty purr was as good as medicine.

The door opened and Elizabeth stepped back into the room, recoiling immediately and covering her nose with one hand. "Ooof." Her eyes swept the room, landing on me as I tugged on my sneakers. "Everythin' alright?"

"Yeah, uh… family emergency. I need to get home."

"Is it your kitty?"

I wanted to hug this woman who worried as much—or more —about her furry clients than her human ones, and I felt bad lying to her. But it was easier than trying to explain what'd really happened.

"Yeah, it's just…" Before I could finish answering, the pain in the back of my head swelled to a crescendo. I rested the tips of my fingers on my temples and hissed through my teeth.

Elizabeth frowned. "I've heard about you. Folks say you're a psychic, and not one of these pretenders 'round here. Is that true?"

I winced as I nodded.

"I have somethin' that might help." She led me to the counter in her waiting room, retrieved a necklace from a drawer there, and handed it to me.

A single black stone, about the size of my pinky finger and wrapped in silver wire, hung from a long piece of braided leather. On closer inspection, the stone looked like a small piece of charred wood, but it was rock-hard and reflected the surrounding light.

"Put it on," Elizabeth said.

"What is it?" I asked, squinting at the crystal rod.

"Black tourmaline. Blocks negative energy. Keeps my customers' emotions from seepin' into me as I treat them." She held up her wrists, shaking the black stones that dangled from each one.

"Do they work?" I asked, unable to keep the doubt out of my voice as I slipped the necklace over my head.

She arched a pale eyebrow and frowned at me. The meaning was clear; Elizabeth Monk wasted no time with nonsense that didn't work.

I slipped the necklace on over my head. The stone rested against my sternum, just over my heart.

She watched me intently. "Can you feel it?"

"I don't know. How long… wait." As I spoke, the pain at the back of my skull subsided. The dull buzzing I'd been hearing since our trip to Cambion's Camp quieted. All at once, I could hear my own thoughts again. I stared at Elizabeth with wide eyes.

She chuckled. "Good."

"Thank you," I breathed. "What do I owe you?"

"Nothin' today. Come back another time, finish that massage. Stone's a gift. I like knowin' there's another true Empath in this town."

This time, I did hug her. She returned the gesture, squeezing me tightly against her tall frame and wishing me luck with the "family emergency" before I left.

My phone buzzed in my pocket as I hustled down the stairs and onto the narrow footpath. *Graham*, I thought eagerly, looking at the screen. But it was an unknown number. I nearly pressed the button to ignore it when a pang of paranoia convinced me it might be someone calling *about* Graham. Like a police officer. Or the hospital. I stopped halfway to the street and answered the phone.

"Hello?" I panted.

"This call will be recorded and monitored. I have a collect call from—"

There was a pause, followed by static. Then a familiar voice with a light Spanish accent said, "Gabrielle Suntador."

CHAPTER THIRTY-THREE

The recording continued, "—an inmate at a Driscoll County detention facility. To accept this call and associated charges, press '1.' To—"

I nearly dropped my phone in my rush to press 1. "Gabrielle? Hello?"

"Mackenzie!" Gabrielle sighed into the phone. "Thank God. I wasn't sure if you would pick up."

A thousand questions crammed into my mind at once, but my brain was too overloaded to process them. Gabrielle was calling me. My old friend. My mentor.

And thief.

And murderer.

Not a murderer, my gut protested. Not technically. She hadn't gone to trial yet, but I'd heard from Deputy Wallace that the charges would probably be reduced to manslaughter by the time Gabrielle faced a jury. She hadn't intended to kill anyone, but she was undoubtedly a criminal.

"I just got your letter," she told me. "There wasn't time to respond to you in writing. This is too urgent. You must stop trying to reach anyone on the other side. You've opened yourself up in a very dangerous way."

"I know. I wasn't even trying to contact the other side just now, and he appeared to me again."

The silence on the other end of the phone unnerved me.

"Are you still there?"

"Yes, yes," she said. "I'm thinking. You're sure you weren't reaching out? Your mind does unexpected things when it wanders."

I knew exactly what she was referring to. Once, I'd accidentally thought about a particular spirit during a séance. He'd just flitted briefly through my mind, but that'd been enough to summon him into the room, where he'd proceeded to wreak havoc.

"Positive," I said. "I was just relaxing, getting a massage."

A lot of good it had done. My shoulders were back to their regular tricks, trying to flank my ears, and the thick knots of stress and anxiety were already twisting back into place. But despite that, my thoughts were steady. Focused.

I realized how desperately I'd missed having a teacher, someone to guide me through the minefield of talking to the dead.

"Do you think he's a poltergeist?" I asked.

"No. I don't know what he is. There has never been such a spirit in my house before. His claim that he died there isn't true. He's lying to you, Mackenzie."

"Ghosts can lie?" It was one thing to hear Yuri, Amari, and my dreams tell me it was possible. It was another thing entirely to hear it come out of Gabrielle's mouth.

"I have never known one to do so. It's very troubling. You also mentioned his red eyes. That's not something I have ever seen before."

"They freak me out," I admitted. "I keep seeing them in my nightmares."

"This is why I'm concerned. The way you've described him... He might not be a spirit. There's something familiar about this, but I can't recall why. It's something a friend wrote to me about a very long time ago. I saved a collection of letters and notes from my correspondence with other intuitives over the years and hid it beneath the floorboards in my attic."

"Penelope found all your secret cupboards. Maybe she—"

"She didn't find this one," Gabrielle interrupted. "I didn't include it in my list, and she would have told me if she found it on her own. The documents are all very personal. She would not have done anything with them without doing me the courtesy of letting me know, I'm sure of it. How soon can you get to my house?"

Her house. My heart broke to hear her call the Oracle Inn "hers." It didn't belong to her anymore. Even if she got out of prison, she'd never have that home to come back to.

"Not long," I said. "Maybe twenty minutes if I run."

"Good. As I said, this is urgent. I feel you're in danger, Mackenzie. This spirit... he's like nothing I've encountered before."

The full meaning behind each of her words sank in slowly. Horace was a liar. I was in danger. And worst of all, even Gabrielle—the expert that even Yuri had always consulted when he was up against something unexpected—wasn't sure what was happening.

"There are two possibilities. We must—" Her voice was suddenly drowned out by sirens, which wailed painfully in my ear. "Lockdown!" Gabrielle shouted. "Find the box in my attic! I will call again!"

The line went dead.

I stared at the phone in my hand for a moment, paralyzed by the overload of information Gabrielle had just given me. Horace wasn't what he claimed to be, and to find out what he was, I had to return to the attic of the Oracle Inn. For another box. I groaned. She couldn't have known how traumatized I'd be from the last time I'd been tasked with finding one of those.

As I considered her request, Graham's plea from the night before echoed in my mind. There was no way I'd couldn't look for that box of letters, so returning to the inn was a surety. But I didn't have to do it alone. I needed backup. Fight or no fight, I wanted Graham and Striker by my side.

The call went to voicemail. I left him a message. "Hey, it's me. Gabrielle just called. Long story short, I have to go back to the inn. I know what you're thinking, but I won't go alone. Call me when you can."

My mind raced. I had a few options. I could wait until Graham got home, but I had no idea if he was still hours away in Moyard or if he was pulling into the driveway at Primrose House this very second. I needed to find a way to stop Horace from visiting me, and I needed to do it now, or I feared I would never sleep again.

The next best option after Graham would be another psychic. Someone who could help me block Horace out… or better yet, banish him.

There were only three people in town I was sure weren't lying about their abilities. Elizabeth had smelled the scent Horace had left in the room, proving she was sensitive to the paranormal, but I wasn't sure how strong that sensitivity was. I also couldn't picture her saying "yes" to a request from a client—one she'd only met twice—to close up shop early and go on a mad errand to find some old letters.

Stephen's rune reading had felt genuine. But he'd been at the cabin and hadn't seen Horace. Only one other person there had: Daphne. She was strong enough for that, at least. I just had to hope she'd be willing to risk seeing him again. I hustled back up the street to Visions and exploded into her shop.

Her head jerked up from the magazine in her hands. "Mac! What's wrong?"

"I need your help."

She was on her feet in an instant. "What is it? Are you hurt?"

"No, nothing like that." I took a deep breath, trying to gather my thoughts. "Listen, do you have any appointments tonight?"

Her eyes narrowed with suspicion. "Why?"

The words couldn't come out of my mouth fast enough as I explained about seeing Horace upstairs after my massage and Gabrielle's claim that the letterbox in her attic might hold the answer to getting rid of him.

"She said there's a secret place, a hidden compartment in the attic. I need to find it, but I know if I go back there alone, he'll be waiting for me." I swallowed. "Every time I see him, it's like he's more powerful. I can't face him on my own."

Daphne's eyes widened in alarm. "How many times has he visited you?" she asked, her voice a thin whisper.

I counted on my fingers. "That was the third one... maybe more. I've been seeing him in my dreams a lot lately, and I honestly don't know if that's him or just my brain trying to process the memory of him."

She took a deep breath and closed her eyes. "I don't know. I think it's too risky to go back there. For people like us, I mean. He's obviously drawn to intuitives."

"I know. He's said as much, but I have to go. Come with me. Please. I—" My voice cracked, and I covered my face with my hands. "I'm in way over my head. And I'm terrified. I don't blame you if you don't want to get involved, but I have to do something, and I'm too scared to try it alone."

She stared at me for a few moments then stood up, pulled a hair tie off her wrist, and gathered her long hair into a high pony-tail. I recognized the habit from the cabin, and my chest swelled with hope as I realized it was a sign that she was preparing to tackle a difficult task.

"Fine," she said, proving me right. "Let's go."

We took Daphne's car to the Oracle Inn. The parking lot was nearly empty; it'd been days since any new developments in the case had been announced, and the ravenous news cycle had moved on to their next target.

She headed toward the front door, but I grabbed her arm and pulled her toward the back entrance. Despite Gabrielle's confidence that the renovations hadn't unearthed her collection of correspondence, I thought it prudent to check with Penelope before heading up to Horace's domain. We trailed up the long driveway and rounded the corner to the back porch where a small hump of dark fur huddled.

"Striker!" I jogged forward and scooped up my cat. "What are you doing here?"

In answer, she rubbed her face against my chin. I took that as an apology for abandoning me the night before and scratched the top of her head.

"I'm glad you're here," I whispered, feeling slightly silly in front of Daphne. "I've missed you."

Inside the inn, Penelope's office door was locked, and nobody answered when I knocked. At the reservation desk, the clerk shrugged when asked where she'd gone.

"She didn't say." He reached for a notepad. "Can I take a message?"

"Send her up to the attic suite if she gets back before we come down, okay?" I fished around in my bag for the room key then led Daphne upstairs.

The attic suite was exactly as we'd left it after filming my account of Horace appearing to me before we left for Cambion's Camp. The king-sized bed was still made up with a fleet of decorative pillows, and the room smelled faintly of disinfecting cleanser.

We both paused in the doorway before entering, the toes of our shoes inches away from the threshold. As this had been my idea, I decided it was only fair I entered the room first, but it took several seconds of talking up the idea to myself before my body agreed to move.

"Let's start with the floor," I said. "Penelope told me they didn't have to refinish it, so I'm guessing that's where we'll find the compartment. We can check the walls after."

I started in the bathroom at the back, dropping to my hands and knees. Relying on memories from Nancy Drew novels I'd read at least fifteen years before, I prodded and scratched at the floorboards, trying not to think about how the floor is the dirtiest place possible and how much dirtier a bathroom was than any other room.

To distract myself from thoughts of strangers' bare feet, I called a question to Daphne. "Did you ever come here for Gabrielle's séances?"

"Yes." Her answer was faint; I popped my head out of the bathroom and saw that she lingered in the doorway to the landing. "A few times. It was always... marvelous. There's no other word."

"I know what you mean." Finished with the small bathroom, I crawled into the main living space and got to work beside the bed. "I only got to be here once, but it was incredible. She was so in tune with the spirits. Their mouths would move, but the words would come out of her instead."

Daphne finally followed me into the room and mimicked my example, sitting on the floor and pressing on the boards by the door. "You saw them? The spirits who visited?"

"Yeah, didn't you?"

"I've never seen a ghost. Well, before your séance at the

cabin, I mean."

I stopped what I was doing and stared at her. "Really?"

"Is that so weird? From what I understand, the gift you and Gabrielle share is super rare."

"Yeah, but... I don't know. I guess it's weird you could see him but not the others." It bothered me. Why had she been able to see Horace? What made him so special? I quickened my pace, wanting to find Gabrielle's secret stash that much faster.

"I hope it's not under the bed," Daphne said. "We'd probably need help moving it."

"Let's save that for last then, after the couches."

My methodical search took me around the perimeter of the room. Soon I found myself behind the same screen where Raziel had died, and I shuddered. The memory of finding his body tried to invade my mind, but I forced it out. I couldn't allow myself to think of the dead. If I accidentally tried to reach out to Raziel now, I was sure Horace would appear.

It didn't take long for us to run out of unfurnished floor. I narrowed my eyes at the heavy frame supporting the king-sized bed, trying to estimate its weight. I wasn't confident we'd be able to move it without scratching up the hardwood, and Penelope would surely kill me if that happened. Four tall, thin legs supported the frame, leaving about a foot of space beneath the box spring. I lay down on my belly and scooched forward until my head and shoulders were under the bed.

"I think I can squeeze under here," I called from the darkened space.

"Couches first, right?" Daphne reminded me.

"Right."

I wiggled back out into the room and helped her drag the couches and coffee table in opposite directions. As we lifted the faux bearskin to drape it over the bed, Striker shot beneath the rug. She emerged a moment later, shaking a hair tie back and forth with a growl and scampering sideways under the bed with it.

"I need a break." Daphne settled onto one of the couches, now pushed up against the dormer window, and fanned herself with one hand. "This is more exercise than I've gotten in a year."

"Deal." I pulled out my phone and dialed Graham. The call went to voicemail, and I hung up without leaving a message, tossing the phone on the coffee table. He had to have gotten my earlier voicemail, but hadn't called me back and still wasn't answering. He was probably avoiding me. Great.

"There's a coffee shop downstairs, right?" Daphne asked. "Would you mind grabbing me a latte?"

It'd been too long since I'd had a chai. I'd been afraid of encountering Horace at the inn so I'd been going without. Maybe it was the crystal around my neck or Daphne's company, but I didn't feel nervous about him right now. The headache that'd plagued me for the past week, a sensation I now associated with both Horace and the jewelry box, was nowhere to be found. That alone was worth celebrating with my favorite beverage.

"Definitely. Come on, Striker. Let's grab a snack."

Usually, the S-word brought her running, but she remained under the bed, growling at her toy.

"She can stay with me," Daphne said.

"Okay."

As I turned to leave the room, Striker made a high-pitched "mew" sound I'd never heard her make before. I walked back to the bed and got on the floor to look at her. She'd caught one of her claws between two of the floorboards and was tugging desperately to unhook herself. Her eyes were wide and panicked as she looked at me and mewed again.

"Stop pulling!" I told her, dragging myself along the floor on my belly.

She ignored me, yanking on her paw in a way that made me

wince in sympathy. When I reached her and moved her body forward so I could release her claw, she rewarded me by swiping at the back of my hand. A thin line of blood appeared by my knuckles and I hissed in pain.

"Everything okay?" Daphne asked.

"Fine. Just typical feline gratitude."

I reached for Striker again, meaning to pull her out from under the bed with me, but she growled and clawed at the same floorboard she'd gotten stuck on.

"Stop it! You'll catch your claw again." I grabbed at her, and she swiped at me a second time before going back to scratching at the floor.

Realizing she might be onto something, I gently shoved her aside and ran my hand over the floorboards. One was raised slightly higher than the others, just enough to register on my fingertips but not my eyes. I used my fingernails like claws to pry the board away from the floor. Once it was out of the way, the two on either side lifted away also, and the familiar scent of Gabrielle's favorite nag champa incense wafted up from the space. The outline of a shoebox was just visible in the darkness. I dragged it with me as I pushed myself back out from under the bed.

"You found it!" Daphne hurried off the couch and knelt beside me.

I lifted the lid and the smell of nag champa grew stronger. It was as if the folded papers and envelopes had been bathed in the scent, and I imagined Gabrielle reviewing the contents down in the bookstore while the Doobie Brothers played on the stereo.

Striker rubbed her face against the box then started running laps around the attic suite. She'd always liked Gabrielle. The smell of our old friend seemed to energize my cat and make her forget about the pain from a moment before.

Leaning against the bed frame, I gingerly pulled a handful of envelopes out of the box. Stamped with postage from Spain and addressed to Gabrielle in New York City, the contents proved to be written in Spanish. The cursive handwriting was so loopy and overlapped that even if I'd spoken the language, I wasn't sure I'd be able to read them. The only parts I could make out were the dates at the top, from the 1980s, and the signature at the end: Rosanna Suntador.

"These are from Gabrielle's sister," I said, passing a few to Daphne. "She must have sent them before following Gabrielle here."

"Oh, Rosanna?" She accepted the letters from me and scanned them. "I knew her. She was the sweetest woman."

"Can you read them?"

She shook her head and put the letters in the shoebox's upturned lid. "I took French in school."

I kept pawing through the box, looking for anything with a United States postmark while silently cursing myself for never studying a foreign language. Halfway through the pile, I found a return address that made my heart stop.

Daphne peered over my shoulder and read the name in the upper left corner of the envelope. "Who's Evelyn Clair?"

I swallowed down the hard lump of sadness that'd formed in my throat at the familiar sight of the slanted handwriting. "My mom."

CHAPTER THIRTY-FOUR

I'd suspected these letters existed from the moment Gabrielle had produced a set of photographs my mother had mailed her when I was a child. Gabrielle had confirmed those suspicions when she offered to show me my mother's old correspondence... but only in return for my silence about her crimes. When I'd refused and she'd been arrested, I accepted that I'd never get to see the things my mother wrote to her.

My hands shook as I pulled the first letter out of its envelope. Nostalgia washed over me at the sight of so much of my mother's handwriting, sloping upward on the unlined stationary. A watermark of a hummingbird filled the lower corner of the page.

The letter was dated three years before I'd been born and was postmarked from Springdale, Utah. My hungry eyes took in my mother's thoughts about the feeling in the canyons at Zion National Park.

I think it's a spiritual nexus, like Donn's Hill. Somewhere the dead have an easier time crossing over. I wish you could be here to explore it with me. You'd love the desert.

It looks so dry and desolate, but I can feel the energy swirling around me every time I close my eyes.

There have to be thousands of other places like this in the world, right? Is it foolish to want to find them all? I feel more connected to my family here than I've felt since you helped me say goodbye to my mother. I know it's selfish to chase that feeling... but what else can I do?

The next letter was postmarked two years after the first and mailed from Crestone, Colorado. My mother began the letter by complaining she hadn't been able to find another "nexus" in the area then switched topics to something that made my breath catch.

Also, I took your advice and let Henry take me to dinner. He's a nice guy, but we're too different to make it work. He laughed when I asked him if he believes in ghosts. He thought I was joking when I said that's why I'm here.

It's moot anyway. He'll be finishing his dig here in a couple of weeks and then going back to Denver to wrap up his doctorate.

"Who's Henry?" Daphne asked, still reading over my shoulder.

"My dad."

I hurriedly rifled through the next few letters, hoping to find one that explained if they'd gone on a second date, but everything was woefully disorganized. I skimmed pages, getting sucked into pockets of time in my mother's life and then moving on once I realized they weren't about her relationship with my father. A timeline began to take shape as I ordered the letters based on the dates in the upper corner of each page.

There was so much I'd never known before. She worked her way across the United States over a period of two years, taking odd jobs or waitressing as she hunted for other places of spiritual power. She returned to Donn's Hill every April, and the subsequent letters were typically dated in June or July. I imagined she'd stay with Gabrielle and Rosanna for a month or two, studying and laughing with her friends before venturing back out into the world on her spiritual quest.

Striker pawed at the box, hooking a single claw into a crinkled envelope.

I shooed her away. "These aren't your toys. Where'd your hair tie go?"

She made her annoyance clear by jumping up on the bed and glaring at me. I ignored her and turned my attention back to the letters.

"Find anything about Horace yet?" Daphne asked.

"Hmmm?" I looked up from the letter in my hands, feeling dazed. "Oh, sorry. I got distracted."

She'd been picking through the letters as I put them down, and I handed her a stack of ones I hadn't gotten to yet.

"Here, take these. I don't have to be the first to look at this stuff."

"Are you sure? You seem pretty engrossed. I don't want to throw off your groove."

I shook my head. "You won't. Sorry. It's just…"

"I get it. I never even knew your mom, and it's still fascinating stuff. I can't imagine what it's like for you."

She pulled open a letter and skimmed its contents. I dove back into my mother's history. A few months after her first date with my dad, she wrote to Gabrielle from Seattle with news that she'd met another medium named Anson Monroe who could help develop her powers.

He's been doing this for decades, just like you. He's studied all over the world. Between the two of you, I think I can cross over.

My eyebrows drew together. Cross over to where? She couldn't mean the other side. The living couldn't go there... could they?

That was exactly what she meant. In her next letter, she vented about the difficulties of astral projection and complained she didn't feel powerful enough to do it. That was one of the few supernatural things she'd talked to me about when I'd been young: the magic of the astral plane.

"I thought she was kidding," I muttered aloud.

"What's that?" Daphne looked up from the letter she was reading.

"Oh, nothing."

I read on, and more details about my mother's journeys and personality emerged. She drank her coffee black and loathed tea. She celebrated every time she found a new job by saluting the sunset with a gin and tonic, and fortified herself against the jobs she really hated with a nightly glass of red wine.

The lump rose in my throat again. She'd had a glass of red wine every night until she died. She must have hated her job, but she'd kept it.

For me.

Daphne poked me in the arm. "Hey, I think I've got something. Listen to this." She read aloud from a heavy sheet of ivory-colored paper:

"You owe me a night on the town next time I see you, darling. I was right. The so-called 'Banshee of Braxton' was a hoax. The

red-eyed demon was nothing more than a prank. Of course, you were partially correct. There was an element of the paranormal involved. The young Betsy, as it turns out, is a psychic of prodigious skill. She bypassed the locked doors via astral projection."

"Wait, I just read something else about that." I pulled the letter from Daphne's hands and skimmed it. It was dated in 1975 and signed "affectionately yours, Alfie."

"What do you know about it?" Daphne asked.

"Not much. I didn't even know astral projection was real. But look at this." I passed her the letter from my mother where she shared how difficult it was to do. "My mom was studying it before I was born."

"I didn't think it was real, either." She frowned. "But this thing about a 'red-eyed demon' really being an astral traveler...."

She didn't finish her sentence, but I immediately knew what she meant. Horace's eyes had glowed red at the cabin, and though they'd faded to black the next two times I'd seen him, they'd started out red then too.

It fit. Daphne had been able to see him but had never seen a ghost at one of Gabrielle's séances. Did you need some level of psychic ability to see someone traveling through the astral plane and a higher level to see ghosts?

The questions piled up in my mind like a mudslide. If Horace was astral projecting, where was he projecting from? Was there a limit to the distance? How did he know who I was? And how did he know *where* I was so that he could project right into whatever room I was in?

"Mac, your phone's ringing."

"What?" I ripped my attention away from the letter and checked my phone, which buzzed on the coffee table where I'd left it. Graham's name blinked on the screen, and I stepped out onto the landing to talk to him.

"Is Striker with you?" he asked without preamble.

"Yeah, why?"

He sighed into the mouthpiece. "I could have sworn I left her in my apartment when I left this morning, but she wasn't there when I got back. After last night... I was just worried."

I didn't know what to say to that. My emotional feathers were still ruffled by his cold anger the night before and his absence all day today. An awkward silence stretched across several long moments.

"Where are you?" he finally asked.

"I'm at the inn with Daphne. We found a box of Gabrielle's old letters in the attic." I paused, wishing he and I weren't fighting so this moment could be full of pure happiness instead of muddled by sadness and regret. "A bunch of them are from my mom."

His voice was hesitant. "Do you mind if I join you?"

I sagged against the banister, relieved to hear him ask. "I would love that."

"I'll be there soon."

When I came back into the room, Striker was darting excitedly around the suite with a slightly puffed tail as though chasing an invisible bird, and Daphne was climbing out from beneath the bed.

"Find anything else down there?" I asked.

"No." She put her hands into her hoodie pocket, pulled out a tissue, and blew her nose. "Sorry. Allergies. Striker got all hyper, and I was worried she might try to climb in the hole, so I closed it up."

"Oh, thanks." I settled myself back on the floor and pulled the box of letters onto my lap.

"I hate to leave you, but I should be going."

"What? But we're so close!"

She dusted her hands off on her jeans. "We're more than

close. We've solved it. This Horace guy isn't a ghost. He's just some psychic messing with you from somewhere."

"But we don't know who he really is or why he's doing it." How she could walk away in the middle of this baffled me until I remembered Horace wasn't stalking her. She had the benefit of some distance from the problem. But still… I would stay for her.

I'd stay to help a friend.

A flash of annoyance warmed my face. This was the curse of the jewelry box all over again, but subtler. Even my newest friends were abandoning me. Well, fine. I'd finish this alone then.

Almost alone. Striker still zoomed around the room like a pinball in a machine, threatening to knock over the lamps on the night tables and the desk.

"Thanks for your help," I forced myself to say, turning my back on Daphne to focus on the shoebox in my lap.

"Let me know if you find anything else."

Her footsteps crossed the room. A moment later, a loud *THUMP* and a crash jolted me to my feet, sending the box of letters flying. I spun around to see Daphne sprawled on the floor in front of the door.

"Oh, my God!" I rushed to her side. "Are you okay?"

"I think so." She let me pull her into a sitting position, rubbed her ankle, and winced. "I think it's sprained."

"What happened?"

"I tripped"—she lifted her chin toward my cat, who was now cleaning one of her front paws with cool detachment—"on Ms. Jetpack."

"I am so sorry." I rounded on my cat. "Striker! You could've killed her!"

Striker ignored my scolding, forcing me to walk over and pick her up. She'd been sitting on something; the glass face of a cell phone reflected the bright light above us. I bent down to retrieve it, telling Daphne, "I think you dropped this."

The other woman struggled to find her feet on her twisted ankle and hobbled over to me, hand outstretched. I turned the phone over in my hands, moving to give it to her, then stopped.

Raziel's face glowered at me from the back of the case. I recognized the stylized art from when I'd seen his phone at the cabin, and it had the same red flames and blue "veritas vincat" lettering I'd noticed when he'd been texting Amari.

"Is this Raziel's phone?" I asked.

"No, it's mine."

She reached for it, but I stepped away from her.

"You hated Raziel. You'd never have his face on your phone. Why do you have this?" My eyes flicked to the bed. "Was it in the hidey-hole?"

"I told you, it's mine. I changed the case."

The lie was obvious to the point of being insulting. I backed away from Daphne, Striker in one arm and the phone in the other, and swiped to unlock the device. It asked me for a code, but the lock screen featured a photo I recognized from the news coverage of Raziel's death: a rare picture of Raziel smiling with his mother at his side.

"Cut the crap, Daphne. This is definitely Raziel's phone. Why did you take it?"

She narrowed her eyes at me. "It doesn't matter. Just give it back."

"No." I slipped it into the pocket of my jeans and circled around her toward the door. "Deputy Wallace was looking for it. The police need it."

"*I* need it," she growled, wobbling slightly as she took a few steps toward me. "Don't make me hurt you, Mac."

I edged closer to the door. Would she really hurt me? An hour ago, I'd have been sure she wouldn't. But this woman in front of me didn't wear the face of my friend. Her eyes held no light, and her mouth was set in a determined line.

"Just talk to me." The door was only a few feet to my left now. "Let me help you. Whatever's going on, we can work through it."

"No. We can't."

She dove for me.

With a surprised shriek, I lunged for the door. Striker launched off me, landing on the desk and sending the lamp clattering to the floor. Daphne had the benefit of a long reach and grabbed my hair, yanking me backward. I stumbled and lost my footing, toppling to the ground.

She was on me in an instant, knocking my face into the hard-wood floor and kneeling on my back. Her hands fumbled at my pockets, then she grabbed the edge of the phone and pulled the device to freedom.

As soon as her weight lightened on my body, I rolled, knocking her off balance while she tried to stand. I yanked on her injured ankle, dragged her to her knees, and knocked the phone out of her hands. It skittered across the floor and under the bed. Striker soared after it, her dark shape distracting me long enough for Daphne's good foot to smash into my chest, knocking the wind out of my lungs. As I gasped for air, she scrambled around on the floor and got behind me, grabbed the string that held the crystal around my neck, and yanked.

Lights popped in my eyes. I scratched at my neck, trying desperately to find a finger-hold. Then, the braided leather snapped, and she flew backward, hitting her head on the displaced coffee table with a thump.

The instant the little black stone left my neck, the migraine that'd been plaguing me for the past week and a half surged back into place. Pain flooded my sinuses, squeezing my skull from every direction. I cried out, pressing a hand against the back of my head, and Daphne did the same.

The door to the attic suite banged open. Graham's tall figure momentarily filled the doorway, and shock registered on his face as he loped toward me.

"Police," I croaked. "Now."

He wasted no time pulling out his phone and dialing. Daphne's limbs collapsed beneath her body, and her defeated sobs filled the room.

CHAPTER THIRTY-FIVE

The Driscoll County Sheriff's Department buzzed with activity. From my seat in the waiting room, I watched through the heavily tinted windows as Sheriff Harris fended off reporters on the front steps. He kept holding up his hands and shaking his head, and I wondered what he might be telling them about my involvement with the case.

At least now, I was confident he wouldn't use the word "suspect" to describe me.

We'd been sitting here for over two hours. Graham had tried to convince the deputies to let us go home until they were ready to take our statements, but they'd insisted we stay at the station. Soon after we got there, Kit and Amari had arrived and been immediately whisked into a conference room. Every time I got up to use the bathroom or the drinking fountain, I'd slowed my pace at the conference room windows, trying unsuccessfully to hear any snatches of conversation.

After a long while, Kit and Amari emerged back into the open. I intercepted them as they left the station. Kit wrapped me in a hug, checked my face and my neck for any lingering signs of injury, then punched me on the shoulder.

"Ow!" I rubbed the spot where her small fist had connected with my bone. "What was that for?"

"For being an idiot." Kit glared at me. "That nutbag could've killed you!"

Amari's face bore the signs of strain and exhaustion, but she shot me a weak smile. "I'm so relieved you're not injured. I hope they don't keep you waiting much longer."

I nodded toward the conference room. "What happened in there?"

Kit opened her mouth to answer, and Amari rested a hand on her arm.

"I'm sorry," she said. "They asked us not to speak to anyone about it until all the interviews are completed."

"I get it," I said. "Go home, get some rest. We'll catch up later."

They left, and we continued waiting. To kill the time, I watched the deputies at their desks as they pored over case files and made phone calls. The hum of their conversations filled the air, their words merging into a mass of unintelligible chatter. I rubbed my temples, wishing they'd taken us straight to the conference room or even that cold interrogation room. Either place would be quiet. It was difficult to think with all this noise.

"Is your migraine back?" Graham asked from beside me.

I shook my head. "No, thank goodness. This just feels like a regular headache."

"You must be exhausted." He put an arm around me and inclined his head toward the piece of black tourmaline hanging from my neck. "That's new."

"Yeah." I pulled away from him and lifted the stone from my chest, taking care not to break the leather cord again. I'd hastily re-tied it in the attic suite before the deputies had escorted us out of the inn, and the large knot jutted awkwardly outward at the back of my neck. "Elizabeth Monk gave it to me after my massage. Jeez, that was just this afternoon. It feels like days ago."

"I like it."

"Thanks. This will sound crazy, but I think it's the reason my migraine is finally gone. I think...." I bit my lip. Here, in this busy place, my theory seemed too ridiculous to say aloud.

Graham nudged me. "You think what?"

I shook my head. "It's stupid."

"You don't have to tell me if you don't want to, but whatever you're thinking, you're probably right. I'm sorry for calling you reckless. I just worry about you." He shot a glare toward the door to the holding cells where Daphne had been taken. "And I won't apologize for wanting to know you're safe, because trouble seems to follow you around. But you have good instincts, and I'm always here to listen to your theories, okay?"

"Okay." I let the stone fall back against my t-shirt and took a deep breath. "Before Daphne attacked me, we found some letters Gabrielle had hidden in her attic. One of them described a person who was astral projecting as having red eyes, and I think that's what Horace is doing. He's not a ghost. He's not dead. He's just a psychic. A really, really powerful one."

Graham's eyes went wide behind his glasses. "What? How is that even possible?"

"I don't know. I guess it's something my mom was working on before she had me. I'm not super familiar with it, but from what I understand, it's possible to displace your own spirit. You can disconnect yourself from your body and use the astral plane to travel around."

"That sounds... dangerous."

I nodded. "I know. I can't imagine doing it. But that's what Horace was doing. He said he'd been looking for another psychic like me. What if everything he told me was at least a half-truth?

He claimed he'd been drawn to me while I was calling out to Richard Franklin's ghost. What if that's true, and Horace just happened to hear me while he was on the astral plane?"

He frowned. "I guess that makes sense."

"I think the same thing happened when I reached out to Raziel. Horace heard me, and then he found me. Then he sent me to Cambion's Camp after that jewelry box, and that's when the migraines really started." I rubbed the back of my head. "You know how you can sort of feel eyes on the back of your head when someone's watching you? It's like that, but so strong it hurts."

I paused. We were now leaving "I think" territory and barreling straight into the truly unknown. Until I could confirm my theories with someone like Gabrielle, all I had from this point forward was pure conjecture.

"What if he was spying on me somehow, maybe watching me from the astral plane? And that's how he knew everything that was going on? And this"—I lifted the black tourmaline necklace again—"stops him from seeing me?"

Before Graham could react to that, the door to the interrogation room opened. Deputy Wallace stepped out of the room, glancing toward us before motioning to someone behind her. The pale, shaking figure of Stephen Hastain followed her to her desk, where she handed him a business card. Then, with a clap on the back, she pointed him toward the door.

Instead of heading for the exit, Stephen raised his hand in greeting and made his way toward the row of chairs where Graham and I sat.

"Hey!" Wallace barked. "Not 'til I'm done with them."

Stephen winced, glanced back at the deputy, then tossed us an apologetic shrug.

"We'll see you later," Graham called to him.

The rune caster nodded and left the station, and Deputy Wallace beckoned for us to join her at her desk.

"Sorry for the wait," she said. "There's a lot to sort through. Follow me."

I expected her to lead us back into the same interrogation room where she'd just met with Stephen, but instead she led us to a small conference room at the back of the station. It was the same room where I'd told her about my psychic abilities earlier that year, and I smiled at the memory of her warm reaction to the news.

She flopped into a chair at the head of the oblong table with a deep sigh, tossing a laptop and a manila folder onto the surface in front of her. "Lord, I'm tired. You guys want coffee?"

"We're okay," I said, speaking for Graham as we sat down beside her. I'd had the station coffee before and loved him enough to spare him from it.

"Okee-dokee then. Down to business." She reached forward and switched on a recording device in the center of the table, then flipped open the folder and scanned the contents briefly. "Let's start with you, Mac. Why were you at the Oracle Inn with Daphne Martin today?"

I took her through my day, starting with the visitation from Horace at the massage parlor and ending with the wrestling match I'd had with Daphne on the floor of the attic suite. Deputy Wallace asked me to clarify a few things for the sake of the recording, like last names and approximate times, and I was grateful Sheriff Harris wasn't in the room this time to glare at me from behind his beard.

"Well, that explains why your fingerprints are all over the phone," Wallace said when I'd finished. "And it lines up with the account Daphne gave us. Okay, Graham. Your turn."

Graham explained that he'd come to the inn to see me and heard Daphne and I yelling at each other while he'd been climbing the stairs. He described the scene he'd walked in on after throwing himself against the door. "Daphne was on the floor, crying. They both looked hurt. Mac asked me to call you guys, so I did."

"And Mrs. Martin made no attempt to flee while you were waiting for the authorities to arrive?" Wallace asked.

Graham shook his head. "No, I blocked the door with my body in case she tried to leave, but she just laid there."

"She wouldn't talk to us," I added.

"Well, she had plenty to say once she got here," Wallace said.

I stiffened. What had Daphne told them? How much of it had been the truth? Wallace had mentioned fingerprints a moment ago. Had Daphne said something to them that somehow made me *more* of a suspect than I'd been before?

Wallace reached out and patted my shoulder. "Relax, Mac. You're in the clear. Daphne confessed to killing Raziel Santos. From what she told us, and from the evidence we've gathered, she acted alone."

"She really killed him?" I tried to square the Daphne I knew with the idea of taking a life. "Why?"

"Because of this." Deputy Wallace opened the laptop and pulled up a video file.

Despite the muddy darkness of the footage, I recognized the interior of the cabin. It was the night of the séance. Dozens of flickering candles dimly illuminated a circle of faces, and I heard myself screaming. The sound sent a bolt of icy terror through my veins, and I remembered seeing Horace smile for the first time.

Raziel's phone didn't capture Horace's face. For a few moments, the video was completely black. Then Graham re-lit the first candle, passed the flame around, and Stephen pulled Daphne to her feet.

"I need to lie down," she said.

The camera swept the room, recording my team as they

switched on the battery-powered lanterns we'd brought along and started tearing down our equipment. Then, a few minutes, later, Raziel moved down the hallway toward the back of the house.

Light from another electric lantern spilled out from around the nearly closed door of the back bedroom. Raziel's pace slowed, and it took an agonizing few minutes before the camera reached the door. A muffled scratching overtook the audio for a moment and the angle shifted sharply a few times as Raziel took the phone out of his pocket and slid it through the narrow opening between the door and the frame.

Daphne and Stephen sat on the floor of the bedroom, their backs to the door. A lantern glowed between them. Daphne rubbed Stephen's back and nestled her face into his neck.

He shoved her away. "No, Daph. There's a half dozen people out there. Someone will hear us."

"They're all distracted," she said. "It's fine."

"How are you not terrified right now?" he asked. "You heard Mac's scream. And you saw... Well, what did you see?"

She snorted. "Oh, relax. There was nothing there. She was faking it for their show, just like everybody else."

"I think she saw something." Stephen shifted, repositioning himself on the floor a few inches farther away from her. "I felt something in that room. I can't wait to get out of here."

"I'm not a customer, you know. You don't have to pretend you've got some kind of psychic gift in front of me."

"I'm not pretending."

"Sure. Then I'm not, either." She stretched her arms above her head then hugged herself and squealed. "I can't wait for this episode to air. The timing is perfect. People will freak, and the *cirque d'letrange* will get a huge publicity boost."

More muffled scratching drowned out Stephen's reply, and the camera returned to a height that made me assume Raziel had put the phone back in his breast pocket. His thin, tattooed hand pushed the door open.

Stephen and Daphne turned toward the camera. He flinched. She glared.

"Cozy place you two have," Raziel said. "Don't hide back here too long. You'll miss the show."

The video stopped, the screen went black, and Deputy Wallace closed the laptop.

"That's one small piece of Raziel's recording from that evening," she said. "His manager, Amari Botha, helped us unlock the phone."

Exhaustion made my mind slow to process what I'd seen, but eventually the reality sank in. Daphne *hadn't* seen Horace. She'd made it up for the benefit of the cameras. She'd lied to me about it, then lied to me again. And worse than that…

She'd killed Raziel to keep her secret.

"Why?" I whispered. "Why did she do it?"

Wallace raised a quizzical eyebrow. "Did you watch the clip? She was a fraud, Mac. When Raziel told you he'd been recording all night, she realized he had everything he needed to ruin her career."

"But couldn't she just… *talk* to him?" I'd been in Daphne's exact position, and I hadn't wanted to kill him. Sure, I'd tried to punch him. But taking a life…

"She claims she tried to, at first. She went to his hotel room that night and begged him to delete the video." Wallace pursed her lips. "She says he just laughed at her, so she snapped and yanked a cord off the curtains."

Every word out of the deputy's mouth sent my mind deeper into a tailspin. I tried to picture Daphne strangling the life out of Raziel, but the image refused to take shape in my head. Nick had called me naïve; had he known just how right he was?

"Did Nick know?" I asked at last. "Or Stephen?"

"Stephen seemed genuinely shocked when we questioned him. As for Nick"—she shrugged—"we're not sure."

"But you said Mac's good, right?" Graham asked. "She's not a suspect?"

"No, not anymore." Wallace looked me in the eyes. "You understand, right? I have to follow every lead, every time. Even if they take me somewhere I don't want to go."

"I get it." I stood and offered her my hand.

She followed suit, getting to her feet. Instead of shaking my hand, she pulled me into a hug, releasing me after a few seconds. "Good. Now get out of here. I've got a pile of paperwork a mile high and lots more statements to gather."

"Hey," Graham said. "Any leads on the break-in at our house?"

Wallace shook her head. "No. I'll level with you guys. The murder investigation has been taking up most of our resources. We'll keep looking into it, though. You have my word."

We left her to her duties and snuck out a side door to avoid the press then settled into Graham's Geo. I exhaled, putting my feet up onto the dashboard and stretching my arms above my head. Despite the shock of discovering Daphne's true nature, the relief of knowing the real killer had been found made my spirit feel light. I felt like I could float up out of the car, drift over the farmland, and sail away on the breeze.

"I haven't seen you smile like that in a while." Graham squeezed my knee. "How's it feel to be a free woman?"

"Amazing. I want to celebrate."

"Well, you don't have to stick close to Donn's Hill anymore. Want to take advantage? Drive to Moyard, get some food?"

I stared at him. "You don't want to do that drive twice in one day."

He tapped the tiny digital clock next to Baxter's ancient tape deck. "It's after midnight, so technically it's not the same day.

Come on, there's a great all-night diner we used to hang out at after concerts when I was younger. They had the best pancakes and the worst coffee."

"Who can resist that?"

"Excellent." He grinned and gunned the engine playfully then headed for the highway.

I marveled at the changes we passed on the way out of town. The old Main Street Diner, which had previously occupied a run-down rail-car-style building, had been transformed into the new Café on Main. Bunting hung from the restaurant's windows, and despite the late hour, Penelope's staff was visible through the brightly lit windows making last-minute preparations for the grand opening in the morning.

At the edge of town, a pile of rubble marked the place where the E-Z Sleep Motel had stood. I'd started my life in Donn's Hill in that seedy place, and now it was nothing more than bricks and dust. A large sign promised that modern, luxury accommodations were on the way.

"It's so different," I said.

"This town never seemed to change at all until you got here. Now..." He glanced at me with a smile. "Everything is better."

Ahead of us, the road curved gently. The Geo's headlights swept the tree line, illuminating a broken-down van on the side of the road. The other vehicle's hazard lights blinked slowly, and its brake lights glowed crimson against the darkness.

"That's not Kit, is it?" I asked irrationally. She and Amari had looked beat. They wouldn't be out on the road.

"I don't think so."

Graham pulled over, bringing the Geo to a stop a few yards away from the van. We climbed out and approached it, getting close enough to confirm it wasn't Kit's. It was a much newer model, tall and white, with yellow New Mexico plates.

"Hello?" Graham called. "Need a hand?"

No one answered. A light hissing filled the air, and I unconsciously touched the spot on my chest where my seatbelt had bruised me during the accident at Cambion's Camp. Something about the van—and that sound—was uncomfortably familiar.

As we rounded the corner of the vehicle, my breath caught. Steam poured out of the hissing engine. One of the van's headlight's was blocked by the enormous boulder it'd smashed into.

The other illuminated two bodies lying face down in the gravel ahead.

"Call 911!" I shouted, sprinting forward. I knelt beside each man, checking for any signs of life.

Neither had a pulse in their neck or their wrists. Their bodies twisted into strange positions, as though they'd tumbled a few times before stopping. I stood and backed away from them, gagging into my elbow.

"I think they're dead," I croaked to Graham as he caught up to me.

He spoke into his cell phone, describing the scene as he double-checked each body for a pulse. "Two men," he told the emergency operator. "Both dead."

His calm demeanor baffled me. How was he not vomiting all over the asphalt? How was he not screaming at the dark trees, like I wanted to do?

I didn't want to look at their faces. I was sure they'd be badly lacerated from the impact with the road. But I couldn't help it. I needed to know if these bodies belonged to someone I knew, if their spirits were likely to linger.

Gathering all my willpower, I forced myself to look at their faces. I'd been right; their injuries made them unrecognizable. But as I backed away, something about them struck me as familiar.

One was tall and oddly skinny. The other was much shorter and heavyset. I didn't know them, but I'd seen them before.

Twice, I realized. Once at the Oracle Inn, just before we left for Cambion's Camp. And again, in the security video from Graham's studio.

These were the men who'd broken into the garage.

These were the two who'd taken the jewelry box.

I clutched the black stone around my neck and bolted back toward the van, skidding on the loose gravel as I rounded the vehicle. My hands, slick with sweat, fumbled with the handles on the cargo doors at the back before finally pulling them open.

Old, rotted, wooden cabinets filled the space. They smelled of mildew and campfire smoke. Lewd graffiti covered their doors. I'd recognize them anywhere. They'd been taken from Richard Franklin's cabin.

And atop one of the overturned cupboards, I recognized something else: Yuri's mirror-lined box.

It was open.

And the little wooden jewelry box it contained was open too.

The hissing in the air combined with the hissing in my ears, rising to a deafening volume. Dimly, I heard Graham calling my name, but my own screams drowned out all but that awful, snake-like sound.

Then, his body collided into mine. He half-carried, half-dragged me back toward Baxter, shouting something in my ear. As we passed the Geo, the van caught fire.

"Duck!" he yelled, not giving me any opportunity to do anything else as he dove behind his car, pulling me to the ground with him.

We cowered there for several minutes, waiting for an explosion that never came.

"Did you notice the license plates?" I whispered after a while.

"No, why?"

"They were from New Mexico." I sat up and pulled my knees

into my chest. "And those guys…. They're the ones who stole the box from your studio."

Graham stared at me. "What? Are you sure?"

"Positive."

The reflection from the flames now engulfing the van glowed in his pupils as he stared at me. "New Mexico, and they knew about the box that Horace asked you to find. That can't be a coincidence."

I inched my head around Baxter's rusty bumper to stare at the van. Experimentally, I took off my necklace. As soon as the braided cord cleared my head, I felt it.

Richard Franklin's foul, dark energy crashed into me like a tidal wave. But like a wave, it washed over me, passing around my body as though I was a stone on the beach.

There was a second energy in there, too, mingled with the poltergeist. It grazed my cheeks as though grasping for a handhold.

As the flames consumed the van and its wooden cargo, both energies faded away like smoke drifting into a starry sky. My eyes misted over and something hitched in my throat. There was no denying it; Richard Franklin had crossed over, taking the spirit from the jewelry box with him.

I blinked tears out of my eyes and focused back on the van. Graham was right. It couldn't be a coincidence that the men who stole the box were driving a vehicle with New Mexico plates. Horace had been at Richard Franklin's cabin, and he'd been the one to send me looking for that jewelry box. He'd known when it'd been stolen because it had been stolen on his orders, and his lackeys obviously couldn't handle the spiritual energy they'd packed for the drive home.

A strange smile spread over my face as I realized Stephen was right. I *had* to go back to New Mexico. What other choice did I have? I'd find Horace there; I could feel it.

The importance of finding him dwarfed everything else. Suddenly, I didn't worry about Kit leaving the show or if we could continue on without her.

Those things lay behind me.

New Mexico, and answers, lay ahead.

How do you catch a killer who moves like a ghost?

DONN'S
LEGACY

THE SOUL SEARCHERS MYSTERIES, BOOK THREE
CARYN LARRINAGA

Thank you for reading *Donn's Shadow*! If you enjoyed the book, I would deeply appreciate a short review wherever you bought this book. Reviews are crucial for any author, and even a line or two can help another reader discover this story.

Want to know when the next book is on the way and other big news? Join my email list and get a free ebook!

http://carynlarrinaga.com/free-ebook

Join me on Facebook and Twitter to chat about books, cats, horror, and anything else that strikes your fancy!

https://www.facebook.com/carynwrites
https://twitter.com/carynlarrinaga

ACKNOWLEDGMENTS

First, I always need to thank my wonderful husband, Kelly. You encourage me, push me forward, and comfort me when stories don't sell or characters don't cooperate. You listen to every awful first draft and help me develop my ideas. In short, I wouldn't be where I am without you, in my writing or in anything else. I love you!

Thank you, Mom, for once again reading through each draft and helping me make them better. I don't know how you can stand to read and re-read my books, but you always give me the confidence to keep going.

Thank you, Dad, for never getting tired of theorizing about the nature of the soul and the possibilities of the afterlife. And for the last time: no, you're not Mac's father.

This book would literally not exist without the help and guidance of my incomparable friend, Jerry McPhee. Thanks for being the machete I needed to cut through the nonsense and clear a path for the future.

Enormous thanks to my editing team: Kelley Lynn and Jolene Perry at Cookie Lynn Publication Services. You help me learn and improve with every pass. Thanks also to my proofreader, Beverly Bernard, for your diligence and expertise. I wouldn't have the confidence to put this book in front of readers without all three of you.

Huge thanks also to Stephanie Feldman, Brandy Rood, Steve Matney, and Martin McConnell who helped me track down last-minute issues in the book.

Thank you, Lexi Johnson, for reading through this and reassuring me that I wasn't about to make an enormous ass out of myself.

And thank you to my real-life reiki masseuse, Kim. You helped me heal in difficult times.

Finally, thank you to all the readers and friends who encouraged me to keep Mac and Striker's story going. You know who you are, but you'll never know how much it meant to me that you reached out to let me know how you felt about the first book. Thank you for talking to me at events, for sending me messages, and for telling others about Donn's Hill.

Thanks for being part of the magic!

ABOUT THE AUTHOR

Caryn Larrinaga is an award-winning mystery, horror, and urban fantasy writer. Her debut novel, *Donn's Hill*, was awarded the League of Utah Writers 2017 Silver Quill in the adult novel category and was a 2017 Dragon Award finalist.

Watching scary movies through split fingers terrified Caryn as a child, and those nightmares inspire her to write now. Her 90-year-old house has a colorful history, and the creaking walls and narrow hallways send her running (never walking) up the stairs. Exploring her fears through writing makes Caryn feel a little less foolish for wanting a buddy to accompany her into the tool shed.

Caryn lives near Salt Lake City, Utah, with her husband and their clowder of cats. Visit www.carynlarrinaga.com for free short fiction and true tales of haunted places.

facebook.com/carynwrites

twitter.com/carynlarrinaga

instagram.com/carynlarrinaga

amazon.com/author/carynlarrinaga

goodreads.com/carynlarrinaga

bookbub.com/authors/caryn-larrinaga

SUPERHERO SYNDROME

Tess McBray was dying. The Solstice Syndrome had no cure, and she resigned herself to an early grave. But just when she gave up on survival, all her symptoms mysteriously disappeared.

All but one symptom, anyway. Something is wrong with Tess's hands. They absorb any material they touch, and her skin turns to wood, or steel, or concrete. It doesn't take this comic-book obsessed 21-year-old long to figure out what's going on: somehow, she's developed super powers. And she's not the only one; across the country, people are coming forward and sharing their gifts with the world. In her own city, where the police are battling a human trafficking operation, a masked vigilante called The Fox is saving lives and stopping criminals.

Tess doesn't know where she fits into this new, super-powered world. But when people around her start disappearing, she can't just sit on the sidelines. Teaming up with The Fox to create the world's first superhero duo might be the only way to rid her city of evil and save the people she loves most.

HIDE AND SEEK

Agatha isn't looking forward to Christmas. While other eight-year-olds are hoping for a pile of presents, she just wants her evil stepsisters to leave her alone. Summer and Rain have a cruel idea of what passes for fun, and it always involves tormenting Agatha.

When the three of them get stuck inside their house on Christmas Eve, the twins force Agatha to play a twisted version of Hide and Seek. But they aren't the only things hiding in the house, and someone is about to get more than they bargained for beneath the tree...

GALTZAGORRIAK AND OTHER CREATURES: STORIES INSPIRED BY BASQUE FOLKLORE

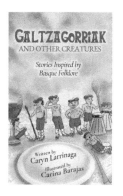

Dive into stories about love, loss, greed, and revenge. Meet creatures like the mischievous *Galtzagorriak*, the deadly *Gaueko*, the beautiful *Lamiak*, the legendary *Erensuge*, and the wicked *Sorginak*.

The captivating tales in *Galtzagorriak and Other Creatures* are accompanied by breathtaking illustrations by artist Carina Barajas, and are sure to delight the whole family. Whether you're already familiar with the Basque Country or this is your first introduction, you don't want to miss this collection.

"A FRIEND IN NEED," FEATURED IN A YEAR OF THE MONKEYS

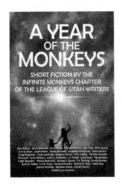

There is a theory that says if you give typewriters to one hundred monkeys, and let them type for one hundred years, they will eventually reproduce the works of Shakespeare. We decided to put that theory to the test - with a few minor modifications.

We didn't have one hundred monkeys - but we did have the membership of a League of Utah Writers chapter that calls itself "The Infinite Monkeys." Most of them didn't have typewriters, but worked on laptop or desktop computers, smartphones, and tablets. And instead of one hundred years to perfect their prose, we gave them one year to get from blank page to published anthology. So while you won't find any reproductions of Shakespeare here, what you will find are thirty-five short stories that will make you laugh, make you cry, make you think, and sometimes make you glad you don't live in the unsettling worlds of the imagination.

Featuring #1 Amazon bestselling author Michael Darling's "Sailing on the Sands of Burning Tides," the award-winning stories, "What We Leave Behind" from Masha Shukovich, and "Stone Soup" from Leigh Saunders, together with a brand new story, "A Friend in Need," from the award-winning Caryn Larrinaga. Also includes stories by: Jenn Adams, Jenna Bowman, Scott Bryan, Julie Frost, Effie Graves, Joni B. Haws, Laurie Heath, Sariah Horowitz, Jonathan Humphries, Norm Jenson, Craig Kingsman, Gregory Lemon, C.H. Lindsay, Victoria Lisowski, Terra Luft, Anna Marasco, Justin C. Matthews, J.T. Moore, Jared Quan, Talysa Sainz, Rachael J. Sparks, P.A. Sterling, Jennie Stevens, Scott E. Tarbet, L.D.B. Taylor, Richard Timothy, Patrick M. Tracy, Heidi Voss, Johnny Worthen, Rashelle Yeates, and Daniel Yocom.

"THE FISHERMEN," FEATURED IN APOCALYPSE UTAH

From the Creators of *Old Scratch and Owl Hoots* and *It Came from the Great Salt Lake,* comes the next installment of new Utah horror, *Apocalypse Utah: a Collection of Utah Horror.*

Twelve Apocalyptic horsemen of the Rocky Mountains have come together in this terrifying anthology of Utah Horror. After years of dystopian fiction, these twelve writers won the challenge to portray how the apocalypse would occur.

Questionable kittens, ritualistic killing, destroying angels, ancient gods seeking punishment, lawless renegades, practitioners of the dark arts, and zombies will haunt every corner of your mind as you read these thrilling accounts of what could happen during the end of days in Utah.

Reanimated corpses of religious fanatics proclaiming salvation are the least of your worries...

Printed in Great Britain
by Amazon

40222361R00182